PLAYING POSSUM

Editor: Cynthia Brackett-Vincent
Cover design by Christopher Wait
Cover illustrations © Getty Images

Published by:

Encircle Publications
PO Box 187
Farmington, ME 04938

info@encirclepub.com
http://encirclepub.com

To My Daughter, Samantha—
You've Always Made Me Proud

Also by Lois Schmitt:

Monkey Business
Something Fishy

PLAYING POSSUM

A Kristy Farrell Mystery

LOIS SCHMITT

Encircle Publications
Farmington, Maine, U.S.A.

CHAPTER 1

"A chicken hawk, muskrat, red fox, and a litter of squirrels." My daughter Abby shook her head. "Why would anyone steal them?"

"It doesn't make sense to me either," I said after sipping my coffee.

Abby, who lived with her fiancé in a house on the beach, had stopped by for an early breakfast before work. We were talking about my latest assignment—an article about the Pendwell Wildlife Refuge I was writing for *Animal Advocate Magazine*. The refuge housed a wildlife rehabilitation center. Last week, several animals under medical care went missing.

"Don't the police have any clues?" Abby asked.

"All I know is the animal enclosures were cut with a sharp instrument. The thief broke the security cameras too."

Abby swallowed the last of her coffee and grabbed a second chocolate donut. I marveled at how someone who lived on pizza, chips, and chocolate remained a size six.

"I'd better get to work." Abby glanced at her watch and grinned. "The boss is a real curmudgeon about coming in late."

I grinned back. Abby, a veterinarian, worked at her father's veterinary practice. My husband Matt was a sweetheart. Definitely not a curmudgeon.

After Abby left, I opened the back door and called in my two dogs, Brandy, a collie, and Archie, a large black dog of uncertain heritage who looks like a small bear. They had been outside for a short morning romp.

Once they were back in the house, I poured another cup of coffee as my thoughts wandered to the Pendwell Wildlife Refuge, and questions

1

began flashing through my mind. What happened to the missing animals? Were they safe or had they met a nefarious end?

* * * * *

Traveling on the Long Island Expressway during the morning rush is better than caffeine at jolting me awake. It was normally a thirty-minute drive from my home to the refuge, but today it was taking close to an hour.

My destination was located in the Village of Wateredge, part of Long Island's infamous Gold Coast. As I exited the expressway, the scenery soon became horse farms, where sleek thoroughbreds grazed in grassy paddocks, abutting estates whose upkeep could support entire third world nations.

Moments later, I pulled into the dirt parking lot by the entrance to the Pendwell Wildlife Refuge and made my way up the wooded path toward the main building. As I inhaled the scent of pine amid the cool spring breeze, I felt my blood pressure lower.

Suddenly, I spotted a woman rushing down the path. Her thumbs moved across her phone like two bugs on Prozac. With her head down, she wasn't paying attention to her surroundings.

"Watch out," I yelled as she came within a few feet of me. I jumped to the side, avoiding a head on collision, but our bodies brushed together.

It is illegal in New York State to text while driving. The law should apply to texting while walking too.

"I'm so sorry," she said without looking up while she continued texting. She finished and stuffed the phone in her pocket. "Oh, are you the reporter who's writing a story about the refuge?"

I was impressed until I realized she probably spotted the *Animal Advocate Magazine* logo on my tote bag.

"Yes. I'm Kristy Farrell, and I'm here to—"

"Victoria Buckley Pendwell," she interrupted. "This place is named after my late husband's family. He donated the land, and I'm chair of the board of trustees. We're the governing board."

I quickly sized up Victoria Pendwell. She looked to be in her early fifties, but I'd read somewhere she was sixty-two. Her short ash-blonde hair was perfectly coiffed, her make-up impeccable, and her sea-green silk top and cream colored linen pants fit beautifully on her tall, slender body.

"Everyone here is talking about the feature story you're writing." Victoria's face clouded. "But I hope you are going to focus on more than the missing animals. Besides rehabilitating injured wildlife, we have nearly three hundred acres of unspoiled woods, a conservation center, and a world class education program."

"Don't worry," I assured her. "My article is about the wildlife refuge as a whole. The rehabilitation center and missing animals are only a small part." But I silently admitted the disappearance of these creatures was what my readers would be most curious about—as was I.

Victoria reached into her designer handbag and pulled out a business card. "Call me. There's a lot I can tell you about this place. We can do lunch."

"I'll be in touch. But now, I better get going. I have an interview with the director in less than five minutes, and—"

"Don't worry." Victoria waved her hand dismissively as she turned away. "If you're late, tell her you were talking with me."

Victoria's phone beeped. She grabbed it from her pocket and strutted back down the path to the parking lot, her head down, thumbs moving.

When I entered the administration building, no one was behind the reception counter, but there was a bell next to a sign that read, *Ring for Help*. That's what I did.

A young woman emerged from one of three glass-enclosed cubicles located about twenty feet behind the counter. She made her way toward the front. I judged her age to be early thirties.

"I'm Melissa Modica, the director," she said. "You must be the magazine writer." As she popped open the counter gate, I noticed she was smaller than me, which is rare, since I'm only five feet.

I introduced myself and trailed her to the middle cubicle, the largest of the three. The other two offices were unoccupied. Melissa motioned me to a seat in front of her desk while she slid into a chair behind it. "Now, how can I help you?"

"Your biography on the refuge's website is impressive," I said. "It appears you rapidly climbed up the career ladder when you were at the

United States Fish and Wildlife Service. But you left two years ago to become director here. Why did you give up a spot in big federal agency with lots of room for advancement to run this place?"

Melissa sat back. "My next promotion at Fish and Wildlife required me to move to Washington D.C., where I would have been nothing more than a pencil pusher. Here, I'm hands on, which I love."

I asked Melissa to tell me more about her responsibilities at the wildlife refuge as well as the duties of other staff members.

"We're mostly staffed by volunteers," she said. "There are only three part timers and three full-time employees, including myself. The other full timers are Elena Salazar, our education coordinator, and George Grogin, who works as our wildlife rehabilitator and animal care director. Elena and George they have the offices on either side of me."

"I have an appointment to see George after I finish interviewing you."

"I'm sorry. George is out sick today. He should have called you," she said in a matter of fact tone.

"Nothing serious, I hope."

Melissa shook her head, her sandy colored hair moving side to side. "No. He's a little under the weather. He promised me he'd be here tomorrow at ten to release a turtle back into its pond. The turtle had injured his foot, but it's now healed. Why don't you come and take a picture for your magazine? Then I can reschedule you for a interview with him after the release."

"Perfect. And perhaps I could also talk to Elena Salazar. I've been trying to make an appointment, but she hasn't called me back yet."

Melissa frowned, shook her head, and mumbled two curse words under her breath. "She should have called you," she said. "I'll make sure she does."

Melissa seemed much more upset about Elena's failure to contact me than about George's failure to let me know he would be out today. I found that strange.

She then talked about the three part-time employees. Two were animal care attendants, and the other was a wildlife rehabilitator who covered when George was not here.

I changed the topic. "Are there any suspects in the case of the missing animals?" I asked.

4

"Not so far."

"Where were these animals kept?"

"Right inside this building. The wildlife rehabilitation facility is down the left wing." Melissa picked up a paper clip, straightened it out, and bent it back and forth until it snapped.

"How could someone get in?"

"The building is locked at night. When I arrived the morning after the break-in, I found a broken window on the side of the building. The police think that's how the thief entered." She fiddled with the silver owl pendant on her necklace.

"Was the thief able to get the animals out that window?" I asked.

"No. The police believe that once inside the building, the thief unlocked the front door and carried the animals out that way."

"I heard on the news that not all the animals were taken."

"That's true. The ones stolen all had the most serious injuries and health problems." Melissa sighed as she adjusted the collar on her jade-green shirt. "The animals almost ready for release such as the turtle were left alone. I've no idea why."

I couldn't think of a reason either. I asked a few more questions and then ended the interview.

"See you tomorrow at the turtle release," Melissa said, escorting me out of her office.

I started to head for the path back to the parking lot when a young, dark-haired woman rushed past me. She was frowning and muttering under her breath. She blew into the administration building, slamming the door behind her.

I scurried back inside and peeked.

Melissa and the dark haired woman stood in front of Melissa's office. Their backs were to me, but they talked loudly, and I could hear their conversation.

"She gave me her commitment," the dark-haired woman said.

"No way, Elena. She wouldn't dare," Melissa replied. "If you or she tries, it will be over my dead body."

* * * * *

The next morning I drove to the Pendwell Wildlife Refuge for the turtle release and interview with wildlife rehabilitator George Grogin. Upon arrival, I noted a police car and a crime scene investigation vehicle.

Is this about the missing animals?

Within seconds, that thought disappeared.

The County Medical Examiner's van pulled into the parking lot.

CHAPTER 2

I waited until a man and a woman emerged from the van. I followed, maintaining a discreet distance, while wondering what happened. Did a jogger succumb to a heart attack? Did a child fall into a pond and drown? I inhaled deeply, hoping to steady my nerves.

I passed the clearing on my right where the administration building was located. I continued trailing the two members of medical examiner's staff until another clearing came into view—this one bordered by yellow crime scene tape.

I gasped.

Not far from where I stood, spread out in full view, was a body with blood covering much of the head. The body was face down, but I recognized the small build, sandy hair, and jade-green shirt.

Melissa Modica.

I tasted bile. I wanted to scream, but I slapped my hand in front of my mouth.

After regaining my composure, I surveyed my surroundings. Three people wearing jackets, emblazoned in the back with the words *Crime Scene Investigator*, were near the front of the clearing. One was bent over the body, and the other two appeared to be examining the ground near Melissa. When the medical examiner's team approached, the investigator next to the body rose up and started talking. I couldn't make it all out, but I did hear him say, "Blow to the head."

"Oh, no" I mumbled when I spied two homicide detectives I knew.

Detective Adrian Fox, a thirty-something African American, stood on the side of the clearing, near a large pond. He was talking with the woman I saw yesterday outside Melissa's office. Melissa had called this woman Elena, so I assumed this was Elena Salazar, the education coordinator.

I couldn't hear what they were saying, but Elena was gesturing wildly with her arms. I flashed back to Melissa's comment yesterday to Elena—"over my dead body"—and, I shuddered.

The other detective, Steve Wolfe, had marched over to the body and was now barking orders to the medical examiner's staff, who didn't seem pleased. As Wolfe turned around, the woman in the medical examiner's jacket shook her head.

I sighed. Wolfe and I had a history. He was a bully who had gone to school with my younger brother Tim, constantly picking on him. Granted Tim was the classic nerd who might as well have worn the sign "Kick Me" on his back. I had recently solved two of Wolfe's murder cases, which only irritated him more.

Wolfe spied me and headed in my direction, his face turning the color of a beet. His gray pants hung below his pot belly, his glacier-blue eyes as cold as ever, and he wore the same annoying grin as when he was a kid that made me want to slap his face.

"What happened?" I asked.

"I'm here about a dead squirrel," he said. "What do you think happened?"

"That's Melissa Modica," I said.

He narrowed his eyes. "You know her—"

"I'm doing a story on the wildlife refuge and—"

"How come whenever you do a story, people die?"

Not really a nice way to put it.

"Who found the body?" I asked.

"Three hikers."

"What caused—"

"This is none of your business. This is a crime scene." He pointed a fat finger at me. "You need to leave."

"I'm behind the yellow tape," I argued.

I didn't think his face could get any redder, but it did. "Stay out of my way." He spun around and stomped off toward the side where Detective Fox appeared to be jotting something in a notepad. Elena Salazar was no longer there. I had no idea where she went.

I had lots of questions, but I wasn't getting answers from Wolfe. The crime scene investigators were packing up. Maybe I'd have better luck with them.

"When was she killed?" I asked the one investigator, who looked young enough to appear on an acne remedy commercial.

"We need to wait for the autopsy."

"Do you have an approximate time of death?"

"Sorry. We can't talk to the public."

I sighed. I'd have to get the answers somewhere else.

I wondered why Melissa had been at the clearing. I glanced at the pond, guessing this was where the rehabilitated turtle would be released. Did Melissa come here early to check things out before the release? But what would she be checking?

My thoughts were interrupted as the medical examiner's team passed by me carrying a stretcher with the covered body. I figured I might learn something if I listened to their conversation. Eavesdropping was one of my talents.

I scratched my theory that Melissa had arrived early to check conditions for the turtle release when one of the attendants said, "I can't imagine why anyone would be here at midnight."

CHAPTER 3

I headed back to the administration building, hoping someone would be there—someone who might offer an explanation as to why Melissa Modica ventured into the woods late last night.

When I arrived, the building door was unlocked. I stepped inside and upon seeing no one, I rang the bell on the reception counter.

"Be with you in a minute," a booming voice called back.

I was about to ring again when a rail-thin African American with a gray beard approached the reception counter. I judged him to be in his early sixties.

"I'm Kristy Farrell." I extended my arm across the counter for a handshake. "I'm the reporter from *Animal Advocate Magazine*."

"George Grogin, wildlife rehabilitator," he said. "We have an interview today." As he spoke, I noticed a large gap between his two top front teeth.

He popped open the latch to the counter gate and motioned me to enter.

"I didn't know if today's interview would be canceled because of Melissa," I said.

George shook his head. "Nope. As they say, the show must go on."

"But if you're upset—"

"I'm okay. Follow me."

As George spun around, he stumbled and almost fell into a metal shelf holding what appeared to be cleaning supplies.

"I better watch where I'm going," he said, grinning sheepishly.

I wondered if George could provide information about the murder, but he seemed anxious to get down to our interview. I'd need to weave questions about Melissa's death into our conversation.

We headed toward the back and veered down the left wing of the building, where I heard chirping. Upon entering a large room, I spotted an aviary housing four fuzzy baby birds, the source of the noise.

While my nose adjusted to the smell of animals in a closed environment, I glanced around, noting five baby possums, three young rabbits, a woodchuck, owl, woodpecker, and turtle. I also spotted a boarded up window on the side. Probably the window where the thief had entered.

A thought flashed through my mind. I asked George, "Could Melissa's death be related to the missing animals?"

I recalled how she had fidgeted with her necklace and fiddled with the collar on her shirt when we discussed the topic. Before this, she hadn't appeared nervous.

"What if she received a ransom note about the animals and was meeting someone in the clearing?" I asked.

The look on his face said I probably watched too many reruns of *Murder, She Wrote.*

"I doubt it," he said. "Melissa was a 'by the book' person. If she received a note, she would have contacted the police."

A "by the book" person wouldn't be in the forest at midnight.

"Our patients fall into two categories." George changed the subject before I could ask another question. "The owl, woodpecker, woodchuck, and turtle had been injured. The baby possums, the rabbits, and birds are orphans who can't yet survive on their own.

"In the case of the possums, the dead mother was discovered on a road outside the refuge. She'd been hit by a car. Someone driving by called us. The babies were still in her pouch, and by some miracle, still alive. I bottle fed them and kept them warm. They'll be released in another few weeks."

George told me about all the animals and what brought each one here. He expected them all to be released back in the wild except for the owl. Merlin, as he had named him, had damaged his wing and would not be able to fly again. He'd have a permanent home here.

"Merlin will serve as a goodwill ambassador as part of Elena's education program."

"What's happening with the turtle release?"

"Since the pond is in the midst of the crime scene, I can't do anything today. Hopefully, I can release him tomorrow. If you want pictures, call me in the morning, and I'll tell you if it's on."

"Thanks. I was also wondering if there's any news regarding the missing animals."

He frowned. "From what I hear, the police haven't a clue."

"Are steps being taken to prevent this from happening again?" I asked. "Repairing the security cameras, which I understand were broken? Installing alarms?"

"The security cameras have been fixed." He snorted. "As for alarms, that all depends on the new director. Melissa didn't seem overly concerned. She did nothing."

"That surprises me. When I interviewed Melissa, she seemed caring and concerned. She said she accepted the position here because she wanted to be hands-on."

"Hands on." He clenched his fists, and his voice got louder. Several animals scurried to the back of their cages. "She came here because she didn't want to leave Long Island. She takes care of her parents and moving away would create hardships."

He paused, and then continued in a normal voice. "When Melissa started here as director, she was okay, but recently she changed. She spent most of her time recently arguing with everyone, including Victoria Pendwell."

"The chair of the board of trustees?"

He nodded. "Yup."

I had read the information on the Pendwell Wildlife Refuge's website, so I had a general idea of how the place operated. "Wasn't Melissa appointed director by the board of the trustees?"

"Yup."

"Didn't they have the power to fire her?"

"Yes and no."

I smiled. "What does that mean?"

"She was appointed by the trustees, but they gave her a three-year contract. Without a major reason, they couldn't fire her until that contract ended."

"What was Melissa's problem with Victoria?"

"They differed on how to run the facility, especially on how to spend the money. Personally, I think it had to do with Victoria's son."

"Her son?"

"Yeah. Austin Pendwell. I think Austin and Melissa dated when she first started here, but I'm not entirely sure. Anyway, Austin started going with Elena Salazar, the education coordinator, about a year ago, and they became engaged last November. The engagement happened about the same time Melissa and Victoria started butting heads. Rumor is Victoria now wanted Elena to be the director."

"But if Melissa had a contract—"

"The chair of the board of trustees has a lot of power. She could make life difficult for Melissa." He shook his head. "But Melissa gave as well as she got."

"What did she do?"

"Melissa questioned Victoria publicly about how the board approved certain contracts. She even suggested at one point that the one of the bids was…" He paused and frowned. "Sorry it's on the tip of my tongue." Finally, he said, "Rigged."

"That's a serious accusation," I said. "Bid rigging is criminal."

Was the accusation true?

CHAPTER 4

The next morning, after phoning George Grogin and confirming the time and place of the turtle release, I sped off to the Pendwell Wildlife Refuge. I wondered who would be the new director. My story would now include how the murder affected the operation of the refuge and its programs.

Since I arrived early, I made my way to the administration building to see what I could find out from the staff. Sitting in the middle cubicle—Melissa's old office—was Victoria Pendwell, who appeared to be rummaging through the desk.

I rang the bell. She turned her head, rose from her chair, and strutted to the counter.

"I'm so glad you're here," she gushed while unlatching the counter gate. "I want you to know there will be no change in our daily operations. Our rehabilitation center and education program will continue, and we will make sure the woods stays in its current pristine condition."

"Who will take over the duties of the director until a new one is appointed?" I asked once we reached Melissa's old cubicle.

"A permanent director will be appointed at the board of trustees meeting next Wednesday." Victoria slid into the swivel chair behind the desk.

"Wednesday? A week from today?" I plopped down in a straight-back chair facing her. "Is that enough time to call for résumés and schedule interviews?"

"That's not always necessary. We have someone here at the preserve to fill Melissa's shoes. Elena Salazar is perfectly qualified, and it would be an easy transition. We also have a retired teacher who is currently

14

a volunteer here. We plan to hire her to take over Elena's education duties."

"Will the board members support this?"

Her grin reminded me of the Cheshire cat. "I don't anticipate a problem."

"Isn't Elena engaged to your son?"

Victoria's eyes darkened to black, her lips tightened, and her face froze. But she quickly regained her composure and smiled. "Yes. That's how I got to know Elena and discover what wonderful talents she has. She shouldn't be denied an opportunity because of her relationship with my son."

"What about the future of this place?" I asked, changing topics. "Do you think you'll lose visitors because of a murder on its grounds?"

Victoria appeared to mull this over. "Maybe initially. But after a few weeks, I'm sure everything will be back to normal. After all, the murder had nothing to do with the refuge."

"But the body was found here."

"What I mean is it has nothing to do with anyone connected here. I understand the number one suspect is Melissa's ex-boyfriend, Jeremy Toth."

"I didn't know the police had a suspect yet."

"They do now. Jeremy and Melissa broke up nearly three months ago. Supposedly, he wasn't happy about it and wanted to get back together. I heard he was stalking her, and that she sought an order of protection." Victoria waved her hand dismissively. "I'm sure he's the one."

Before I could ask another question, Victoria called out, "We were just talking about you. Come in."

Elena Salazar strolled into the cubicle.

Victoria introduced us and explained how I wanted to interview the staff for my story on the wildlife refuge.

"I'm free now," Elena volunteered.

"Then why don't you conduct the interview in here?" Victoria winked at her future daughter-in-law. "This will be your office soon enough."

Victoria rose from her chair and motioned for Elena to sit there. "I have an appointment with the caterer regarding our next fund raiser, so I have to leave now. Kristy, don't hesitate to call me."

With that, she was gone, and Elena started talking about her education program. She invited me to a presentation she was making next week to a fourth grade class.

I wanted to ask Elena about the fight she had the other day with Melissa, but I didn't. Instinct told me she would clam up. Right now, she was a talker, and I needed that.

"I hear congrats are in order," I said. "Victoria Pendwell told me you're slated to be the new director."

"Yes, and I can't wait to get started. I've got lots of plans."

"Such as?"

"Melissa spent most of our budget on intra-structure. I want to focus on outreach. I'm going to start an 'adopt an animal' program in the schools as well as a contest to select a forest animal who will serve as a symbol of the wildlife refuge. Both activities will require a major marketing campaign."

"Sounds like you thought about this for some time."

She frowned. I wondered if she thought she had said too much.

"Truth be told," she finally said, "Victoria wasn't happy with Melissa lately. Victoria was talking about making changes way before Melissa's death. So, yes, I'd been planning this for a while."

"What types of changes?"

"She planned on having the board of trustees adjust the budget and put a large percentage directly into my education and outreach program. This way, Melissa couldn't touch it."

CHAPTER 5

It was five minutes past ten o'clock when I left Elena and hurried to the clearing for the turtle release. I hoped George would wait until I arrived, so I could get a good picture for the magazine.

George was the only one by the pond. Next to him was a large container, which I assumed held the turtle.

"Take your time," he said with a grin as I waved to him and picked up my pace. "It's just you, me, and Freemont here."

Freemont? It seemed George liked to give names to his patients.

George opened the container, picked up Freemont, and set him down about two feet from the pond. I grabbed my phone from my tote bag and pressed the photo icon as the turtle slowly made his way into the water.

"This was an easy release," George said as the turtle submerged out of sight. "I once rehabilitated a young eagle and had to capture him in order to put him in a transporter cage to take him to be released. I chased him around his pen, but he did not want to be caught. He kept flying back and forth way above my head. Finally, he landed in a spot where I could nab him."

With Freemont back in his natural habitat, George and I made our way down the path back toward the administration building.

"I was talking to Elena Salazar before I got here," I told him. "That's why I was late. She doesn't seem to be a fan of Melissa either."

George furrowed his brow. "I don't want to give you the wrong impression. When Melissa first started here, she was fine. It's only lately that she became a problem."

"In what way?"

"During the last few months, she criticized everything I did. She was especially concerned with how I filled out my paperwork. I work hard, and my job is to save animals. So, maybe sometimes I do something incorrectly on a form."

He shook his head. "Something was bothering her. But I haven't a clue what it was. Enough talk about Melissa. Let me show you our newest addition."

Upon our arrival at the rehabilitation wing, George pointed out his newest patient—another turtle. This turtle had been brought in with a badly cracked shell. It had been found in the middle of a road about a mile and a half from the wildlife refuge. The turtle was in bad shape, but if it survived, it would be released in the woods off the side of the road where it had been discovered.

"Why not bring it to the pond in the refuge?" I asked.

"Turtles never travel beyond a mile of where they're born. They should be released back into their home environment."

I spent the remaining morning with George in the rehabilitation wing. He seemed dedicated and knowledgeable, but he was a little clumsy. He spilled the birdseed and dropped a water bowl he had just refilled.

George also provided me with his background although most of what he told me was on the refuge website. In addition to being a wildlife rehabilitator, he was also a veterinary technician. He'd worked in that capacity for Mancuso Veterinary Clinic for twenty years before taking this job.

At around noon, I left the building and made my way to the parking lot as the clouds overhead darkened and the wind began swirling leaves. A bolt of lightning flashed in the sky followed by the boom of thunder. I made it to my car seconds before the charcoal sky exploded with torrential rain.

I drove at a snail's pace out onto the main road. I had driven about a mile when I noticed a tailgater. He honked, obviously anxious for me to go faster. But Long Island's winding north shore roads were slippery when wet. I continued driving slowly. He honked again and came even closer.

I gripped the steering wheel tightly. The last thing I needed was a road rage incident.

The next intersection held a traffic light. I approached as the light switched to red. If I slammed on my brakes, the tailgater would rear-end me. Noting there were no cars on the crossroads, I made a quick decision and blew the red light. My tailgater did too.

There was a clearing off to the right, so I pulled over and let him pass. I sat shaking for a moment, then pulled back on the road and continued home.

"Crazy driver," I mumbled. "We both could have been killed."

CHAPTER 6

"Glad you're home early," I said to my husband as he sauntered into the house early evening. I was sitting by the kitchen table, my laptop in front. "Abby and Jason are coming for dinner."

"Pizza?"

"Sweet and sour shrimp and fried rice. Eggrolls, too. No pizza."

The two dogs, sprawled out on the floor on either side of me, began whimpering. Brandy flattened her ears against her head. I swear they understood what I said. Both dogs loved pizza.

"When will Abby and Jason be here?" Matt asked, glancing at his watch.

"I'm here now." Abby paraded into the house, the wind slamming the kitchen door behind her. "Jason's coming directly from work."

Abby stretched up to kiss her father who, at more than six feet tall, towered over her. I smiled. With her ebony hair, olive skin, molasses-colored eyes, and aquiline nose, our daughter had inherited her Greek looks as well as her height all from me.

Abby pulled up a chair after kissing me hello. "Half of Jason's family hasn't responded to the engagement party. What should we do?"

"RSVPs aren't due till the end of next week. The party is more than three weeks away, and some people always wait till the last day," I said to my normally easy-going daughter who I hoped wasn't becoming a bridezilla. "If anyone hasn't responded by the due date, you can make calls then."

"I also wanted to talk to you about my ring."

"Your engagement ring?"

Abby nodded and glanced down at her hand. "Since it's a family heirloom, everyone is telling me I should get an appraisal."

The ring was gorgeous. It belonged to Jason's grandmother, a feisty eighty year-old. Her only child, Jason's mom, had died five years ago. Jason was her only grandchild.

"You would inherit it anyway," she had told Jason. "I want you to have it now so I can see Abby enjoy it."

"An appraisal is a good idea," Matt said. "It probably increased in value over the years, so you need to be sure you have the right coverage."

Abby rose up and poured two glasses of red wine. She handed one to me and then slid back into her chair. "Now that the wedding business is out of the way, I want to hear more about the murder. Any clues? Theories?"

I shook my head. "No clues. As for theories, I'm wondering if it is connected to the missing animals."

"Why?"

"Because they're both crimes." I shrugged. "I don't know. Just a theory."

"What about suspects?" She sipped her wine.

"Supposedly, Melissa broke off a relationship with a guy named Jeremy Toth. I hear she was going to file an order of protection against him because he was stalking her. I don't know if the police are looking at anyone else, but I have some additional suspects is mind."

I told Abby and Matt about the fight I witnessed between Melissa Modica and Elena Salazar.

"I need to tell Detective Wolfe about their argument, but for the time being, I'm holding off. I want to get more information from Elena first."

"But you have to let him know," Matt said emphatically.

"I will. I promise. I just need a few days." I sipped my wine. "Then there is the wildlife rehabilitator, George Grogin. He had issues with Melissa too, and he didn't seem upset at her death."

"But is that enough reason to kill someone?" Abby asked.

I shrugged.

"Anyone else you consider under suspicion, Mom?"

My interview with George Grogin flashed through my mind.

"Yes." I nodded. "Melissa had an open feud with Victoria Pendwell.

21

Melissa publicly criticized the way Victoria, as chair of the board of trustees, was allocating money, especially when it came to contracts."

"But administrators like Melissa often have disagreement with members of the boards who oversee them," Abby argued.

"There's more to the story. Victoria was trying to push Melissa out as director so Elena could take that position. This all started after Elena became engaged to Austin Pendwell, Victoria's son."

"Austin Pendwell?" a booming voice called. My daughter's fiancé, Jason, stepped through the kitchen doorway.

"Do you know Austin?" I asked. Jason was an attorney as was Austin Pendwell.

"I met him, but I don't know him well." Jason grinned as he opened the refrigerator door and grabbed a beer. "We run in different social circles. But we do have a small overlap of acquaintances."

Jason had begun work two months ago as an assistant district attorney in white-collar crimes. Austin Pendwell was a partner in a major Long Island law firm that had been founded by his late father, Clifton Pendwell.

Jason pulled up a chair next to us. "Austin is almost certainly going to get the nod to run for the state senate seat being vacated by Senator Ridgeback who is retiring. I heard the announcement will be made within the next few weeks."

"Have you heard about his engagement to Elena?"

Jason nodded. "It's going to be a politically positive marriage for him. Senator Ridgeback's district has a heavy working class population. Elena's father was a plumber and her mother was a waitress. Elena Salazar would help him garner that vote."

"Fine. But she doesn't need to be the director of the wildlife refuge to do that."

"No. But as director, she could actively cultivate a large environmental vote too. Victoria is chair of the board. But everyone knows it's because her family donated the land and got a big tax write-off. Elena comes across as a true environmentalist and has lots of friends connected to environmental organizations."

"So, she can get support from the rank and file which Victoria probably can't do." I added.

I flashed back to what Elena had said about strengthening outreach and spending more on marketing. By doing so she would make a name for herself as well as the wildlife refuge.

I realized there was more to Victoria's motive for obtaining the directorship for Elena than just helping her future daughter-in-law.

"Are you investigating the murder?" Jason asked me.

"Of course, she's investigating," Abby said before I could reply.

Jason chuckled and said, "I thought she would. That's why—"

Jason's cell phone rang. He answered his call. "Wow!" he said after a few moments of listening to the person on the other end. "Thanks."

He ended the call and looked directly at me. "That was the medical examiner's office. I asked them to keep me posted on Melissa Modica's autopsy, because I knew you would be interested. The autopsy is finished, and it's now public information."

"She died from a blow to the head, right?" I asked, putting down my wine glass.

"Yes. But that's not all. She was pregnant."

CHAPTER 7

" So, what's the scoop on the murder?" called out Clara Schultheis as I stepped inside the *Animal Advocate* office the next morning. Clara was the resident gossip and conspiracy theorist. She was also administrative assistant to the editor, Olivia Johnson.

"And good morning to you," I said. I poured coffee from the office coffee pot into my mug.

"It's all over the news." Clara scratched her head oblivious to the mess it made of her short gray hair. "The medical examiner pinpoints the death between midnight and four. But the victim's watch, which broke when she fell, shows the time as twelve-fifteen. I have a theory. I think—"

"I better get to work." With coffee in hand, I scooted off to my cubicle.

I spent the next hour organizing my interview notes. I was about to get myself another mug of coffee when Clara barged into my office.

Clara never used the intercom when face-to-face was possible.

"There's someone here to see you, Kristy. She says her name is Linda Lau."

"Linda Lau?" I furrowed my brows. "I don't know a Linda Lau. What does she want?"

"She says it's about the murder. Oh, she also said to tell you she's Mei Lau's cousin."

"Ask her to come in."

Mei Lau was a former student of mine back from when I taught high school English. While I was writing an article on the Rocky Cove Zoo last year, Mei worked at the zoo as an intern. She had been murdered, and I discovered the identity of her killer.

Clara vanished from my office and a few seconds later returned with a woman who appeared to be in her early thirties.

"This is Linda Lau," Clara said.

"Please sit down."

Clara sat down.

"I meant Linda should sit down," I said smiling. "Shouldn't you get back in case Olivia needs you, Clara?"

"Right." Clara rose and scooted out of the office. Linda slid into the chair in front of my desk.

"I didn't know who else to talk to, but Mei always spoke so highly of you Mrs. Farrell. And you solved her murder." Linda brushed a tear from her eye.

"I didn't know Mei had a cousin. Were you at her funeral?" I asked.

"No. I was in Hong Kong, visiting other relatives. I couldn't get back in time. Mei had emailed me about you two days before she died. She told me you worked for *Animal Advocate*. That's why I was able to find you."

I nodded. "Is there a reason you wanted to find me?"

"Melissa Modica was my college roommate," Linda continued. "We were best friends. We always confided in each other."

"Did she tell you something that might explain her murder?"

"No. Not specifically. But despite what's all over the news, I know Jeremy Toth didn't do it."

"He's only a person of interest. The police haven't arrested him yet." I leaned forward. "But how can you be so sure he's not guilty?"

"I got to know Jeremy really well while he and Melissa were dating. Trust me. He's not a killer."

"That's not evidence."

"The news story about her seeking an order of protection against Jeremy is blown out of proportion. It's true that right after their break-up, Jeremy still reached out to Melissa, trying to get her back. Maybe he was too persistent. But after time, he realized it was over. He has a new girlfriend and is happy."

"Maybe he isn't as happy as you think."

Linda shook her head. "His social media posts for the last month have all been about Chloe—his new girlfriend. And I ran into Jeremy at a coffee shop about two weeks ago. We sat down and talked. Jeremy was getting on with his life."

"What about Melissa's pregnancy?" The autopsy results had been released to the media this morning, and her condition was a major item being broadcast across local news. "Was it Jeremy's baby?"

Linda's face clouded. "I didn't know she was pregnant until I saw today's news. I've been in San Francisco for an eight-week training course for work, and I returned yesterday. Sure, Melissa and I texted and phoned while I was away, but this isn't the type of thing you put in a message or talk about on a call."

"But it's likely he's the father, isn't it?"

"No. The timing doesn't work. According to the autopsy, she was six weeks pregnant. Jeremy and Melissa broke off more than three months ago. I'm positive they didn't have physical contact after that."

Then who was the father?

"I know Jeremy didn't commit the murder," Linda said after a brief silence. "And if the police arrest him, and he's convicted, the real killer will get away."

"Have you gone to the police with your, um, er, theories?"

She nodded. "I spoke with a Detective Wolfe. He didn't seem interested. He's looking at the easiest target."

"Occam's razor," I muttered.

"What?" Linda stared at me quizzically.

"It's a problem solving principal meaning the simplest explanation is usually the right one?"

"Apparently, that is the philosophy of the police in this case. That's why I'm coming to you."

"Me?"

She nodded. "You solved Mei's murder. I'm asking you to please help find out who killed Melissa."

I leaned back. If Melissa's murder tied into the preserve, it would be important for my story. If it didn't… well, instinct told me, it did. I flashed back to my daughter's comment last night. "Of course, she's investigating." I smiled. Abby knew me well.

"Okay, Linda. I only met Melissa once. First impressions aren't always correct. Tell me about the Melissa you knew."

"Melissa is—was serious. In college, some of my other friends didn't think she was a fun person. She studied while others partied. She was dedicated to the environment and her career. Her only other outlet was hiking and running. She was a track star in high school and college. She still ran every morning before work."

"What about dating? Had there ever been someone besides Jeremy? A serious relationship?"

Linda shook her head. "No. She dated, but her dates were few and far between until Jeremy came onto the scene. With the exception of Jeremy, I've never known her to go out with the same guy more than three or four times. They never lived up to her expectations."

Linda sat back and smiled. "I remember when she went out once with Austin Pendwell. It was about two years ago, when she first started working at the wildlife refuge. He was considered one of Long Island's most eligible bachelors. She found him boring."

"Did she have any other friends she might have confided in about her pregnancy? If we had an idea about the father—"

My intercom rang. It was Clara.

"Just a reminder," she said. "The staff meeting in the conference room begins in two minutes. Olivia is headed in there now."

"I have to go," I said to Linda while rising from my chair. "But we'll talk more." We exchanged phone numbers.

"I'll try to think of anyone Melissa may have told about her pregnancy," Linda said. "But I think her murder may have to do with her problems at work."

I wanted to ask Linda what she meant, but I couldn't be late to the staff meeting. My editor was a stickler for punctuality. I would question Linda at another time.

"Are you going to the wake?" I asked as we headed out of my cubicle. "It's tomorrow evening."

"Yes. Are you going? You didn't know her that well."

"I'll be there. I want to pay respects. Plus, people let their guard down at a wake. It's a good place to uncover secrets."

CHAPTER 8

I pulled into the parking lot of Abbott Funeral Home. It was the first night of the wake for Melissa.

I signed the visitor's book and stepped into a room where the smell of lilies wafted through the air. I estimated more than two dozen people in attendance.

An elderly couple, who were standing near the casket, greeted those in line. The woman was dabbing her eyes with her handkerchief. The man stood stoically, but I could see the grief spread across his face. I guessed they were Melissa's parents.

I offered my condolences and said a short prayer in front of the closed coffin. As I turned and started towards the back, I spotted Victoria Pendwell and Elena Salazar seated in the second row.

A man, wearing an expensively tailored gray suit, sat between them. I assumed it was Austin Pendwell. With his wavy, dark-brown hair and chiseled features, he possessed that perfect look—the type you see on a television anchorman.

Linda Lau sat in the fifth row. We made eye contact. She rose from her chair, and made her way toward me.

"Let's go in the back so we can talk," she said.

As we wandered toward the rear, she whispered, "Can you believe the hypocrisy of the Pendwells and Elena sitting up front like that. Despite their solemn expressions, I'm sure Victoria and Elena are doing their happy dances."

Linda nodded to a freckled faced young woman with short, curly red hair. The woman, who had just risen from a seat and was heading toward the door, nodded back, stopped, and said, "It's good to see you again,

Linda, but, oh, how I wish it wasn't here."

"Me too." They hugged.

The red head wiped a tear from her face and said, "We'll stay in touch. I'm leaving Monday on a two week camping trip, but when I get back we'll get together." She exited the room.

"That's Erin Leahy. She's Melissa's friend from high school," Linda said.

"Are you friends too?"

"Erin and I had gone out together a few times with Melissa but not a lot. Two different groups—high school and college. I know Erin said we'll keep in touch, but don't people always say things like that at funerals?"

"Do you think Melissa confided in Erin? Either about the pregnancy or the problems at the wildlife refuge?"

Linda shrugged. "I don't think so, but I don't know. I'm pretty sure their friendship consisted of getting together to run. Erin was on the high school track team with Linda. Occasionally, they got together for dinner. But I don't think their relationship was deeper than that."

"In my office, you said Melissa's murder could be related to problems at work. What type of problems?"

"People problems," she said as we sat down in the back row. "Her staff. The board of trustees."

I was about to ask her to be more specific when I spotted George Grogin entering the room. As he headed to pay his respects, I leaned over to Linda. "George told me Melissa only took the job at the wildlife refuge so she could stay on Long Island and take care of her parents. Is that true?"

"That was one reason, but she also thought running the refuge was a fantastic opportunity. She'd be a big fish in a little pond. She felt she could really change things. It was her dream job."

"George said she changed."

"Not at all." Linda sighed. "George changed. And there was friction between the two. Melissa talked to me about it. I'm director of human resources for a big international company, so I deal with lots of issues relating to supervision."

"What was the problem?"

"Melissa told me George had been excellent when she first came to the wildlife refuge, but suddenly his work became sloppy. Once he forgot to hand in an order form for a specific type of bird feed, and the refuge almost ran out of it. Another time he checked the wrong box on a requisition form and wound up ordering incorrect medical supplies. Melissa also said a volunteer had to remind him twice to give an injured fox its medicine."

Linda paused before continuing. "There was another issue too. George was suddenly having temper outbursts. He supposedly blew up at one of the animal care attendants. He claimed this man was making too much noise when he chewed gum." Linda shook her head. "Can you believe that?"

"And Melissa had no idea what caused this change?"

"No. I'm guessing he was distracted by a personal problem. That's often what causes it. It could also be burnout from seeing so many animals die because of human cruelty or carelessness. Whatever it was, I told her to talk to him and document everything. If things didn't get better, she might have to take disciplinary action, including firing him."

"Tell me about Austin," I said. "You said Melissa went out with him once and found him boring."

"Melissa claimed it was one of the worst dates of her life. She said he was full of himself. He asked her out again, and she refused."

I guessed he wasn't the father of her unborn child.

"What about Elena Salazar?"

"Elena wanted Melissa's job, and she made no bones about it." Linda looked up. "Oh, here's Jeremy Toth."

I turned my head and spotted a young man, slight of build, with light brown shaggy hair and thick-rimmed glasses. He appeared to be in his early thirties.

"I'm glad he was able to come," Linda added. "Jeremy owns a food truck and was scheduled to be at the Community Council's Spring Festival tonight and the rest of this weekend."

"A food truck?"

"*Crepes Galore*. He does all types of crepes, but his specialty is dessert crepes. It's gotten great reviews. The food bloggers love it."

"Does he have someone to run it when he's not there?"

Linda nodded. "Jeremy has a partner, who gave him half the money to start up the business, but he only works in the truck when Jeremy has an emergency. He's probably there now. Or maybe his new girlfriend, Chloe, is running it. I heard she works the truck with him."

Jeremy embraced both of Melissa's parents, knelt in front of the casket, and made the sign of the cross. He stayed there a few minutes until he finally leaned over and kissed the closed coffin. He rose up to leave.

"Jeremy," Linda called softly as he passed by us. "I want you to meet—"

"Not now, Linda." He held up his hand. "Call me." He wiped a tear from under his glasses and exited the room. "I can't bear to be here."

CHAPTER 9

The smell of burning bread permeated the kitchen. I was leaning over the sink, scraping off the black top of an English muffin when my phone chimed. Abby's name popped up.

I grabbed the phone. "Hold on, Abby."

I placed the phone back on the counter, broke the muffin in half, and palmed the two pieces to Archie and Brandy, who never complained about my culinary ability.

"A few more guests have responded to the engagement party," Abby said when I returned to the phone. "But there's still a half dozen we haven't heard from. One of them is Jason's college roommate. Can you believe that?"

"You still have a week until responses are due."

"But I think—"

"I have an idea for the party," I interrupted.

"What idea?" She sounded suspicious.

"Instead of a traditional bakery cake for dessert, how would you like a crepe truck?"

"A what?"

"Crepe truck. A food truck specializing in crepes. There's one called *Crepes Galore* that makes delicious dessert crepes. My treat. Since we're having the party in the backyard, it's perfect. The truck pulls into the driveway and the guests—"

"I like it," Abby interrupted. "You've heard that they're good?"

"Yes. But I still want to check them out. The truck is participating in the Community Council Spring Festival today. Your dad and I were planning on going there tonight. Why don't you and Jason join us?"

"Perfect. Let's meet at five by the Ferris wheel. It's the easiest place to find."

I agreed and said good-bye. About ten minutes later, my phone trilled.

"And what happens if the crepe truck owner lands in jail before my engagement party?" Abby asked. "MOM, did you really think I wouldn't check out the website for *Crepes Galore?* I saw it's owned by Jeremy Toth and—"

"He has a partner. If he did get arrested, his partner would fill in."

"But hiring him for the party is just a pretense so you can question him about Melissa, right?"

"Consider it multi-tasking."

"I don't know—"

"It's a great idea for the party, but I'd like to try out some of the crepes first," I interrupted before she could reject the idea. "And, yes, I also thought I might get some answers about Melissa's murder."

"You intend to question him at the festival?" Abby asked. "Don't you think he'll be too busy?"

"Of course. But I can set up an appointment for a later date to discuss catering your party. That's when I can question him."

"But you don't need to set up the appointment in person. That's what phones and computers are for."

"I've heard that Jeremy's new girlfriend works with him on the truck. I want to see how the two mesh together at work. Body language tells a lot. It was obvious from the funeral that Jeremy still had deep feelings for Melissa. Does he really love this new woman? Or is he still pining for Melissa?"

"But why does this matter?" I heard the skepticism in my daughter's voice.

"What if Jeremy isn't over Melissa? He might feel that if he can't have her no one should. Or perhaps his new girlfriend was jealous and committed the murder."

"Especially if Melissa's baby was his," Abby added.

* * * * *

I knew something was wrong the minute Matt stepped into the house that afternoon, and I saw his face. He had returned from his veterinary office. I had been working from home all day, and was now in the living room reading my new mystery.

"What happened?" I asked, placing my book on the coffee table.

"I'm just so sick of these puppy mills." He slumped down into his favorite armchair.

"I had two cases today," he continued. "The first was a ten-month old golden retriever who stopped growing. It turns out the poor dog has pituitary dwarfism. He'll probably never get larger than the size of a beagle. And it also affects his organs. He'll be on hormone treatment the rest of his life, which probably won't be longer than five years. His littermates may have this too."

"This is because he's a puppy mill dog?" I asked.

"Yes. It could have been avoided if the puppy mill owner had conducted genetic testing before breeding the parents."

"Where did they get this pup from?"

"They purchased him from someone called 'Clay' on the Internet. He's a puppy mill broker."

"You had a second case today?"

He nodded. "The Millers got a rescue cocker spaniel that at one time was a puppy mill breeding dog. She is nearly blind, has two abscesses in her mouth, and spinal degeneration. It's so bad she can hardly walk."

My editor, Olivia Johnson, had wanted me to do another story—in addition to the one on the wildlife refuge. We had bantered around several ideas at the last staff meeting, but no decision had been made. Puppy mills might be just the topic.

I left Matt in the living room and headed into the kitchen where I booted up my computer. I composed a short email and sent it to Olivia.

* * * * *

The Community Council Spring Festival had been held every May for the past five years, and each year it appeared to get larger. The money raised was donated to worthy causes in town, such as the food pantry, the school scholarship fund, the historical society's restoration program, and the "no kill" animal shelter.

The railroad parking lot was filled with carnival rides and games as well as more than a dozen food trucks. The adjacent streets were lined with merchants selling products ranging from T-shirts to sea shell art to bath oils. Community and charitable organizations also had booths promoting their causes.

Abby and Jason met us at the Ferris wheel, and we headed out to find *Crepes Galore*. When we located the food truck, there were two lines, each about seven people deep. We joined the line that had Jeremy Toth at the other end. He was taking food orders.

Handling the customers on the second line was a woman who appeared to be in her early twenties. Her dark blonde hair was pulled back in a ponytail. I assumed this was his new girlfriend, Chloe.

"What can I get you?" Jeremy asked when it was our turn.

The posted menu offered a large selection. We all ordered a different type of crepe. I wanted coffee mascarpone cream. Matt selected peanut butter chocolate, while Abby chose fruit salsa, and Jason decided on a crepe with s'mores filling.

"Your website says you do private parties," I said while Jeremy poured the batter

He nodded. "That's a big part of my business."

"I'd like to talk to you about catering my daughter's engagement party."

"You want to talk now?" He made a sweeping gesture with his hands pointing to the crowd on both lines.

"Of course not. I just want to make an appointment for you to come to my house and discuss it."

"Why don't you make an appointment online?" he asked, grinning. "You could get it done now in the time it takes me to finish your crepes."

"Okay." I grabbed my phone. I'd just finished scheduling Monday night at seven when the young woman with the ponytail dropped a paper plate with a crepe while attempting to hand it to a customer.

"That was your fault," yelled the customer, a tall man with a scarecrow build.

"I know. I'm sorry. I'll make another."

"But now I have to wait."

"Hey buddy, accidents happen," Jeremy called. "How about we throw in a second crepe for free?"

"Yeah, okay."

Jeremy winked at the young woman. "Don't worry, Chloe. I've dropped plenty in my time."

She smiled and then mouthed, "I love you."

"Hey, hurry up with my pancakes," the customer yelled to Chloe.

Chloe went back to making crepes and Jeremy finished ours. As he handed me my plate, he stared at me for the first time, his eyes narrowing. "You look familiar. Do I know you?"

"I don't think so." I had been sitting next to Linda at the funeral wake when she spoke to Jeremy, but we hadn't been introduced. I didn't think he had noticed me, but perhaps I was wrong.

"This looks yummy." I grabbed the plate and hurried away. I didn't want to tip my hand.

"How are you going to do it, Mom?" Abby asked as the four of us found a nearby table and sat down.

"Do what?" I bit into my crepe. It was delicious.

"How are you going to bring up the topic of Melissa's murder when we meet with Jeremy?"

"Good question," Jason added. "I don't think Jeremy will want to talk about that to a stranger. Especially, since he's a suspect."

"I don't know yet. But I have two days to come up with a plan."

CHAPTER 10

After church on Sunday, I headed out to pick up Linda Lau for a visit with Melissa Modica's parents.

"They're private people," Linda said as we pulled away from her house. "But they want to know what happened to their daughter, and they trust me. I've known them for nearly fifteen years."

"How do they feel about you bringing me along?"

"Mr. Modica said no at first. But I reminded him of how you solved the murder of my cousin Mei, and he agreed to speak with you. Reluctantly."

I told Linda what type of information I wanted to solicit, figuring if she asked the tough questions, the Modicas would be more likely to answer.

The Modicas lived in a small Cape Cod home. When Linda and I arrived, Mr. Modica answered the door and ushered us into the living room filled with shelves overflowing with figurines. Framed family photographs hung on the wall. I sank into an upholstered chair that looked older than me. There were lace doilies on the arms.

As I glanced at my surroundings, my eyes focused on the giant, plasma television hanging on the opposite wall. It seemed out of place in this room that screamed 1950s.

Linda had told me that the Modicas were both in their early sixties, but they looked much older. I thought of the contrast with my septuagenarian mother, the "unofficial mayor" of her retirement community in Florida, who was now vacationing with friends in Las Vegas.

"You want to speak to us about Melissa's death," Mr. Modica said after we offered our condolences.

"How was Melissa acting recently?" Linda asked. "Did she seem worried or upset?"

"Yes." Mrs. Modica nodded. "She'd been upset for a while."

"Because she was ashamed," her husband added. "And she shamed us."

The pregnancy.

I took a deep breath. This was a touchy subject. I hadn't wanted to bring it up until the end of the visit after I had gained some rapport with the parents. But it looked as if the topic had to be addressed now. I nodded to Linda. She knew what to do.

"Did you know she was pregnant?" Linda asked

"No. I saw it in the papers. Not something a parent wants to read." Mr. Modica frowned.

"Do you have any idea who the father is?"

"The only one she was seeing was Jeremy Toth," said Mrs. Modica. "But they broke off before this would have happened. He seemed like such a nice boy."

Mr. Modica muttered something under his breath.

"Do you know why they broke off?"

"He was pushing for marriage, and she wasn't in love," Mrs. Modica said.

"After she broke with Jeremy, was there anyone new?"

Mrs. Modica shook her head. "No one. I wanted to introduce her to the nephew of an old friend of mine, but she wasn't interested. She came home every night at around six o'clock and stayed here."

"Can we change the subject?" Mr. Modica said. It was not a request.

"What about the refuge?" I asked. "Did Melissa ever talk about problems with the people where she worked?"

"No," Mr. Modica answered.

"She told me a little." His wife spoke softly. "She was frustrated with her staff. She wanted to fire someone whose name I don't remember. Melissa said this man was making lots of mistakes and taking time off."

George Grogin.

"But I think there was another person who bothered her more. A woman. Her name was Helene or Elaine."

"Elena?"

"That's it. Melissa said this woman wanted her job. She was undermining my daughter's work. Constantly criticizing her."

"Did Melissa ever mention Victoria Pendwell?" I asked.

"Yes. The chair of the board of trustees. At first, Victoria was trying to take my daughter's job away and give it to Elena."

"At first? What do you mean by that?"

"I think things got better at work."

Mr. Modica, who had been sitting quietly, spoke up. "Probably because of the raise. You don't give someone a raise and then take their job away."

"Raise? Melissa got a raise?"

Mrs. Modica pointed to the plasma television screen. "She had this installed for us three days before her death. She also bought us a brand new washer and dryer. When we asked her where she got the money, she said she had been given a big raise."

Linda and I exchanged glances.

"She planned to buy an expensive camera too," Mrs. Modica added. "She wanted to take good pictures when she hiked. Melissa loved to hike."

* * * * *

During the drive back home, Linda said, "Do you think she got a raise?"

I shook my head. "I've done tons of research on the Pendwell Wildlife Refuge. I know how it operates. If any member of staff received a raise it had to be approved by the board of trustees at their monthly meetings."

"How do you know it wasn't?"

"Because when I first received the assignment to write about the place, I read all of last year's board minutes. There were no raises."

CHAPTER 11

After draining my third cup of coffee, I palmed what remained from my bagel to the ever hopeful Brandy and Archie who had been waiting by the table, one on either side of me. As they gobbled the food, I booted up my laptop and headed to the website of *Crepes Galore* to find out more about Jeremy Toth.

According to the online biography, Jeremy had attended a prestigious culinary arts school in Chicago and after graduation worked for a small restaurant in that city. Originally from Long Island, he moved back five years ago and found employment as a chef at Noir Chat, a French café located in a community a few minutes from here. He left the café about a year ago to start his food truck business.

Next I Googled Noir Chat and found their exact location as well as the owner's name.

"Perfect," I mumbled as Matt sauntered into the kitchen. He worked at his veterinary hospital on weekends, so he usually took Mondays off. He poured a cup of coffee and sat down across from me.

"How would you feel about lunch at a charming French café today?" I asked.

He eyed me suspiciously. "What are you up to?"

"What makes you think I'm up to anything?"

"Whenever you're hatching a plan, you twirl your hair. You're doing that now. So, I repeat, what are you up to?" He grinned.

"I'd hardly call it hatching a plan. But I decided to lunch at the café where Jeremy Toth was employed. I want to talk to the staff. Maybe I can dig up more background."

"Sorry. I'd love to go, but I'm leaving for work soon. Abby needed time off, so I'm covering for her today."

I remembered. Abby had a ten o'clock dental appointment for a cleaning this morning.

Matt and I had coffee together, and he told me he was seeing a puppy purchased from the Bay Cove Pet Shop. The buyers had been told this pup was from a breeder. She wasn't. This four-month old Yorkshire terrier had been born in a puppy mill and had a terrible cough and respiratory problems.

A little while later, I phoned Abby, realizing she should be done at the dentist by now.

"Since you're off today how would you like lunch at a charming French café?" I asked. "My treat."

"What are you up to, Mom?"

Why does everyone say that?

I told her my plan.

"Okay. Sounds good. I just need to be back by three o'clock. Since I'm off work, I have an appointment to get my ring appraised."

"I'll pick you up in an hour. After we ended the conversation, I checked my email, deleting at least five from retailers selling merchandise. Finally, I came across an email from my editor. My suggestion to do a story on puppy mills had been approved.

I grabbed my phone and called a contact I had at the SANAN Society. SANAN stood for Stop Animal Neglect and Abuse Now.

Alan Dysart, the organization's director, picked up on the first ring. I explained about the puppy mill story I would be writing. There had been a lot written about the horrors of puppy mills, so he suggested I focus on the distribution chain. He claimed the public needed to know how these puppies were sold.

"People buy puppies thinking they come from legitimate breeders," he said. "The sellers are good at disguising a dog's origins. If we want to stop puppy mills, we need to wipe out the profit."

"Pet stores are a big source, right?" I asked.

"Yes. But there's been some success with these shops. Many no longer sell puppies but instead work with humane groups in offering rescue dogs for free. Unfortunately, there are still stores that do business with puppy mills. Bay Cove Pet Shop, located in the Bay Cove Mall on

Long Island, is one of them."

The Bay Cove Mall was about ten minutes from my house.

Alan continued. "Law enforcement can't legally stop the flow of dogs from puppy mills to pet stores. That will take legislation. But law enforcement can stop cruelty and abuse."

"I remember reading about an SPCA raid on a local pet store last year," I said.

"That's right. The Society for the Prevention of Cruelty to Animals conducts investigations of pet stores. On Long Island, it has the authority to seize dogs that are unhealthy, mistreated, or living under appalling conditions. In some states, their power is limited, and they work in conjunction with other branches of law enforcement."

"The SPCA is diligent and does a great job." He sighed. "Unfortunately, places like the Bay Cove Pet Shop often squeak through the cracks. The reputation of Bay Cove is that the standard of care is not what it should be, but no one has been able to get concrete evidence—yet."

As he talked, I jotted down information about the Bay Cove Pet Shop. It would be the first place I checked.

We continued talking. I heard the weariness in Alan's voice as he told me internet sales of dogs were increasing.

"Puppy brokers, who get the dogs they sell directly from puppy mills, put up websites where they often out and out lie about their dogs."

We talked for a few more minutes. When we finished, I went online and began my research into puppies for sale.

The first site I reached offered golden retriever puppies. According to the information posted, the dogs were all registered and came from top quality parents who were raised in a loving home. Interested parties were told to contact Clay at 555-1294.

The name struck a familiar chord. I recalled that one of Matt's clients had purchased a golden retriever from someone called Clay. This was the puppy that had pituitary dwarfism and would grow no bigger than a beagle.

I continued my search and came across sites for other breeds, ranging from teacup Yorkshire terriers to Great Danes. But several of these ads had something in common with the golden retriever web page. They all said, "Contact Clay at 555-1294."

I also found and checked out a site devoted to complaints from people who purchased puppies through Clay. These complaints included parasites, respiratory infections, bone issues, and aggressive temperaments. What shocked me most was that nearly a quarter of the people on this site had puppies that died within a month of purchase.

Business done over the internet is fast and faceless. With a click of a button, a puppy broker could reach thousands of potential customers. And the ability to disappear and pop up later made cyber commerce difficult to regulate.

I would ask Matt if his client who purchased the golden retriever from Clay would be willing to talk to me. But my story would also focus on pet stores. Later this week, I would check out the Bay Cove Pet Shop.

Right now, I shut down my computer, grabbed my tote bag, and headed out the door to pick up Abby for our lunch at the Noir Chat Café. Hopefully we would find out more about Jeremy Toth.

CHAPTER 12

"There it is," Abby pointed to a sign up the road. The sign featured a picture of a black cat, or in French, a Noir Chat.

We pulled into the parking lot. Since it was a warm spring day, we decided to eat outside. Noir Chat Café featured outdoor dining overlooking a garden ablaze with pink, purple, and crimson azalea.

"So, how are you bringing up Jeremy Toth?" Abby asked as we unfolded our white linen napkins and picked up our menus.

"By casual conversation with the wait staff."

"Do you really think they'll talk to us about him?"

I smiled. "You'd be surprised. If given the opportunity, people really do love to gossip. Here comes someone now."

A petite young woman with short ebony hair and piercing blue eyes poured water into our glasses. "I'm Sophia, and I'll be your server. Do you have any questions about the menu?"

"I'm thinking about one of the crepes. I just had one this weekend from a food truck called *Crepes Galore*. I believe the owner of that food truck worked here. Jeremy Toth?"

She nodded. "I started working here about two weeks before he left. He made great crepes but so does our current chef."

"Now what?" Abby asked after we gave our order, and Sophia headed toward the kitchen. "She wasn't here long enough to know him."

"I'm thinking." I furrowed my brow. "Got it."

"What?"

"Do you see that man in the navy blazer and white turtleneck talking to the couple at the corner table?"

Abby turned her head, and then nodded.

"I recognize him from the picture on the café's website. That's Philip Dubois. He's the owner of this place, and he's going table to table, greeting everyone. When he comes here, I'll pump him for information."

Philip left the table where he was talking and went inside.

"I'm sure he'll be out again," I said. "If not, I'll find him before we leave."

We both decided to go with soufflés instead of crepes. Once our entrees arrived, I told Abby about my visit with Melissa's parents and how it appeared that Melissa had come into money.

"Her parents claim she got a big raise, but I know that's not true," I said.

"Where do you think the money came from?" Abby asked.

"I'm not sure, but blackmail popped into my head."

"You're kidding?"

"I'm not. George Grogin told me Melissa accused Victoria of bid rigging. I'm thinking Victoria paid off Melissa to keep her quiet?"

"I guess it's possible, but how can you find out?" Abby took a bite of her cheese soufflé.

"I'm attending this week's board of trustees meeting. I'm hoping to ferret out information there." I shrugged. "It's a long shot."

"Could the blackmail have to do with her pregnancy? Maybe she wasn't blackmailing Victoria? Maybe Melissa was blackmailing Jeremy?"

"I don't think Jeremy got her pregnant. I'm told the timing doesn't work. But even if he is the father, he doesn't fit a blackmail victim's profile. He's a single guy. Plus, he just started a business, so I'm assuming he doesn't have a lot of extra cash."

"That means there's an unknown suspect? The man who got Melissa pregnant. He could be your blackmail victim."

"If Melissa was blackmailing someone, it's not going to be easy to find out." I shook my head and went back to devouring more of my lunch.

"You could mention your blackmail theory to Detective Wolfe," Abby suggested. "He might be able to trace the money."

"I know. But he'll probably dismiss my theory. He doesn't take kindly to suggestions." I grinned. "Especially coming from me."

"But Melissa's parents can verify that their daughter suddenly came into money. He's got to believe that."

"Maybe. I'll mention it to him. But even if he does investigate, I don't think he'll share what he finds."

We went back to our food and had finished eating when Phillip Dubois approached our table.

"*Bon Jour.* I hope you ladies enjoyed your meals," he said.

"Delicious," I replied. "I told our server I met your former chef last weekend at *Crepes Galore.*"

Philip's face darkened.

"Yes. I understand he has a food truck," Philip said, his nose wrinkling as if he smelled a skunk.

"It was actually very good. I guess you miss him here."

Philip took his time to respond. He appeared to choose his words carefully. "Jeremy was a decent chef. However, I think our current chef is better. I'm glad you enjoyed your lunch, ladies."

"He didn't seem enamored of Jeremy," Abby said after Philip departed.

"Jeremy may have left on bad terms."

"That's an understatement," muttered Sophia as she handed us the check.

"What do you mean?"

Sophia shook her head. "Nothing. I shouldn't have said anything."

"Please, it's important. His girlfriend is a friend of mine," Abby lied. "I want to make sure he's an okay guy."

Sophia paused. I didn't think she would answer. "Let's just say Jeremy's departure was a mutual decision. A week before he left, he and Philip had a huge argument."

"What happened?" I asked.

"We have a customer who is particularly demanding—a real pain in the neck. He has a strawberry allergy that causes him to break out in an itchy rash. Anyway, one night he complained that the onion soup didn't have enough cheese, and he sent it back. Philip overheard Jeremy saying he was going to put a bit of strawberry syrup in this man's dessert."

I gasped. "That's horrible."

"Jeremy said he was only kidding and would never do that. Most of the wait staff, including me, believed him. We knew he was joking. But Philip was horrified. He said if he ever heard Jeremy say something like that again, he'd call the police."

Abby and I exchanged glances. Whether he was kidding or not, it appeared Jeremy Toth had a vengeful streak.

CHAPTER 13

At home that evening, I quickly vacuumed the fur off the furniture—Brandy and Archie were in full shedding mode. Jeremy Toth, as well as my daughter and her fiancé, were expected in less than an hour. Abby and Jason arrived first.

"Do you have aspirin?" Abby asked. She ignored Archie and Brandy who milled around her legs vying for attention. "I have a mild headache."

"Sure. In the upstairs bathroom."

"Is everything okay?" I asked Jason as Abby left us to get the medicine. Abby rarely had headaches.

"Abby told me that other than the headache she feels fine, but I don't know." He greeted the two dogs who had turned their focus on to him. "She's been quiet since she got home tonight. Distracted."

The doorbell rang as Abby came back downstairs.

I swung open the door, and Jeremy Toth stepped into the room. Brandy and Archie bounded toward him, tails wagging.

"Hi guys, I'm glad to see you too." He put his briefcase on the floor, crouched down, and rubbed the dogs under their chins. Their tails wagged faster, and Archie began giving our visitor a thorough face washing.

I smiled. This was a good sign. In my opinion, dogs are great judges of character, although Brandy and Archie would probably befriend a serial killer.

"I'll put them in the back," I said. "Otherwise we will get nothing done. Let's go to the kitchen."

I pulled doggie treats out of the jar in the kitchen, opened the side door, threw out the treats, and the dogs scampered into the yard.

Matt, who had been rearranging things in the garage, joined us, and we sat around the kitchen table. I still didn't have a plan on how I'd bring up Jeremy's relationship with Melissa. I would have to wing it.

Jeremy pulled up his website on the iPad he had been carrying in his briefcase. He started talking about the various party packages available. Jason, Matt, and I asked questions, but Abby was not paying attention. She appeared to be focused on her ring.

Was she having second thoughts about the marriage?

"I like package C and D the best. What about you, Abby and Jason?" I asked. "It's your party."

"They're both great, but I think I prefer C. It includes the s'mores crepes. They're delicious," Jason answered. "Abby?"

"Either is fine." She was not enthusiastic.

"Before we sign a contract, there's something I'd like to discuss with you, Jeremy. I was at Noir Chat Café for lunch today. I heard about the incident you had with the owner about putting strawberry syrup in the dessert of a customer with an allergy—"

Jeremy slammed his hand on the table. His face turned purple and his eyes narrowed. "If Phillip Dubois is talking about this, I'll sue. It was all a joke, and he should know that."

""Whoa!" I held up my hands. "It wasn't Phillip who told me. The person who brought this up said everyone knew it was a joke. But still, isn't this in bad taste?"

Jeremy sighed and shook his head. "Maybe. But people in the food industry do joke about this. It's our way of taking out our frustrations with demanding and cranky customers. But we would never do it."

He paused. "Look, it would be stupid of me to do something like this. If that customer became sick and commented on social media, it would hurt me and the restaurant. And the police could bring charges against me."

"That makes sense," I admitted

I signed the contract for the crepe truck and wrote a check for the deposit. Jason thanked me, and Abby followed suit.

"By the way, Jeremy, you asked me the other day if we met before," I said, thinking this might be the best way to segue into the murder. "We were never introduced, but I was with Linda Lau at Melissa's wake."

"I knew you looked familiar. How do you know Linda and Melissa?"

"Linda's cousin was a former student of mine, and I met Melissa when I interviewed her for a story I'm writing on the Pendwell Wildlife Refuge. I work for a magazine called *Animal Advocate Magazine*." I hesitated. "I know you dated Melissa."

"Everyone knows that," he said drily. "It's been in the news."

I nodded. "You'd been mentioned as a person of interest because of your relationship. Linda told me you were over Melissa. But it didn't look like that at the wake."

He sighed. "I loved her. But I was over her if you can understand that. I moved on. I have a new girlfriend. Her name is Chloe."

"She's the young lady who works *Crepes Galore* with you, right?" I asked.

"Yes. Will she replace Melissa? Probably not. But how many people do you know who are happily married but still have feelings for their first love?"

"You're right." I took a deep breath, not knowing how he would react to my next question. "What about Melissa's pregnancy? Are you the father?"

Jeremy's face darkened. "No. Actually, I'm glad you asked because I want people to know this. We were through several weeks before she conceived. Our only contact after our break-up was through text, email, and phone. We never physically met up after we split."

"You didn't stalk her?" I raised an eyebrow, remembering what Victoria had said about Melissa seeking an order of protection.

Jeremy ran his fingers through his hair. "I sent a lot of text messages after the break-up. And I tried phoning her several times. Looking back, I shouldn't have done that. But I never contacted her in person. We finally came to an understanding, and she never filed an order of protection."

"Do you have any idea who the father of her child might be?"

He shook his head. "Not a clue. From what her friends say, she wasn't going with anyone after we broke up."

"Well, at least you're clear."

"Not totally. I'm not the father, but the police think I still could be the murderer. They consider my alibi weak." He scowled.

"What's your alibi?"

"I had been working a private party in Bay Shore the evening of the murder. That's a little more than an hour away from the wildlife refuge. The party ended at eleven, and I left there a few minutes later. According to Melissa's broken watch at the scene, the murder occurred at fifteen minutes after midnight."

"So, technically you could have still gotten to the refuge in time to commit the murder."

He shook his head as he rose from the chair and made his way toward the door, obviously becoming agitated at my slew of questions. "But why would I meet Melissa at the refuge? I've no connection to that place. Melissa's murderer has to be someone who worked there."

It made sense to me.

After he left, Matt asked Jason to help him move some large dog crates in the garage. Once they departed, I turned to Abby.

"What's wrong, honey? Are you and Jason okay?"

"There's something I need to tell him, and I don't know how."

"What?"

"My engagement ring is a fake."

CHAPTER 14

"It's a good fake, but it's a fake." Abby sighed loudly. "I wouldn't care if he gave me a decoder ring from a cereal box. It's not about the ring. It's about how upset he'll be when I tell him."

"When are you planning to do this?"

"I'm waiting for the right moment, but there doesn't seem to be one." Abby buried her fingers in Archie's fur and massaged his huge neck. The big dog, sensitive to stress in our voices, had laid his huge head on her lap. "But I can't hold it in anymore. I'll tell Jason tonight."

"Do you think Jason's grandmother knows it's a fake?"

Abby shook her head. "Absolutely not. She's always talking about how Jason's grandfather worked two jobs to save up for the ring. This will break her heart."

"That means the diamond was probably switched." I poured myself another glass of wine. Abby grabbed a bottle of water. Since she and Jason came here separately, she would need to drive home. "Did Jason's grandmother wear the ring recently or did it sit somewhere in a drawer?"

"It definitely sat somewhere. Jason's grandmother has severe arthritis and can't get the ring past her knuckles. I've been dating Jason for nearly three years, and I never saw her wear it. I assumed it was in a safe deposit box." Abby shrugged. "But maybe not."

"Someone may have taken the ring, replaced the diamond with a fake, and put the phony ring back. That could be done in a day or two. If it had been sitting in a drawer, she wouldn't have noticed it was gone."

"But who?"

I shrugged. "Someone with access to her house."

"She has someone come in once a week to clean. But Lily has worked for her for years." Abby shook her head. "I can't imagine Lily did it."

"Wait a minute. Didn't she have her bathroom remodeled less than a year ago? There were strangers working in her house every day for two weeks."

"You're right."

"You need to tell Jason. And he needs to question his grandmother. If someone stole the diamond, maybe you can identify the thief and get it back."

* * * * *

Abby phoned me the next morning before I left for work.

"I told Jason last night," she said. "He's outraged and wants to catch the thief. He says the district attorney's office can start an investigation. But he's reluctant to talk to his grandmother because he knows how much this will upset her."

"He doesn't need to tell her yet. I have an idea." I quickly moved my corn muffin away from the edge of the table where Brandy and Archie were sniffing. "You invited Jason's father and grandmother along with dad and me to your house Saturday night for dinner, right?"

"Yes. It will be the six of us."

"I'll have a casual conversation with Jason's grandmother about her bathroom remodel. Who was working there? Where was she at the time? I can ask a dozen questions without her knowing the real reason."

"Okay," Abby agreed. "Whatever you find out, Jason can take to his boss. Then the office can check it out, maybe set up a sting. I guess we're lucky Jason works in the white-collar crimes division."

"I know it's a long shot, but let's try it this way before Jason mentions it to his grandmother."

* * * * *

"A Detective Wolfe phoned," Clara called out the moment I stepped inside the office. "He said he'll call back later today. What do you think he wants?"

53

"I haven't a clue." I really didn't have any idea. Wolfe was not about to share his findings with me, so why would he call?

"He seemed angry. What did you do?" Clara winked over the top of her half-moon glasses and smiled.

"Nothing." I shrugged. "I'll find out when he calls back."

"Keep me posted."

I grabbed a mug of coffee and bee-lined for my office. Once inside my cubicle, I booted up my computer and began reorganizing my notes. But I couldn't concentrate. I kept conjuring up images of Melissa's dead body.

I hit another button on the keyboard and brought up a blank screen. I posted my list of suspects, leaving enough space between each name to jot down my thoughts.

JEREMY TOTH. Ex-boyfriend but not the father of her child. Although he appeared happy with his new girlfriend, he still carried a torch for Melissa. But he also had no connection to the wildlife refuge, and it seemed like an odd place for them to meet.

ELENA SALAZAR. She wanted Melissa's job. But murder is a drastic move to speed up one's career. Melissa had once dated Elena's fiancé, Austin Pendwell, although it was a long time ago. But was Elena jealous? Enough to kill? And what were Melissa and Elena arguing about the day before Melissa's murder?

VICTORIA PENDWELL. Melissa claimed Victoria was rigging bids—a criminal charge. Was the accusation true? Was Melissa blackmailing her? Did Victoria need to shut Melissa up permanently?

GEORGE GROGIN. Melissa had problems with his work. She was documenting evidence in case she needed to fire him. George didn't appear to shed any tears over Melissa's death, but I didn't see him having a burning hatred for her either.

All had motive. But what about opportunity? Did any of the suspects have a verifiable alibi for midnight?

I sat back, dissatisfied with what was on my screen. The more I thought, the more I realized that the key to Melissa's death would be centered on Melissa. Who was the father of her unborn child? Where did the money that Melissa acquired come from? The case of the missing animals might be connected too.

As I pondered various scenarios, the intercom buzzed.

"Detective Wolfe is here for you." Clara said.

"What line is he on?"

"He's not on the phone. He's—"

"I'm here." Wolfe stomped into my cubicle.

"Have a seat." I pointed to a chair in the corner.

"I'm not staying that long. But I decided to deliver my message in person."

"Which is?"

"Stay away from my case." He slammed his hands on my desk and leaned forward. His face was inches from mine, and his ice blue eyes met my brown ones. "I went back to ask more questions of that murdered girl's parents today and found out you had been there this weekend. I don't like that you questioned the Modicas, even though they had nothing to add to the investigation."

Nothing to add?

I stood up, not about to let him intimidate me. "I'm not interfering. I'm writing about the wildlife refuge. The murder will be a part of my story," I said. "By the way, did the parents tell you about the plasma television Melissa bought them?"

"Plasma television," he sputtered. "No. And they didn't tell me about their favorite ice cream flavor either."

Apparently Wolfe didn't realize there was a recent influx of money into the Modica household.

Wolfe turned around and made his way to exit. "I'm warning you," he said while standing in the doorway of the cubicle. He waved a fat finger. "If you obstruct my investigation in any way or don't disclose evidence, I'll arrest you."

"Where's your partner today?" I asked before he stomped out.

"Detective Fox is back at headquarters finishing paperwork. Not that it is any of your business."

Once he left, I sat back down, grabbed the phone, and punched in the number for the county's police headquarters. I asked for Detective Fox in homicide. After a surprisingly short runaround I connected to him.

"What can I do for you, Mrs. Farrell?" he asked.

Unlike Wolfe, Detective Fox was reasonable and, more importantly, not a bully. Unfortunately, Wolfe was the senior partner and called the shots. But Wolfe was at least thirty minutes away from police headquarters, so I had a chance.

I decided it was time to tell the police about the argument I'd overheard between Elena and Melissa.

"You should have told us this before." I heard the anger in his voice. "She actually used the words 'over my dead body?'"

"People say that all the time."

"Still, this information—"

"I have more," I interrupted, before he could continue his lecture. "I believe Melissa Modica recently came into money."

"How much money?"

"I don't know how much, and I don't know where it came from. But it could be from blackmail. That would be a motive for murder."

Silence. "Okay. Thanks for the tip," he said. "I'll check it out."

"Will you let me know what you find out?"

"No. This is a murder investigation. Good-bye Mrs. Farrell."

Once off the phone, I smiled. The police would dig into Melissa's finances. Now all I had to do was to somehow get them to share that information.

On my way home, I decided to stop at *The Scarlett Noose,* a bookstore specializing in mysteries and crime stories. I parked in front and began wandering through the store, finally selecting two books. While a clerk processed my credit card, I spotted a small poem taped to the cash register.

Pick any mystery.

And remember when you read

Three motives for murder

Lust, Revenge, and Greed

Which one would prove to be the reason for the killing of Melissa Modica?

CHAPTER 15

The next morning, I peered through the window. The shop seemed large and bright.

I entered the Bay Cove Pet Shop. This was the store that Alan Dysart from SANAN said was suspected of animal neglect, but there was no hard proof. This was also the place where one of Matt's clients had purchased their puppy mill dog.

The right side of the shop featured fish-laden aquariums. Further up were snakes and lizards, followed by hamsters, mice, and gerbils. Pet supplies filled the back wall.

But it was the left side that drew my attention. Here were puppies ranging from toy poodles to Bernese Mountain dogs. They sat in cages with barely enough room to turn.

"May I help you?" asked a blonde, overly made-up woman.

A small, apricot poodle coughed.

"That dog sounds sick."

The woman smiled, showing teeth worthy of toothpaste commercials. "Just a small respiratory infection. He's on antibiotics. He'll be perfect in a day or two. Are you interested in him?"

"Just looking." The puppy coughed again.

"Well, we have a great sale going on for some of our puppies if you buy today. Come with me." She led me to three cages near the front, featuring a German shepherd, basset hound, and a Morkie—a designer dog that was a mix of Maltese and Yorkshire terrier.

"Anyone of these dogs would be perfect for you."

"Why are they so cheap?" I asked. "These three are selling for half the price of the other dogs in the store."

"We want to make them available to animal lovers who otherwise could not afford the purchase price."

I doubted that. According to the sign attached to each cage, these dogs were all between eight and nine months old. The store needed to make room for a shipment of younger puppies.

"All these dogs are pedigree and come with papers," the saleswoman said. "They're perfect."

"Pedigree. You mean they don't come from puppy mills?"

"No puppy mills," she said emphatically. "They all come from breeders."

This was a lie. Matt had been able to trace the origin of the dog his client purchased here. It came from a puppy mill in Missouri.

"All our puppies have been examined by a veterinarian. They are in perfect condition."

I surveyed the cages. A tan cocker spaniel puppy sat listlessly in a corner cage whining. Pus oozed from its right eye.

"What's wrong with that puppy's eye?"

"A little eye infection. He's on antibiotics."

I stood silently staring at the puppy.

"He'll be fine," she said. "He's perfect."

Had she been instructed to say "perfect" each time she opened her mouth?

The saleswoman frowned. "Billy," she called to a young man with a bad case of acne who was mopping the floor nearby. He appeared to be in his late teens. "Would you take the tan cocker spaniel pup and the apricot poodle into the back?"

"Huh," he said.

"Put the dogs in one of the holding cages. We don't want customers to walk away because they think our dogs are sick."

The saleswoman turned back to me after Billy wandered off to retrieve the puppies. "Now, do you see any dog that catches your eye?" she asked. "Do you prefer big or small dogs?"

Before I could respond, Billy returned. I noticed he walked with a slight limp.

"Eliot said to tell you he's leaving for lunch now," he said to the saleswoman. "He should be back in an hour."

"Eliot is our store owner," the saleswoman said to me.

"He told me to put this sign in the window." Billy held up a sign that read: *Help Wanted. See Owner.*

"You're hiring?" I asked.

The saleswoman nodded. "Today is my last day. My husband and I are moving to Florida. When my shift ends in a little less than an hour I'll be gone for good."

"And the manager has only started looking now for your replacement now?"

She shook her head. "The person replacing me called earlier today and said he'd gotten another job. He was supposed to start Friday. I'm part-time. I only work two days a week." She turned around as if looking to see if anyone was in hearing distance, and then whispered, "I make a commission, so I'd love you to buy from me."

"I need to think about it." I turned and made my way out of the store.

I headed five stores down to a coffee shop, where I ordered a tomato soup and grilled cheese sandwich. I needed comfort food, and I needed to bide my time.

Since it was way before the traditional lunch hour, the coffee shop wasn't particularly busy, and they didn't pressure me to hurry up. I pulled my book out of my bag and read as I ate my lunch.

I glanced at my watch. More than an hour had gone by. The blonde sales associate would be gone by now. I strolled back to the pet shop and stepped through the doorway.

"May I help you?" asked a middle-aged man who was wearing a black toupee with way too much hair. "I'm Eliot, the store owner."

"Yes. I'm here about the "*Help Wanted*" sign in the window."

* * * * *

I got the job!

Visiting the pet shop and questioning the salesperson provided insight for my story. But nothing would give me the inside scoop like working at the pet store.

Later that day when I stepped inside the *Animal Advocate* office, the first person to greet me was Clara, who said, "Olivia wants to see you immediately."

My spirits dropped. An unscheduled session with my editor usually meant trouble.

"Do you know why?"

"I have no idea. She received a phone call earlier. And since then, she's been pacing around here like a caged animal. She went back into her office about ten minutes ago."

Olivia's door was ajar. Experiencing that sinking feeling in the pit of my stomach, I peeked in. "You wanted to see me?"

"Come in." She barely acknowledged me as she stared at her computer. I stepped into her inner sanctum. She hadn't told me to sit, so I remained standing. After a few seconds that seemed like minutes, she rose from her chair.

At nearly six feet in height with broad shoulders, Olivia was an imposing figure. With skin the color of deep French roast coffee and silver hair fashioned in a short, no nonsense style, she favored dark-colored conservative suits, like the navy blue pinstripe she wore today.

"Does the murder at the Pendwell Wildlife Refuge have anything to do with the missing animals?" she asked, getting straight to the point.

"I don't know," I answered. "It could be related. But it might not. There are other motives that might be the cause."

"Personal or relating to the wildlife refuge?"

"Both. It could have to do with the victim's pregnancy, which is personal. Or it might have to do with a turf war going on at the refuge." I didn't mention the money Melissa appeared to have acquired, but I did tell my editor about Melissa's accusation that Victoria was involved in bid rigging.

"Bid rigging is a serious charge." Olivia came around to the front of her desk. She stared down at me like a lioness sizing up its prey.

"I know you are investigating the murder." she said. "I got a call from an annoyed Detective Wolfe."

I opened my mouth to speak, but she held up her hand and said, "I don't care one bit about him. But Victoria Pendwell is another story. It's only a matter of time until she realizes what you're doing, and she will not be pleased. Anything that provides bad publicity to the wildlife refuge incurs her wrath."

Olivia chuckled. "You're too young to remember, Kristy, but Victoria came from the wrong side of the tracks. She was a B-grade actress when she met Clifton Pendwell and mesmerized him with her stunning good looks."

Olivia turned her head away and appeared to stare at a picture on the wall of a falcon in flight. "Our magazine is no longer an independent publication. We're now part of a conglomerate. And our focus is wildlife, not crime. Although no one from corporate has interfered with us yet, I don't know how far Victoria's tentacles reach. She is one of the most powerful women in this state."

"Are you saying I shouldn't pursue this?" I'm sure my voice showed my shock. My editor had worked her way up from the streets of the south Bronx. She was not one to back down.

Olivia slipped into her chair, leaned back, and crossed her arms. At least, she no longer looked like she was ready to pounce.

"My advice," she said. "If the police discover that the killer and the motive relate to the wildlife refuge, you can and should include that in your story. I'll back you one hundred percent. But until you know, play it smart. Stick to the refuge's operations and its accomplishments. Focus on the new director and the missing animals. Let the police investigate the murder." She paused. "You can go now."

As I made my way out the door, she called, "But if you don't heed my advice and you continue to investigate, at least be discreet."

CHAPTER 16

That evening, I pulled into the parking lot of Blackthorne Manor—an English Tudor style mansion located directly across the road from the Pendwell Wildlife Refuge. This was where the board of trustees meeting would be held tonight.

The mansion had recently been bequeathed to the wildlife refuge by Josiah Blackthorne, an avid wildlife enthusiast and a supporter of the environment. The plan was to turn the manor home into a wildlife conservation education center. Bedrooms would be converted into classrooms and the downstairs renovated so conferences could be held. This renovation contract was on the agenda for tonight.

Tonight's board meeting was set up in the library. Behind a long table were five seats for the board members with name plates and microphones on the table in front of each place. Facing the table were twenty folding chairs in four rows—seating for the audience. As of now, only four chairs were filled.

Elena Salazar was one of the attendees, and she was sitting in the front row. I waved. She mouthed "hello" and went back to staring at her phone. Further down her row were two men in dark, gray business suits. One clutched an iPad and the other held onto a portable screen.

Power Point presentation?

The last attendee was a young man, who was probably in his early twenties. He wore a black turtleneck and khakis and sported a small, blond mustache. I made my way along the second row and slid into a chair, two seats down from where he sat.

"I'm Kristy. I'm a writer for *Animal Advocate Magazine,*" I said. "I'm doing a story on the wildlife refuge. What brings you here?"

"My name is Brian," he said. "I'm a graduate student at Decker University. I'm taking a course in "not-for-profits" and my term project is an in-depth report on the operation of this place."

"This room is pretty empty. Think more of an audience will show?" I asked.

"I doubt it. These meetings are open to the public, but I've never seen more than a handful of people. It's pretty much attended only by those who are doing business with the refuge."

"I take it you've attended board meetings before?"

He nodded. "This is my sixth. The first four were pretty dull, but the last meeting had a tense undercurrent."

"What happened?"

"You see those two guys in suits?" He pointed to the men in the front row.

I nodded.

"Victoria Pendwell wanted to push the contract to renovate this house into an education center. The guy on the right is the builder, the other one is his attorney. At the last meeting, one of the board members, Susan Hanson, said she needed more information before she would vote on the contract. Victoria was furious—you could see it in her face— but she agreed to a postponement. That's why those two are doing a presentation tonight."

Having done my homework on the board members, I knew Susan Hanson was chair of the biology department at a local high school and a noted ornithologist who had authored several articles on birds native to Long Island. She was the only Pendwell Wildlife Refuge trustee with a background in wildlife. The other board members were a retired public relations executive, the CEO of a local technology firm, and a socialite/ philanthropist. They all had close ties to the Pendwell family.

"But even if Susan Hanson cast a 'no' vote, it would still be a four to one decision," I argued.

Brian shrugged. "I know, but Victoria wanted a unanimous vote."

When I read last month's minutes, the tabling of the renovation appeared to be a formality. It simply seemed that the board wanted more information. By not attending the meeting in person, I missed the emotions and nuances behind this action.

Brian and I chatted for a few more minutes. Then he glanced at his watch.

"It's late, isn't it?" I said. "Wasn't the meeting supposed to start ten minutes ago?"

He nodded. "I overheard Elena Salazar talking to the attorney for the builder earlier. She said the meeting might be a little late because Victoria was returning from Florida, and her flight had been delayed."

"I didn't know she'd been away?"

He grinned. "I eavesdrop a bit. She was only gone for three days. Apparently, she had business to conduct that's connected to work she's having done on her Palm Beach home. A portion of the house was damaged in a fire a few months ago. Oh, here come the trustees now."

The five board members straggled into the room and took their places behind the table. Victoria was the last to arrive. She nodded to Susan Hanson, but greeted the other trustees enthusiastically.

Susan Hanson was by far the youngest board member. An attractive woman who appeared to be in her mid or late thirties, her skin was ebony and her black hair styled into rows of braids.

The first order of business was the treasury report and budget. The money came in from donations, fundraising events, fees for programs, and private grants.

Under expenses, I noted final payment to Gerber Engineering for restoration and clean-up of the refuge. This included removal of invasive species, dredging to improve pond depth, and installing collection devices to intercept storm water borne sediments. I remembered that the approval for Gerber Engineering to do this work had been given by the board of trustees five months ago.

Although I had read all the minutes for the past year, I couldn't recall all the details of this decision. Brian said he'd been here for the last six meetings, so I leaned over and whispered, "Did Susan have objections to the contractor hired to restore the refuge?"

"When that was approved, Susan was absent." Brian said. "She had the flu."

The next order of business tonight was the vote to make Elena Salazar the director. It was unanimous.

After that, the power point presentation on converting this house into an education center began. Susan asked no questions of the presenters. Neither did any other board member. Victoria called for a vote.

Susan voted for the renovation of the manor house into an education center, but her body language indicated she wasn't happy. During the vote, she sat with her arms folded in front. She scowled, and her eyes appeared to be focused downward.

After the meeting, Brian and I exchanged phone numbers realizing we both might be help to each other. Then I wandered up to the main table.

"Did you get all you needed for your article?" Victoria asked, heading me off before I could reach anyone else on the board.

"Yes. I have plenty of information." I smiled. Elena strutted up to where we were talking and stood next to Victoria.

"Now that my promotion is official, let's get together again, Kristy," Elena said. "I'd love to show you my plans in detail. Perhaps we can meet after my presentation to the fourth grade class tomorrow—the one you're attending."

"Sounds good," I agreed. From the corner of my eye, I spotted Susan Hanson exiting the room.

"Excuse me," I said. While Victoria turned and began chatting with other board members, and Elena beckoned the attorney for the builder to come and see her, I raced out, hoping to catch up with Susan Hanson.

"Ms. Hanson," I called when I sighted her outside the building. She was about twenty feet ahead of me. She stopped and turned.

"Could I talk with you about your vote for the renovation of the manor house into the education center?" I asked.

"Who are you?"

"Kristy Farrell. I'm a write for *Animal Advocate Magazine*—"

"I've nothing to say," she said, cutting me off.

I continued anyway. "During the presentation, I saw from your facial expression that you weren't happy, but you asked no questions nor voiced any objections."

"I'm fine with the contract."

"Really?"

She paused. "No. I'm not fine. But I can't talk here."

"There's a pub down the road," I said. "It's called the Tipsy Toad. We could meet there."

She nodded. "Okay, but only on one condition. What I say is off the record."

CHAPTER 17

Susan Hanson and I arrived within minutes of each other. We found a comfortable booth on the side, far away from the crowded bar and also a good distance from three young men in the back, who were playing darts. Susan insisted on sitting facing the door so she could see who entered.

The Tipsy Toad Pub was about as British as you can get this side of the Atlantic. The menu posted on a chalkboard featured such items as Shepherd's Pie, Bangers and Mash, and Fish and Chips. Susan and I split a Ploughman's Special, which consisted of bread, cheese, onions, and pickles. Although I would have liked one of the pub's famous ales, I had a long drive home. I ordered coffee as did Susan.

"The other board members are all wealthy and possess major fundraising capabilities. I don't," Susan said, getting straight to the point. "But I'm the only trustee with any knowledge of wildlife. The president of my school board is the former law partner of Victoria's late husband, Clifton Pendwell. Victoria wanted one of her trustees to have an environmental background, so he suggested me."

I nodded. "I can see where your background could be helpful."

Susan snickered. "You would think so, but they just wanted to list my credentials. They don't want me to use my knowledge. I'm the only trustee who ever asks questions. At last month's —" Susan stopped mid-sentence while the waitress served our coffee and snack.

"At last's month's meeting, I thought the presentation about renovating the manor house was too vague. I asked for a postponement until we could get more information. Victoria agreed but was furious. The contractor is a major developer on Long Island, and he is a friend of hers."

Susan sipped her coffee and continued. "The next afternoon, my school board president—that's the law partner of Victoria's late husband—called my principal and asked why I was such a trouble maker."

"That's awkward."

"It's more than that." She sighed. "I'm up for a big promotion—assistant superintendent for science curriculum for the entire district. I really want this job. And if I antagonize the school board president, I'm not going to get it."

"Is that why you voted for the contract tonight?"

She nodded. "To be fair, it wasn't that bad, but I still would have liked more detail."

"Such as?"

"I'd like to know more specifics as to the material they're using on the renovation."

"You said the builder is Victoria's friend, right?"

"Yes. He belongs to the same golf club as her late husband, and his wife and Victoria are both part of the horsey set. They participate in the same equestrian events. I understand they've known each other for years."

I mulled this over in my mind. "I heard you were absent for the meeting on the wildlife refuge restoration project. The one where the other trustees approved Gerber Engineering to provide dredging, removal of invasive species, collection—"

"Yes. I was out sick. And it wasn't supposed to be on the agenda that night. I think Victoria added it when she heard I had the flu."

"Because she thought you would object?" I asked.

"I was the only board member who would understand the science behind what was being done. I could ask embarrassing questions." She lowered her voice although no one was near us. "There were high costs involved. Don't get me wrong. Everything may have been fine, but I felt a lot needed an explanation."

"Did you bring any of this up to Victoria?"

Susan shook her head. "No. Since I missed the meeting, there wasn't much I could do. To question Victoria after the contract passed would have just stirred the pot, and at that point, it was too late to change anything."

"Do you have a copy of the proposal?"

"Yes. I did insist on that although Victoria was reluctant to send it to me. But she finally did."

"What did you think?" I popped some cheese in my mouth.

"If I'd been in attendance, I would have asked lots of questions about money. I'm a scientist, but I'm not an environmental engineer. I understand the procedures involved by Gerber Engineering, but I had no idea of the costs."

"Were there other proposals?"

"Two others. I had Victoria send me copies of those proposals also. One was a start-up and didn't have all the equipment necessary. The cost to buy that equipment pushed this company's bid out of the ballpark."

Susan ate one of the pickles on the platter. When she finished chewing, she continued. "The other company didn't specialize in environmental engineering. That meant they would need to sub-contract much of the work. Victoria never got bids from competitors of equal standing to Gerber although there are several on Long Island."

"Can you send me a copy of the Gerber proposal? My future son-in-law's father is a retired engineer. He doesn't specialize in environmental engineering, but I'm sure he has contacts in the field. I'll ask him to have someone look at the proposal and tell me if Gerber padded his costs."

"As long as you don't divulge where you got it."

"I promise." I drained my coffee cup. "I heard that Melissa Modica criticized both the contract and Victoria."

Susan nodded. "Melissa's background was in environmental science. She knew her stuff, and she accused Victoria of bid rigging and receiving kick-backs."

"Kickbacks? But why would Victoria do this?" I shook my head. "She doesn't need the money. I can't believe she's involved in kick-backs."

Susan grinned. "Remember the saying, 'you can never be too rich or too thin'. I think that describes Victoria."

Susan paused while the waitress poured refills. "Victoria isn't as rich as you think. Her late husband was a good man, and he gave generously to charities, including setting up several trust funds. That took a big chunk away from the estate that Victoria inherited. I've also heard some of her investments took a downturn. So, while she has more money than you or I can imagine, it's not enough for her."

During a momentary silence while Susan and I polished off the Ploughman's platter, I processed what had been said. The Pendwells were a prominent family, frequently mentioned in society news. Victoria's Long Island estate, Manhattan condominium, winter home in Palm Beach—the maintenance alone would be more than Matt's and my salary combined.

And now, she was supposedly having work done on the Palm Beach house, although if the damage was from a fire it was probably covered by insurance. I also knew she owned a stable of horses and a large yacht, all of which required heavy upkeep.

Was Victoria Pendwell living in a financial house of cards that was about to come tumbling down?

I decided to throw something else out and see where it landed. "It also makes Victoria a suspect in Melissa's death. If the accusations are true, she has motive."

Susan responded, "I believe the accusations are true."

"Why?"

"A month before her murder, Melissa phoned me. She claimed she had proof of the accusations and would call me later in the week to discuss it in person."

"What did she tell you when she called?" I leaned forward in my seat.

Susan's eyes narrowed. "That's just it. We never met, because she never called back. Three weeks later, I contacted her. Melissa now claimed she'd been mistaken. She claimed there was no proof. I didn't believe her, but she died before we had a chance to talk again. I think Melissa was being pressured by Victoria."

Or Melissa had started blackmailing the Pendwells.

* * *

I phoned Melissa's good friend Linda Lau during my drive home from the pub.

"I heard that Melissa confided in one of the refuge's trustees. She claimed she had proof of bid rigging. Did she ever mention this to you?" I asked.

"No," Linda responded. "She made vague accusations, but she never had proof. Remember, I was in California for a training course for eight weeks before her death, so I don't know if she uncovered something then. During that time, our contact was only by text and a few phone calls."

"She never said anything to you during the phone conversations?"

"Nothing specific." Linda paused. "But there was a change in her attitude. The first few weeks I was away, she sounded depressed whenever we talked. Right before her death, however, she seemed happy. I'm thinking it had to do with her newly found riches."

CHAPTER 18

The next morning, I sped off to the Pendwell Wildlife Refuge to attend Elena's wildlife presentation to a fourth grade class.

It had rained last night, and the smell of wet pines and damp earth filled the air. The presentation was being held in the grassy area behind the administration building, so I trudged back there.

The class had not yet arrived, but I spotted Elena setting up items on a long table. Two cages sat on either end. As I came closer, I saw that one held an owl and the other a squirrel missing one leg.

Hovering around Elena was the man who had been sitting next to her at Melissa's wake.

"Glad you're here early," Elena said as she looked up and spotted me. "I'd like you to meet my fiancé, Austin Pendwell."

"I wanted to be here for Elena's first day as director and watch what may be her last presentation as education coordinator," he said after we exchanged pleasantries.

Elena frowned. "It's not my last presentation. We hired a former volunteer to take on my old job, but I still intend to conduct a few programs each month."

Austin smiled, showing off his beautifully capped teeth.

A sudden rustling of bushes accompanied by voices in the distance caught my attention. I spun around and watched a group of children approaching. Trailing closely behind the group were two women and one man. I presumed they were the teacher and parent chaperones.

The older woman, and most harried looking of the three adults, spread a large blanket on the damp grass. I guessed she was the teacher. The children rushed to sit on the blanket.

"Hello Mrs. D'Angelo," Elena called to the woman. Elena introduced me to the fourth grade teacher. Austin had moved to the side to take a phone call.

Suddenly, there was a piercing scream. It came from where the fourth graders sat.

Austin dropped his phone. Horror spread across Elena's face. I froze. But the scream was quickly followed by a fourth grader yelling, "Eek. It's a spider."

I felt the tension drain from me. *False Alarm.*

"It's harmless," said Elena, who had rushed to see the cause of the commotion. "It's a common house spider."

"I guess we're all on edge," I said when Elena returned to the table. I smiled.

She did not return the smile.

When the program began, I stood next to Mrs. D'Angelo. Elena brought out the owl and explained that the bird's wing had been damaged and could never fly again. Then she talked about the squirrel that lost its leg when it fell out of a tree as a baby.

Elena went on to say that the goal of wildlife rehabilitation is to release animals back into their natural habitat once they heal. Unfortunately, the owl and the squirrel would not survive in the wild, so they had a permanent home here and served as ambassadors.

"She's a natural educator," Mrs. D'Angelo whispered to me as Elena began explaining signs that a baby animal is abandoned. "And she'll be an even better director."

I wondered how she knew about Elena's promotion so soon after yesterday evening's board meeting.

As if reading my mind, Mrs. D'Angelo said, "Elena sent out emails last night to all who participate in her education programs. She wanted us to know about the change and to ensure us that the school programs will not only continue but will be expanded. She told us about the new education coordinator. It sounds as if she and Elena will work well together."

"That's always a plus." I smiled.

Mrs. D'Angelo nodded. "It certainly will be a change for the better. Elena and Melissa were constantly at each other's throats. They created way too much tension."

"At each other's throats? What do you mean?" I asked.

"I bring my class here for presentations, and I use the educational resources, such as videos and activity books. In other words, I'm at this place on a pretty regular basis. Every time I've gone into the administration building, if Elena and Melissa were both there, they would be arguing."

"What about?"

Mrs. D'Angelo smiled wickedly. "Mostly pecking order. It appeared Elena basically did whatever she wished, and Melissa wanted everything cleared through her."

Mrs. D'Angelo paused. "Although the last time I was here—that was two weeks before Melissa was murdered—I think the argument was different. It was much more intense."

"In what way?"

"Not sure. I came in at the tail end, and I couldn't hear what they were saying."

"Then how do you know the argument was more intense than before?"

"Elena slapped Melissa across the face and stomped out of the building."

"Wow!" I processed all that had been said, realizing Elena could have been charged with assault.

The hatred between Melissa and Elena had to be more than professional rivalry.

* * * * *

"Do you have extra time today," Elena asked me at the conclusion of her presentation. "I know we were getting together right after my program, but a pressing matter came up. Could you come back in an hour? Maybe you could get lunch or walk one of our trails."

"That's fine. I'd like to explore the refuge. I'll meet you in your office in an hour."

When she left, I made my way to the clearing where Melissa's murder had taken place. Three squirrels scooted up a tree. I wandered to the pond where I spotted Freemont the turtle and two of his turtle friends.

I sat on a log, pondering the murder scene.

74

Everyone assumed Melissa was meeting someone here at midnight. But what if she wasn't?

What if she was here for a totally different reason?

What if she was here to take night photos? Or just to gaze at the pollution-free sky?

If this was so, did she come upon someone by chance? Had she stumbled on criminal activity?

I shuddered. I remembered a case a few years back when a body had been discovered in a wooded area about an hour from here. It was the result of a gang killing.

But the more I thought about it, I realized that couldn't be it. Gang slayings use guns or knives. They don't smash someone on top of the head.

I recalled Linda Lau's comment about Melissa being a track star in school and how she still ran every morning. Unlike shooting a gun from twenty feet away, you would need to be on top of someone to kill with a blunt instrument. Wouldn't Melissa have run away from any stranger who appeared threatening?

The killer had to be someone Melissa knew. Someone she'd let get up close.

But why meet here? That question remained in my mind.

Sighing, I pushed myself off the log, a task that would have been easier if I were ten years younger and twenty pounds lighter. I made my way back down the trail for my appointment with Elena.

As I approached the administration building, I spotted George Grogin leaving. He carried a big box under his arm.

"Hi George," I called. I had hoped to speak with him after my appointment with Elena, so I added, "Are you leaving for the day?"

"I'm leaving for good. I've been fired."

CHAPTER 19

"You fired George Grogin?" I asked Elena when I entered the building.

"Yes." She popped open the latch and I followed her back to her cubicle. "He made too many mistakes. I hired our part-time wildlife rehabilitator, Cassie Chipperwich, to replace him. I was just on the phone making arrangements to hire another rehabilitator to take the part-time job that Cassie vacates."

She sighed. "I need to call Victoria and let her know, but I can do that after you leave."

"How is she going to feel about this?"

"Victoria will be fine. She knew he was becoming a problem."

Elena plopped down in the chair behind her desk, and I slid into the seat in front. Elena quickly changed the topic, making it obvious the subject of George's termination was closed. She talked about the new programs she hoped to initiate. When I rose to leave, I asked if I could interview the new full time wildlife rehabilitator.

"Cassie is here now, but she's busy for the next few days," Elena said. "If you come here Tuesday afternoon, you can interview her. How's three o'clock?"

"Fine."

"And if you remain here after that, you can attend another of my activities. I'm involved with a youth group in my home community. I promised to take them on a hike through one of our trails. I have that scheduled for four in the afternoon."

I would be working undercover at the Bay Cove Pet Shop on Tuesdays and Fridays. Tuesdays my shift ended at two o'clock. That would give me plenty of time to get here. I wanted to meet the new wildlife rehabilitator. Since she had previously worked part-time at the refuge, she knew all the players.

* * * * *

Matt worked late this evening, performing emergency surgery on a dog hit by a car. He phoned and said the operation was a success and he'd be home soon. Dressed in my pajamas, I was debating whether to tackle a crossword puzzle or settle down with my new mystery, when my front door swung open.

Abby and Jason paraded into the house.

"Did you forget we were coming," Abby asked grinning. Jason stared at my fuzzy mouse slippers that complemented the mice and cheese design on my pajamas.

"No reason I can't be comfortable." I actually had forgotten. The other day, Abby asked if she could borrow my exercise bicycle. Since it had not been used in the last two years, I agreed.

"The bicycle is in the basement," I said.

While Jason headed downstairs, Abby flopped down in a chair and asked what was new with the murder investigation.

"I'm more convinced than ever that Melissa was into blackmail," I said.

"But who was she blackmailing?"

I filled her in on what Mrs. D'Angelo told me about the fight between Elena and Melissa.

"Maybe Melissa was blackmailing Elena. Or Victoria." I shrugged. "I'm not sure. The police are looking into Melissa's financials based on a tip I gave to Detective Fox. I think it's time for me to call Fox and see if he uncovered a money trail."

* * * * *

The next morning, I punched in the number for police headquarters and asked to be connected to Detective Fox. I crossed my fingers, hoping Wolfe wasn't nearby. I didn't know if I could worm information out of Fox, but if Wolfe was around, I'd get nothing.

"Detective Fox," he answered.

"Can you talk?" I asked after identifying myself. "Are you alone?"

"Am I alone?" I could hear him chuckle. "There are about fifty officers on this floor. But if you are asking what I think you are, the answer is yes. Detective Wolfe is not here."

"I assume the tip I gave you to check Melissa's finances panned out." I held my breath. Fox had said he wouldn't tell me anything, but I hoped I could coax some information out of him.

"We checked your info," he said. "We're satisfied."

"Satisfied? What does that mean?"

"It means we found nothing suspicious."

"But Melissa went on a buying spree. Do you mean to tell me that there is no indication of where that money came from?"

"I'm not at liberty to tell you anymore. Once again, we're satisfied. Good-bye, Mrs. Farrell. Have a good day."

I'd no sooner hung up when another call came in. This one was from Linda Lau.

"Jeremy called me early this morning," she said. "The police brought him back in for questioning last night."

"Why?"

"It turns out Jeremy borrowed money from Melissa a few weeks before she died. He needed it for his business but said he'd pay it back. It was due two days before she was killed. She made him sign a loan agreement saying if he didn't repay by that date she was entitled to half of his portion of the business."

"I take it he didn't pay her back."

"Exactly. And that gives him a motive to kill her."

"How did the police discover this?"

"They uncovered an email Melissa sent him."

"Before jumping to conclusions, let me see what I can discover." I said good-bye, booted up my computer, and brought up *Crepes Galore*. Today the food truck would be at a Food Expo in a community park only a few miles from here. I shut off the computer, drained my coffee mug, and zoomed out of the house.

Upon my arrival at the community park, I quickly spotted Jeremy's vehicle among more than a dozen exhibitors. He was wedged between a taco truck and a barbecue wagon. Since the Expo didn't open officially for another twenty-five minutes, I was able to grab Jeremy's attention.

"Why do I think you're not here to sample more crepes," he said when he saw me. "I'm guessing you heard about the loan."

I nodded. "Is it true?"

"It's really none of your business."

"I believe you're innocent, and I want to help."

He hesitated. "I spoke with Linda Lau. She told me a little about your crime solving history. I guess I can trust you."

"Then tell me about the loan."

"We had some unexpected repairs needed on the truck. I was okay with signing her agreement, because I knew I could pay her back."

"But you didn't pay her back?"

"Unfortunately, we had several storms in the following weeks. We don't get a lot of customers during heavy rains, so when the money was due, I was still a bit short. I told her all I needed was another week, and she agreed."

An unpleasant thought flashed through my mind. "Jeremy, you told me you had no physical contact with Melissa since you broke up."

"That's true. Our communication was text, email, or phone." He sighed. "She made me sign an agreement online because she was brought up to be business-like. But she was a softie. She probably would have forgiven the loan if I needed that."

"When you told her you needed more time, did you do that by email or text?"

"No. I phoned. That's the problem. I can't prove to the police what we said, so they think I have another motive to kill her."

"Apparently, she died before you repaid her."

"Yes. But I have the money. I plan on giving it to her parents."

"Jeremy, as far as the police are concerned, this is a strong motive for murder."

CHAPTER 20

Early that afternoon, I arrived at the mall for my first day working undercover at the Bay Cove Pet Shop. I made my way to the back office where Eliot, the owner, greeted me.

"I wanted to talk to you before you start work," he said while rising from his chair behind his desk. "Let's go over a few important points."

I nodded.

"The puppies sell themselves, but you can help the sale along." He grinned, as we left his office and entered the showroom. "You can bargain. We're like most department stores. We inflate our original prices, and then we lower for a sale. People think they're getting a deal. You can go down two hundred dollars on any dog. If you still need to go lower, see me."

"What about the dogs over there?" I pointed to three cages. According to the birth dates on the signage, these dogs were more than eight months old.

"Ah. I was just going to mention them. We need to get rid of them. As you can see, we slashed the prices. They're about fifty percent lower than the other dogs."

Eliot wiped his nose and continued, "We sold an eleven month old boxer last week. His initial price was $3,000. We let him go for $550. And we still made a profit." He rubbed his hands together gleefully.

I thought about that puppy spending the first eleven months of his life in a cage with little socialization. He would likely have behavioral issues. I hoped his new family would weather the storm and not abandon the dog.

Eliot then introduced me to my three co-workers. Maybe being surrounded by dogs had something to do with it, but Ted, the other sales associate, had a face resembling a bloodhound. The second staff member was the young man Billy that I'd met the other day. He was in charge of cleaning the cages and basic care, such as making sure each animal had food and water. The last employee was June, the cashier.

I spotted the tan cocker spaniel that I'd seen on Tuesday—the one with the eye infection. "That dog still has pus oozing from its eye."

"The eye infection is minor," Eliot said. "We tell customers that these eye infections are common and that the dog is on antibiotics and will be fine in two to three days." Eliot grinned broadly. "Trust me. It works."

I had been told on Tuesday the infection should be gone in two to three days. Today was Friday. It was still there, and it hadn't improved.

As I scanned the cages, I noted the little apricot poodle with the cough was no longer here.

"Is the apricot poodle is the back room?" I asked apprehensively

"No. We sold her."

Was that true? Had she gotten better or had she died? Or, had Eliot and his staff convinced an unsuspecting customer that the dog's cough was normal for a puppy and would get better?

"Let's make some sales today." Eliot adjusted his toupee, then turned and headed to the section of the store that featured the snakes and lizards.

A few minutes later, a young woman entered. She pushed a double stroller, holding twin girls. A boy was skipping next to her. I judged him to be about seven years old.

"Oh, look at this Mom," the boy said, rushing up to a cage with a Dalmatian pup.

I winced. Dalmatians are super active dogs, and they need someone who will spend lots of time on training.

The mother looked at me and smiled sheepishly. "I sort of promised him a puppy if he got a good report card."

Sort of promised him?

"I don't know how he'll find the time for it. He has Little League, Boy Scouts, and travel soccer." The woman sighed. "I don't know how I will find the time either, and my husband's job requires him to travel frequently." She stooped down and picked up a toy bunny that one of the twins had dropped, and handed it back to her. The girl dropped it again.

I hesitated before saying, "Although some breeds are less active than others, all need attention and training. You shouldn't get one until you have the time. Otherwise, the first few months of puppy destruction will last a lifetime."

She put her hand on her son's shoulder. "Michael, maybe we should wait."

"But you promised, Mom!"

"How about two new video games?"

"I guess that would be okay. Can one of them be Z-rangers?"

The mother nodded. She swiveled the stroller and her son followed her out the door. I spun around only to face a scowling Eliot.

"I need to speak with you now," he said.

I followed him to a corner of the store. "Don't ever discourage a buyer," he said. "If they have trouble training a dog, that's not our problem."

"But—"

"No buts. If a customer wants a specific breed, no matter what you think, it is your job to sell."

"But an untrained puppy often winds up in a shelter or worse."

"Not our problem." He stomped off to his office.

I noticed another puppy with a cough. Billy must have noticed it too. He took the pup—a black poodle—out of its cage and was caressing it in his arms.

He genuinely cares for these animals.

I made my way to where he stood.

"I feel so sorry for this little guy," Billy said. "But please don't tell Eliot I took the pup out. He doesn't want me to do anything but my chores."

"I won't say a word. Is this puppy on medication?"

"Yes. But it doesn't always help. You can't believe how many die."

"Did the apricot poodle die?"

He nodded. "The apricot poodle and this poodle were brought here by our delivery service nearly two weeks ago." Billy said bitterly. "They delivered five puppies. Two were dead on arrival. The apricot pup died while here, and this one isn't doing so well."

"What about the fifth puppy?"

"He had a cough too, but we sold him. Don't know what happened after that."

"Was this the first time sick puppies were delivered here?" I was pretty sure I knew the answer, but I wanted to hear it firsthand from Billy.

"No way! Every time we get a delivery, there are puppies with diarrhea, coughs… You name it."

Delivery and acceptance of sick puppies was something the SPCA would want to know about. I would see they did. This might provide the evidence needed to seize the dogs and shut down this operation.

CHAPTER 21

After finishing my shift at the Bay Cove Pet Shop, I hurried home and changed my clothes. Tonight was the thousand dollar a ticket fundraiser for the Pendwell Wildlife Refuge. Victoria invited me as a guest. I knew she hoped I'd include her fundraising efforts in my story.

I asked Victoria if rather than taking photos with my phone, I could bring a photographer. She agreed, so I recruited my daughter. Abby owned an expensive camera, had taken a photography course, and won an award for one of her pictures.

"Did you hear the news?" Abby asked as she hopped into my car. "Austin Pendwell announced his candidacy for the State Senate this morning. Jason told me."

Since I hadn't watched or listened to the news today, I wasn't aware.

"His announcement came on the same day as the big event for the wildlife refuge," I said. "What a coincidence."

"Jason said it was known for weeks that he would run. Austin announced at ten o'clock, and by noon his headquarters were up and running."

We sped off to the fundraiser.

Victoria was hosting the fundraising cocktail party at her estate. I wasn't sure how large her property was, but I knew her community had a minimum zoning requirement of three acres. Passing through the open gate, I continued up the long driveway where valets were waiting to park the incoming cars. Her home overlooked the Long Island Sound, and the lights of Connecticut could be seen across the water.

"So glad you could come," Victoria gushed as soon as she spotted us.

She was dressed in purple silk, and an emerald and diamond choker adorned her neck. "You both look lovely."

We did look good. I wore a black silk skirt with a silver jacket. Abby was in a sea green cocktail dress.

"We have three bars set up," Victoria said. "One by the pool, the second down on the dock, and the third is at the entrance to my rose garden. For food, we're using Enzo Caterers. They're the best on Long Island. We have the food stations sprinkled throughout the property."

"I'd like to take some photos first," I said.

"Wonderful. Take all the candid shots you want. But I'd also like you to take a picture of our new director, Elena Salazar."

Before I could reply, Elena appeared next to Victoria. She looked elegant in a red cocktail suit with her dark hair in a French twist. Accompanying the new director was her fiancé, Austin Pendwell.

"Austin, as Elena's husband to be, you should be in the photo too," Victoria insisted. "My son is going to be the next senator."

After Abby shot the photo, Victoria turned to me. "One of my board members just arrived. I should greet him." She smiled. "I'll catch up with you later."

"Please excuse me too," Austin said. "I see an associate from my law firm, and I need to speak with her."

Austin dashed off and within seconds was conversing with a blonde in a little black dress who was standing by the bar near the Pendwell's Olympic-size swimming pool.

Elena frowned.

"When are you getting married?" I asked to break the silence of an awkward moment.

"We haven't set a date yet." She glared at Austin who was still engaged in conversation with the blonde.

"I better mingle," Elena said, still frowning.

"Trouble in paradise?" Abby asked me after Elena marched off in the direction of her fiancé.

I shrugged. "Let's get some candid shots for the magazine. Then we can relax with a drink and some food."

As we made our way around the estate grounds, I noticed all the trustees were here except for Susan Hanson. Had she not been invited?

After twenty minutes of snapping photos, of which I'd probably only use one, we maneuvered through the crowd to the bar. Abby grabbed a white wine and I ordered a pomegranate martini.

"Pomegranate is loaded with antioxidants," I said to the bartender. "So if I'm imbibing I might as well get some nutrients out of it." That was my theory even if no one else agreed.

Abby shook her head but grinned.

"Kristy, Abby, I haven't seen you in ages," a voice called out.

"Jonathan. What a pleasant surprise," I responded.

Doctor Jonathan Weiss was a prominent veterinarian who specialized in equine medicine. Abby and I had met him through my husband. Last year, Matt and Jonathan had co-chaired a fundraiser to help abused animals.

"I didn't know you were involved with the Pendwell Wildlife Refuge," I said.

"I'm not involved although it's a great cause. Victoria asked me to support tonight's event. I take care of her horses. Did you know she's won several blue ribbons at horse shows? She's an excellent rider."

"I read somewhere that riding was her passion."

He nodded. "She learned to ride as a teenager."

"Did her family own horses?"

"No. Victoria doesn't come from money. She always loved horses and worked part-time in a stable when she was young, so she could ride for free."

"I hear she has quite a stable now."

Dr. Weiss sighed. "In the past she did, but recently the number of horses Victoria owns has dwindled. It always was around six or more, but now it's down to three."

"What happened?"

"She sold the others after her husband died." Doctor Weiss hesitated, looked over his shoulder, and lowered his voice. "Victoria didn't want to do it, but I don't think she could afford the upkeep."

I surveyed the magnificent grounds. It was hard to associate this place with money problems. But Susan Hanson had said the same thing.

We chatted a few more minutes and then took our leave.

"I'm starved," I said to Abby as I placed my empty glass back on the bar. "Let's eat."

"You're always starved." Abby grinned. We made our way toward one of the food stations.

"I can't believe she's here," I said. "But why is she working as wait staff?"

"What are you talking about, Mom?"

"That woman. The one serving up plates at the raw bar. That's Alicia Layne, a professor of theater arts at Decker University. She did several presentations at my school when I was still teaching English. Alicia is also a professional actress. Why is she working here?"

"Maybe she needs extra money."

"Possible, but I doubt it. She's up to something. Let's find out."

Alicia Layne was a large woman who stood out in a crowd. Although tonight she wore the caterer's standard black uniform and white apron, she sported a ring on each finger. Earrings, appearing to be almost five inches in length, dangled below her short, silver streaked black hair.

As we approached the food station, Alicia called out, "Kristy Farrell. How good to see you. Have some clams."

"Alicia, what are you doing here?"

"Serving clams, oysters—"

"I mean, why are you here?"

"Oh. I have a marvelous summer stock role. I play an older woman, down on her luck. She gets a job with a caterer who turns out to be a serial killer who poisons his victims."

"Sounds lovely."

"I need to live the role. I'm a method actress. I took this job so I could feel what it's like to work in the food industry."

A young man in the caterer's uniform appeared. "Enzo said you can have a break now, Alicia. I'll take over. Be back in twenty minutes."

"Purr-fect timing." She whipped off her apron.

"If you want to eat, you must go to the kitchen," the young man said. He stared directly at us. "Enzo's rule is no mingling with the guests. And no drinking."

"Of course." She winked at me. I knew she had no intention of obeying Enzo's rule.

"We'll head in the direction of the kitchen until we're out of sight," she whispered.

"But someone else may see you."

"I don't care if I'm fired. I'm quitting after tonight. I soaked in the background, and I have a feeling for my role." She grabbed a glass of champagne from an unsuspecting waitress passing by.

"How long have you been working for Enzo Caterers?"

"This is my fourth catering assignment." She gulped down the champagne and placed the empty glass on a nearby table. "Have you seen anyone serving caviar canapes?"

"I haven't. Why are you quitting?"

"I just told you. I've garnered enough experience to perform my role in the theatre."

A waiter passed by with more champagne. Alicia snatched another glass.

She took a big swallow and then continued. "I was planning to quit after my last assignment with Enzo, but I stayed on because I was dying to see this place. I'm so glad tonight's event wasn't canceled."

"Why would it have been canceled?"

She gulped more champagne. "Because of all the talk." She winked.

"What talk?"

"I hate to say."

I didn't believe that. The Alicia Layne I knew loved to gossip.

"Please tell me." I pleaded. "It's important."

"Tonight almost didn't happen because Enzo was leery of catering anything involving Victoria Pendwell."

"Why didn't he want to deal with her?"

"Supposedly, he catered a private party for her on July fourth, and she wasn't prompt in paying."

"Don't most caterers require a down payment in advance and then payment in full right before the event?"

"Usually. But since her late husband was one of Enzo's preferred clients, he made an exception. According to one of the other waitresses here, when Victoria told him she had a small cash flow problem and couldn't pay in full until two weeks after the July fourth event, he said that would be okay."

"Let me guess. She didn't pay him."

"Exactly. She didn't cough up the money until three months ago when he threatened to contact a collection agency. If that got out, can you imagine what it would do to the Pendwell reputation?"

CHAPTER 22

"Good morning." Abby slammed the door behind her and blew into the kitchen. "What a beautiful day it is."

I downed what remained of my third cup of coffee before looking up, frowning. "No one should be so cheerful this early in the morning."

"It's nine o'clock. You seem a bit grumpy. What's up?"

"I was sorting through yesterday's mail and found this." I held up an envelope.

After bending to greet Brandy and Archie, who had collided with one another in an attempt to be the first to reach my daughter, Abby grabbed the envelope.

"Uh, oh. Traffic Bureau. This can't be good."

"It's not. I got caught by a red light camera," I grumbled.

"You drive like a snail. How did this happen?"

"About two weeks ago, I sped through a red light on the road about one and a half miles past the wildlife refuge. It was the only way I could prevent a tailgater from rear-ending my car. I didn't realize a red light camera had been installed."

Red light cameras had been placed at many intersections throughout Long Island. Once the traffic signal turned to red, the camera snapped a picture of the license of any car that went through. A few weeks later, the guilty party received a summons in the mail calling for a hefty fine.

Abby nodded as she poured herself a cup of coffee. "The counties love the revenue stream from these cameras. Jason said a new batch was installed two weeks ago."

"This must be one of them. I didn't know it was there." I sighed. "What brings you here?"

"I need to borrow a platter for tonight's dinner. Don't forget. You're asking Jason's grandmother about my ring. Have you decided how you'll bring that up?"

"Not sure yet, but I'll find a way."

Abby made her way to the counter, stretched up, and pulled open the door to the overhead cabinet where I stored my serving dishes. "This one is just right for my Athenian Shrimp," she said, grabbing a platter in the shape of a fish.

Abby pulled out a chair, and plopped down across from me. "What's that?" she asked, pointing to a large Styrofoam poster board she now faced. Earlier, I had propped it up on an easel and placed it near the archway that separated the kitchen from the dining room.

"Oh, I found the easel in the basement. It's back from when I took those painting courses. I decided to bring it up here and use it to mount my suspect board."

"Suspect board?"

"I'm planning to list all the suspects, their motives, and other pertinent information."

"Great idea. Let's do it."

I grabbed a black marker and scribbled five names. Underneath the list, I placed a question mark.

"First is George Grogin. He had been having issues with Melissa. I need to find out how serious the rift between them was.

"Next is Jeremy Toth, who turns out to be more than the jilted lover. If Melissa went through with her contract agreement, allowing her to take over part of *Crepes Galore,* he'd lose his dream. He claims Melissa granted him an extension, but all we have is his word.

"Then we have Elena, who wanted Melissa's job. The two argued frequently. One of their encounters got physical."

Abby read off the fourth name on my list. "Victoria Pendwell. She also wanted Melissa out as director. If Victoria was cooking the books, Melissa may have been blackmailing her."

I held the marker upright while pausing to gather my thoughts. "I added Austin to the suspect list. Now that he has announced his candidacy for the state senate, he has a powerful motive that intertwines with Victoria. If rumors of Victoria's bid rigging are true, that will not only ruin her, but it would destroy Austin politically."

"And Elena's future too. She's marrying into the Pendwell family." Abby pointed to the question mark I'd drawn on the board. "What is that for?"

"Perhaps there is a sixth suspect—one that involves the pregnancy. Jeremy hadn't had physical contact with Melissa since the breakup. Melissa dated Austin once, but that was nearly two years ago. So who is the father? And has he anything to do with Melissa's murder?"

"I don't see how you can find out?"

"I need to delve deeper into Melissa. If you know a little about who was killed, it should tell you a little about who did the killing. I'll call Melissa's old roommate, Linda Lau, later today. Hopefully, if I can pick her brain, she can remember something that will help."

I poured another cup of coffee. "I also need to find out more about the other suspects, especially the Pendwells. Victoria has always been socially prominent and therefore newsworthy. There's lots of information on her, but—"

"It's what's not out in the public eye that you need to uncover." Abby completed the thought.

I moved my marker back to Elena Salazar. "Not a Pendwell yet, but soon to be one. Elena is a puzzle. As Austin's fiancé, the media is now focusing more on her, but little is known about her life before she came to the wildlife refuge.

"The refuge's website has been updated and now gives her in-depth biography," I continued. "It lists Elena Salazar's last job as program coordinator for the Long Island Nature Museum. I'm going to check with their employees to see if anyone remembers her."

"What about Austin? He's always been in society news," Abby admitted. "But since he's running for public office, a lot more information should be available."

"Yes. And I intend to talk to a few campaign workers."

"Jason can probably find out where Austin's campaign headquarter is located," Abby volunteered.

I smiled. "Oh, no. I'm not going to his campaign headquarters. I don't want the sanitized version of Austin Pendwell."

"But I thought you said—"

"I want the dirt. I plan to visit the headquarters of his opponent."

CHAPTER 23

During my internet research, I discovered that Austin Pendwell's opponent was Jennifer Sheridan, a forty-two year-old insurance broker. The website gave the address of her campaign headquarters, so I decided to drive there this morning.

The headquarters appeared busy this Saturday with more than a dozen campaign workers stuffing envelopes while seated around two long tables. A few nodded at me when I entered, but most didn't look up from their work.

"May I help you?" asked a young man, sporting a well-trimmed goatee. He had emerged from a back room and now made his way to a large coffee urn on a side table.

"I wanted to find out more about Jennifer Sheridan and her opponent," I said. "I haven't made up my mind yet." Truth be told, I didn't live in this senatorial district.

"I'd be happy to tell you everything about Jennifer and why she'd be a terrific state senator," he said. "Follow me." He grabbed a paper cup, filled it with coffee, and led me to a side table with stacks of campaign literature. "By the way, I'm Jennifer's campaign coordinator. My name is Stan.

"This tells you all about Jennifer's professional and educational background as well as her involvement in the community." He handed me a brochure.

"And this," he said, picking up another flyer, "talks about what Jennifer stands for and supports."

"Before I make a choice I want to find out about her opponent, Austin Pendwell," I said as casually as possible. Austin was the only reason I was here, but I figured the campaign coordinator might grow suspicious if I didn't show any interest in Jennifer.

Stan's phone chimed. "I have to take this. Why don't you sit down and read these brochures. Have a cup of coffee. I'll be back in a few minutes to answer any questions."

I could never resist an offer of coffee. As Stan headed to the back office, I grabbed a cup and sat down next to an attractive brunette who was stuffing envelopes.

"Hi. I'm Kristy," I said.

"I'm Diana. I overheard your conversation with Stan. I can tell you about Austin Pendwell," the brunette said in a voice not much louder than a whisper.

I turned my head to face her.

"Stan will talk to you about ideology. I'll tell you about character. Austin has none. He's a pig."

"Why do you say that?"

"I dated Austin."

"I take it the relationship didn't end pleasantly?"

"That's an understatement. Austin Pendwell is used to getting his way. When he doesn't… well, let's just say, all his charm disappears. The man has a temper."

"Where did you meet him?"

"In law school. We were in the same study group."

"How long did you go together?"

"About six months." She sighed. "I held two jobs while in law school to make ends meet. At first, I was impressed by all his wealth. But I got over it quickly." She shook her head. "What a narcissist."

The brunette sipped her bottled water and then continued. "Austin won't take no for an answer. On our last date, I wasn't feeling well after dinner and wanted to go home. He said that since he paid for my meal, I owed him some fun back at his apartment. Can you believe that?"

I shook my head. "What happened?"

"We had a huge argument, and I had to fight him off. Finally, he gave up and took me home."

"Why not come out and say something?"

She avoided my eyes and stared at the table. "It happened nearly ten years ago. Times were different then." She shrugged. "And now..." She paused. "Let's just say, I don't think it would be in my best interests. But the least I can do is see he loses this election. I come here every Saturday morning and Wednesday night."

Before I could ask another question, Stan returned.

"Have you looked over the brochures?" he asked.

"No. I was chatting with this lady." I rose from my chair. "I'll take the brochures home and read them. If I have any questions, I'll contact you."

It looked as if he was about to say something when his phone rang. He handed me his business card. "Here's my number. Hope you'll be back."

I said good-bye and made my way to the door.

Although I hadn't learned anything directly related to Melissa's murder, I was beginning to fill in a picture of Austin Pendwell. Perhaps I could draw upon it in the future.

* * * * *

I decided to pick up dessert to bring to Abby's house tonight. Patsy's Pie Place, one of my favorite bakeries, was on the way home, so I decided to stop there.

I found a parking space at the end of the block and trekked back to the store, passing a deli, a dry cleaner, and a small Italian restaurant. Once inside, the bakery, I inhaled the aroma of freshly baked breads and other delights. After making my purchase—a cherry crumb pie—I left the bakery and was about to head back to my car when I spotted a familiar figure emerging from the Italian restaurant.

Austin Pendwell.

His arm was around the blonde he'd been talking with at last night's fundraiser.

* * * * *

Upon arriving home, I grabbed my mail from the box. After tossing aside the bills and junk flyers, I slit open the one from Pendwell Wildlife

Refuge trustee Susan Hanson. As I requested, she'd sent me a copy of Gerber Engineering's proposal for the restoration of the refuge. Although she'd missed the meeting where this was voted upon, she had the good sense to get and keep this document. I sat down and read the first two pages.

"Too technical for me," I said to Brandy and Archie, who had scooted into the kitchen to greet me and were now positioned on either side of my chair. They both cocked their heads.

I stashed the proposal in my bag. Tonight, I'd ask Jason's father, a retired engineer, if he could coax one of his environmental engineering associates to look it over and tell me if the costs were in line with what they should be.

Since I hadn't eaten lunch, I made myself a peanut butter and jelly sandwich. I'd no sooner sat down to eat when my phone chimed. Linda Lau's name popped up.

"I was going to call you later today," I said before she could speak. "We need to know more about the last few weeks of Melissa's life. You were away, but—"

"We may have a break in the case," Linda interrupted.

"What?"

"Melissa's mom called me earlier. She wants to talk to us tomorrow. She found a strange note. It may provide a clue as to why Melissa was murdered."

CHAPTER 24

Matt and I pulled into the driveway of Abby's beach house, which was three miles from our home. As I hopped out of the car, I inhaled the salt-water air—no surprise since the Great South Bay was part of Abby's back yard.

"Are we the first to arrive?" I asked Abby as she ushered us inside.

"Yes. But Jason's dad and grandmother should be here any minute."

"Owl," I called out, delighted to see Abby's cat. The calico had been abandoned a year ago in the trash bin behind Matt's veterinary office. The poor cat was terrified of dogs and didn't respond well to Archie or Brandy's attempt to play, so it was decided she would be better off with Abby. I missed her but knew she was thriving.

Owl scooted over, rubbed her body against my legs, and purred. She did the same with Matt.

"Let's go into the living room for drinks," Jason suggested. He smiled at me. "I made a batch of pomegranate martins for you."

A batch? I was the only one here who drank them.

We settled down in the living room where I made myself comfortable on the sofa facing the sliding glass doors. For a brief moment I watched the wind whip the bay into angry whitecaps. A storm was on its way.

"What's new with the murder case?" Abby asked, jolting me out of my thoughts.

I told my family about seeing Austin and the blonde.

"He had his arm around her," I said. "He's running for public office. You would think he would be more discreet."

"Austin doesn't want to run," Jason said. "This is his mother's idea."

I hadn't realized that. "His mother has that much influence?"

"It's hard to say no to Victoria Buckley Pendwell." Jason said. "One of my associates went to law school with Austin and had dinner with him a few weeks ago. He told me Jason and his mother had a huge argument about the senate seat. And Elena sided with Victoria. But that's to be expected."

"Why?" I asked. Owl hopped on my lap, nearly spilling my drink.

Jason shrugged.

"What aren't you telling me?"

Jason hesitated. "What I'm about to tell you is strictly rumor. I don't know if it's true. I do think—"

"Most rumors contain an element of truth," I interrupted. "But I won't take it as fact without digging further."

"Okay," Jason agreed. "Elena is ambitious. She'd been engaged to someone she worked with before she came to the wildlife refuge, and she broke it off after meeting Austin. The talk is she saw Austin as a way to move up in social status. Now, his run for the senate increases that status even more, and it provides a way to get her environmental agenda enacted into law. She does take that issue seriously."

"You're saying she's marrying him so she can get legislation passed?"

"That and living the life of a Pendwell." Jason grinned. "She likes nice things."

Before Jason could speak further, someone rapped on the front door. Jason's father and grandmother had arrived.

After everyone exchanged pleasantries and were seated with drinks— his grandmother had a pomegranate martini too—we began talking about the wedding plans. Although I wanted to question Jason further, I knew this would have to wait.

Abby announced that dinner would be ready in about ten minutes. She and Jason headed into the kitchen to put the finishing touches on the meal.

Jason's father, Dominick, a distinguished looking man with a mane of silver hair and a matching mustache, had settled in an armchair next to the sofa. He leaned over to me and said, "Jason told me you have something you'd like me to see."

"Yes." I reached into my bag and pulled out the proposal on the clean-up of the wildlife refuge that I received from Susan Hanson. "I'd like to know if the costs listed here are realistic or completely out of the ballpark."

"One of my former associates specializes in environmental engineering. He's a good friend and he's discreet." Dominick took the proposal from me. "But I will tell you, it may be difficult to determine without knowing all the land conditions."

"I appreciate anything you can do."

Abby called us to dinner.

Abby inherited the "cooking genes" from my paternal grandmother—the Greek side of the family. I inherited "cooking genes" from my mother which were basically non-existent. Tonight, Abby had prepared an appetizer of spanakopita followed by the main dish of Athenian Shrimp over rice along with a Greek salad.

I was seated next to Jason's grandmother, waiting for a chance to talk to her privately about Abby's engagement ring. When Abby and Jason were clearing off the plates and Matt and Dom discussing the New York Yankees versus the Mets, I saw my opportunity.

"How did your bathroom renovation turn out?" I asked.

"Wonderful. It was worth the inconvenience."

"I may be doing a renovation in the near future," I lied. "Would you recommend the remodelers that you used?"

"Definitely."

"Besides doing good work, my major concern is how trustworthy they are. Matt and I are gone a lot, and they would be working alone in the house."

"That's always a concern," she admitted. "I was home most days, but there were times I had to go out."

"What did you do?"

"I have a safe in my house. I always keep my cash and jewelry there."

Abby and Jason returned with my cherry crumb pie and the chocolate layer cake Dominick had brought. I decided my questioning needed to head in another direction.

"Abby's ring is gorgeous. It has such a sparkle." I said to Jason's grandmother.

"I had it cleaned two weeks before I gave it to my grandson to give to her."

"Cleaned? Where did you have it done?"

"Krill's Jewelry. That's right up the road from where I live. Convenient, plus they offer free cleanings. I understand a lot of jewelers do that. It's a way of bringing more people into the store. Who knows? Someone may buy something while there."

I nodded. "It makes sense. And the cleaning doesn't take that much time, right?"

"It takes longer than you think. They had so many customers who came because of the offer that it took three days until they finally got to my cleaning."

"How did they handle that? Did they make you come back in three days or did you leave the ring there?"

"Oh, they were most accommodating. They let me leave the ring there."

CHAPTER 25

Sunday afternoon, I picked up Linda Lau and we sped along the highway on our way to visit Melissa Modica's mom.

"Did she say what she found?" I asked as we turned off the highway onto a suburban street.

"No. It was a quick call. Her husband was there, and she didn't want him to know she was speaking to me. That's why she asked us to visit today. He won't be home. He's on a bowling league and plays every Sunday afternoon at four. The last time we saw him, right after Melissa's death, was the first time he missed the games in three years. But according to his wife, he's back to playing."

She paused. "Mel's father is strict. He doesn't believe in drinking—they have no liquor in the house. And he doesn't believe in gambling either. According to what Melissa told me, everyone in his bowling league puts five dollars in a pot each week. The bowler with the highest score gets it all. Her father is the only one who doesn't participate."

When we arrived, Mrs. Modica ushered us into her dark and gloomy living room. Although it was a bright spring day, the heavy drapes were drawn closed, shutting out all sunlight.

"I found a note," Mrs. Modica said, getting right to the point as soon as we were seated. "The police checked Melissa's room and took her computer and phone, but they left everything else alone. At first, I couldn't go in there..." A tear rolled down her cheek.

Linda and I said nothing. Sometimes silence was the most compassionate response to sorrow.

"Finally, I did go in. Melissa had a beautiful designer handbag that my niece, Teresa, had admired. I wanted to give it to her, so she'd have something to remember Melissa. Teresa's been a godsend to me since this nightmare happened."

She paused, apparently needing time to compose herself. "The bag had been a gift from Jeremy. It was hardly used. Melissa wasn't into fancy stuff." Another tear trickled down her face.

Linda and I waited patiently while Mrs. Modica pulled a handkerchief out of her pocket and dabbed at her eyes.

Last time Linda and I were here, Mrs. Modica had still been in shock. Now it looked as if she was facing the brutal reality.

She continued. "I remember Melissa once saying, jokingly, that if she didn't know where to put something, she'd stuff it in that bag. That way she could always find it. Anyway, I was cleaning out Melissa's bag, and I came across this." She grabbed a paper from atop the coffee table and handed it to Linda.

As Linda unfolded the note, I peered over her shoulder.

Scrawled across the note was the following:

Monday Midnight At Clearing
555-0739

"Did you show this to the police?" Linda asked.

"No. My husband wants this all to go away." Mrs. Modica began to cry softly again. "He's a good man. And he loved Melissa. But he's so shocked and disappointed about the pregnancy. And embarrassed. I know it's common in this day and age, but he's old school. I thought you could help—discreetly."

"Have you called the phone number?" I asked.

Mrs. Modica shook her head.

I grabbed my phone and punched in 555-0739.

No ring. It was no longer operating.

"It's a burner phone." I could feel my shoulders sag with disappointment.

"Does that mean you don't know the owner?"

I nodded. Silence permeated the room.

"I'm sorry if I wasted your time," Mrs. Modica said.

"This isn't a waste. I have some questions I'd like to ask."

Mrs. Modica nodded.

"You said after Melissa broke off with Jeremy, she came home around six every night and stayed here," I said, leaning forward in my chair.

"Yes. She never went out at night."

"What about weekends?"

"She stayed home on Friday and Saturday nights, but during the day, I do recall her leaving a lot. I think it was mostly to go hiking or running."

"Did she go with friends?"

"I don't remember." Mrs. Modica frowned and appeared to be mulling over something in her mind. "Wait. A few times she ran with a friend."

Linda leaned forward in her chair. "Do you know what friend?"

"Erin Leahy."

"Erin Leahy was from her high school days," Linda said, turning to face me. "Remember, I ran into her at the funeral wake."

I nodded.

Mrs. Modica's face clouded. "I never liked Erin. She was not like you, Linda. She talked too much."

Linda smiled. "Erin can be a gossip. And she loves posting on social media. I'm surprised Melissa and Erin stayed close friends. Melissa was a very private person, and she hated gossip. Their only connection was their love of running and of the outdoors."

Mrs. Modica nodded in agreement. "I remember you were away at the time. The one Saturday morning before she went out running with Erin, Melissa said she wished she could talk with you. I had a feeling she had something on her mind."

* * * * *

"You were away, and she was here," I said to Linda as we drove away from the Modica house. "Even if Melissa didn't trust Erin the way she trusted you, she still may have confided in her."

"You're right," Linda admitted, pulling out her phone. "It can't hurt to try to talk to her. Oh, no!"

"What's the matter?"

"She's away. Remember at the funeral she said she was going camping for two weeks. She won't be back till the end of this week."

"Can't you call her anyway? We can talk through the phone."

Linda shook her head. "I guarantee she's out of cell range. Erin likes to go deep into the wilderness when she camps."

"I guess we'll have to wait until she gets back."

"You really think she can help?"

I shrugged. "Don't know. But we have to question everyone. Someone out there knows something."

CHAPTER 26

My first stop Monday was the Long Island Nature Museum, Elena Salazar's last place of employment before she began her career at the Pendwell Wildlife Refuge. The museum was housed in a one story, cedar-shingled building in the midst of a county park, and it featured exhibits of Long Island's flora and fauna.

A docent was about to begin a tour of the exhibits, so I joined the six others in the group. Two were senior citizens. The other four, according to their conversation, were young college students studying Long Island's habitats.

When we finished the tour, which ended with a look at a replica of a beaver's dam, the docent made her way across the large lobby and was about to enter the staff office.

"Excuse me," I called, rushing in her direction as she grabbed the doorknob. "I wanted to let you know how much I enjoyed your program. A friend of mine worked here not too long ago and told me about this place. She was right."

"Who's your friend?" The docent smiled. She was a small, middle-aged woman with bird-like eyes and a beakish nose. She wore her gray hair atop her head in a bun.

"Elena Salazar. Do you know her?"

"Yes." Her smile faded. "Elena has become quite a success story around here. She's now director of the Pendwell Wildlife Refuge and engaged to Austin Pendwell." While saying his name, her face took on an expression that looked as if she were eating lemons.

"You don't like Austin?"

"I never met him. It's just…" She paused. "I better not say anything.

You're a friend of Elena."

I decided to come clean. "I'm not really a friend, but I do know her. I'm a writer for *Animal Advocate Magazine*."

"I shouldn't be talking to you at all."

"Please," I begged. "I'm not going to mention you or include anything you say in my story. But I need to find out more about Elena."

"Why?" Her expression was guarded.

"It may have to do with the murder where she worked."

The docent's eyes widened. Her mouth opened as if she was about to say something, but nothing came out.

"The murder?" she finally said. "You think Elena committed the murder? I can't—"

"I don't know who committed the murder," I said, cutting her off. "But understanding the personalities and backgrounds of the people at the Pendwell Wildlife Refuge will help form a picture that could be useful."

"I didn't have much contact with Elena when she worked here," the docent said. "I don't know what I can tell you."

"How did she get along with everyone here?"

"Okay." The docent shrugged. "We're a small operation. The only paid employees are the curator and the program coordinator—that was Elena's position. But the rest of the workers, including me, are volunteers. You have to treat volunteers differently than you do paid employees. If volunteers aren't happy, they'll quit."

Before I could ask a question, the docent added, "Her attitude toward the volunteers was courteous but aloof. No one hated her, but no one loved her, either."

"How did she get along with her boss, the curator?"

The docent grinned. "That's different. Colin, the curator, was once her fiancé, so I'd say they got along fine. At least until they broke up."

"Who broke it off?"

"She did. Once Elena started working at the wildlife refuge and met Austin, she dumped Colin and set her sights on the Pendwell Prince." The docent hesitated. "Elena was passionate about the environment. But she was also passionate about money. She was a bit of a social climber."

This is what Jason had told me, but I needed a clearer picture. Perhaps the docent could fill in some blanks.

"You're saying she wanted Austin because of his money?"

"Money and status. Elena came from a working class family. She attended school on a full scholarship—brilliant girl. When she met Colin, she was straight out of college. Colin's parents were professionals. Mom's a high school principal and dad's an attorney."

"That was important to her?"

"Yes. Their family friends were professionals and in positions that could ultimately help her. For example, Colin's father's best friend owns a car dealership. He got her a great deal on a new luxury model."

"But I'm guessing his connections were not as good as Austin's network."

"When she started working at the preserve and met Austin, she hit the jackpot."

A thought flashed through my mind. "How did Elena get the job at the wildlife refuge?" I asked.

"Well, according to Colin, Elena persuaded one of her old college professors to recommend her. This professor had attended boarding school with Victoria's husband. They go back a long ways." The docent smirked.

She wasn't telling me everything.

I said nothing, aware that an uncomfortable silence will often cause someone to speak up. Plus, I sensed this woman loved to gossip.

It worked.

The docent smiled wickedly. "I heard Elena had an affair with this professor while she was his student."

"I assume the two remained on good terms," I said.

"That's not what I heard." The docent stood there, still smiling. She was waiting for me to probe further.

"What did you hear?"

"Elena and the professor ended their relationship with a rather nasty fight. I understand she hadn't spoken with him since she graduated. That's why Colin was surprised she called the professor for the recommendation."

"This is strange," I admitted. "Maybe she felt enough time had passed, and he no longer was angry."

"Or maybe she threatened to expose him if he didn't recommend her." The docent appeared to be enjoying this conversation. "Having an affair with your student is taboo at most colleges and years later could come back to haunt you."

I mulled over the docent's statement. I was beginning to form a picture of Elena Salazar that was none too flattering. Did Elena pressure her old professor to make a recommendation under threat of exposure?

But more importantly, did Melissa know about this? If so, did Melissa threaten to tell Austin about it?

CHAPTER 27

On the way home, I made a stop at a strip mall shopping center. I rang the doorbell outside Krill's Jewelers and waited to be buzzed inside.

"What may I help you with?" asked a rotund, balding man who was standing behind the counter. He smiled broadly, his teeth glistening.

I don't know why, but the image of the big, bad wolf flashed through my mind.

"I want to have my diamond cleaned." I extended my hand, enabling him to see my engagement ring. "What would it cost?"

"Absolutely nothing." He grinned. "We offer free cleanings."

"That's wonderful. "How long will it take? I need to be at work in an hour."

"Unfortunately, we can't do it now. We're too busy."

There was one other customer in the shop—a middle age man looking at watches. A salesclerk was assisting him, and two additional employees were chatting with each other behind the counter.

The rotund, balding man must have read my thoughts. "Our sales help doesn't handle cleanings. We employ a specialist for cleanings and repairs, but he is not here yet."

"Should I make an appointment for later?"

"Not necessary. Leave the ring. We'll give you a receipt, of course. You can pick the ring back up Tuesday or Wednesday."

I smiled sweetly. "I'd feel naked without my ring for that long. Why don't I make an appointment?"

"Because we are never sure what time he's coming." Was I imagining it, or was he talking through clenched teeth?

"I'm not sure I want to leave it."

The man sighed. "Okay. My cleaner will definitely be here tomorrow morning. If you don't want to leave your ring now, come back here after ten tomorrow, and we can do it while you wait."

"Let me think about it." I departed and headed to my car. I had an idea, but there could be a glitch.

* * * * *

When I arrived home, Matt was sitting at the kitchen table. He was eating a bowl of rocky road ice cream, and the two dogs were on either side of him, hoping something would drop. They would be disappointed. Ice cream doesn't have crumbs.

"What are you doing?" We're having dinner in less than an hour. Abby and Jason are coming over."

"I was starving," he said. "Abby watches me like a hawk at the office. No more jelly donuts."

"She's concerned for your health."

"But she eats like a longshoreman."

"Unlike you, she's hasn't turned fifty." I gave him the once over. "And you have put on a few pounds."

"No I haven't."

"Just a little." I grinned.

"What's for dinner?" Matt asked, changing the subject. "Pizza?"

"No. The kids are bringing sushi."

Jason and Abby arrived a few minutes later. Matt had finished his ice cream.

"I want to hear what Jason's grandmother said to you," Abby grabbed some plates and handed out the sushi.

Abby had texted me yesterday and asked if Jason's grandmother had given any indication during Saturday's dinner of how the diamond might have been switched. I'd texted back saying I was pretty sure I knew, but first I needed to verify something. I promised I would fill her in today.

"Had she left the ring sitting in a drawer?" Abby asked. "Do you think the bathroom remodelers took it?"

110

I shook my head. "No. Before she gave it to you, she took it to Krill's Jewelers for a cleaning. She left it overnight."

"Left it with them! Everyone knows you never do that," Jason sputtered.

"Apparently, she didn't."

Jason shook his head.

"I visited Krill's Jewelers today," I said after taking a bite of my California roll. "The sales clerk wanted me to leave my ring, but when I balked, he said I could come back tomorrow and the cleaning would be done while I waited."

"Of course. It's too risky to switch every ring that comes for a cleaning," Jason admitted. "I'm sure they size up customers."

"You ask lots of questions, Mom," Abby said. "They're not going to take a chance with you. But an elderly lady like Jason's grandmother is the perfect target."

"I think the district attorney's office should do a sting and send an undercover officer into the jewelers with a diamond ring," I said.

"Absolutely." Jason nodded. "I'll talk to my bureau chief tomorrow. We can get a diamond ring from the police evidence room—one that was confiscated during a drug heist. Then we'll have it plotted."

Plotted? I searched my memory for the term, recalling it somewhat.

"That has something to do with blemishes in the diamond, right?" I asked.

Jason finished chewing. "A plotting diagram is a map of a diamond's clarity characteristics, which are one of the factors used in determining the stone's value. Every diamond has some flaws, most not visible to the eye. Plotting makes a map of these inclusions. It's like fingerprinting."

"I get it. This way, when you get the ring back, you can verify if the plotting is the same. If not, it's a different diamond."

"Exactly." Jason leaned forward, placed his elbows on the table, and formed a steeple with his fingers. It looked as if he were praying that what he was about to say would come true. "Since Krill may be targeting seniors, we'll need to use an undercover officer who can be made up to look old and who can act naïve."

"Do you have someone?" Abby asked.

"We'll use someone from the police department. They probably have an investigator who would fit the bill." Jason shrugged. "This could work."

Abby and I exchanged glances. "Could" was the key word in Jason's statement.

What were the odds that Krill's Jewelers would switch the diamond from the ring handed to them by the undercover officer?

I sighed. "Let's hope this works. In the meantime, let's finish eating. We should leave in five minutes. And everyone needs to take a light jacket or sweater tonight. The woods can be cold when it's dark."

"I can't believe you talked us into this," Jason muttered as he rose from his chair.

"Let's go, guys," I said. "Put your plates in the sink. It's time for our next adventure."

CHAPTER 28

A full moon.
The perfect night for an owl prowl.

We piled in the car for our trip to the Pendwell Wildlife Refuge for what was advertised as "a moonlit stroll down one of its many nature trails," otherwise known as an owl prowl. The walk was to be led by Elena Salazar.

When we arrived at the refuge, we were introduced to eleven other people who would be taking the nighttime walk with us.

"Please be as quiet as possible," Elena said as we started off.

The forest is different at night, full of shadows and mystery. The tall pines appeared like dark arrows aimed at the sky. The odor of rich earth and skunk weed seemed stronger now than during the day. Crickets chirped, and I heard the flutter of wings and the rustle of small creatures scurrying nearby.

"Oh, no!" I cried out. I tripped on a small rock, but Matt grabbed me before I fell to the ground.

"Are you okay?" he asked.

"I'm fine. I—"

"Ssh! I know you want to look up in the trees, but you need to watch where you're going," Elena reproached me in hushed tones.

I realized visibility is poor in the woods after dark, even with a full moon. Bumpy roots, holes in the ground, and long, overhanging limbs that suddenly pop up make speed impossible.

Thoughts of Melissa's murder flashed through my brain. I was pretty sure there was only a partial moon in the sky that night, making visibility more difficult than now. Despite being a track star, Melissa would not have been able to run to escape her murderer.

Hiding would be difficult too. The slightest noise is amplified in the woods. Rustling of leaves underfoot. Even the sound that comes from nervous breathing.

Is that why the killer chose to meet her in this place?

But why would Melissa agree to meet someone here? The question haunted me.

I was jolted out of my thoughts when an owl swooped down, and I heard the heart-wrenching cry of some creature who had met its doom.

I was glad I'd worn a sweater as the forest was colder at night than during the day—or maybe it was the sense of eeriness that sent a chill down my spine. A red fox scurried along the forest floor. A possum family waddled into the thicket. Three pairs of eyes peered at us from a hole in a tree.

An hour later, we returned to our starting point.

"I enjoyed this," Matt said with enthusiasm.

"You should get out and hike on a regular basis, Dad," Abby advised.

"Let's not get carried away. I know I need to lose a few pounds. I'll watch what I eat, but my exercise will be shaking my head back and forth when offered a second portion." He grinned.

Abby groaned and shook her head. Jason turned his face away, grinning. I suppressed my smile.

Victoria and Austin, who did not participate in the walk, were waiting for our group in the administration building. They had set up a table with coffee, tea, and cookies, and now they helped Elena serve the refreshments to all Owl Prowl participants.

"What's the matter, Mom?" Abby asked. Victoria and Elena were huddled in conversation with several participants, including Jason. Matt was hovering over the refreshment table eating a cookie. I stood in a corner drinking coffee.

"I may be approaching Melissa's murder from the wrong angle. I keep asking myself the same question. Who would Melissa not fear meeting in the forest? But there is another side to that situation. The woods at night are not for the faint of heart. Which of the suspects would be comfortable rendezvousing there?"

I held up my hand and ticked off my fingers one by one. "First of all, Jeremy is unfamiliar with the woods. Secondly, I can't see Victoria traipsing around the forest in her expensive, designer heels."

Abby grinned. "I'm sure she has other footwear. But you're right. It's out of character. And for Austin too. I think the closest he gets to nature is the golf course."

"That leaves Elena and George." I said. "I don't know enough about them, although Elena navigated through the woods pretty well tonight."

Abby furrowed her brows, appearing deep in thought. "Just because someone is unlikely to do something doesn't mean they won't. I don't think we can eliminate anyone at this point. What's your next step?"

"I'm not sure." As I talked, I scanned the room.

"That's odd," I mumbled.

"What's odd?"

"Victoria and Austin are no longer here," I said. "Let's go outside."

"Why? What about Dad and Jason?"

"They're in the midst of a conversation with that young couple." I nodded in their direction. "I'll explain what I'm up to later. Let's go."

Abby and I padded out of the building with our flashlights.

"Let's head to the back," I said. "I have a hunch."

"I guess the back of the building is better than returning to the nature trail." My daughter's voice dripped with sarcasm.

"Ssh!"

"Mom, what are we doing?"

"I'm pretty sure Victoria would not have departed for the night without saying a big good-bye to everyone. This leads me to believe she went outside with Austin for a private conversation."

My hunch was correct. As we crept along the side of the building, I heard voices. Then I spotted Victoria and Austin.

Abby and I selected a spot to hide along the side of a dumpster where we wouldn't be seen. But we were close enough to hear them talking.

"I can't believe you did that." It was Austin.

"I can't believe what you did either," Victoria snapped back. "You almost destroyed your future."

"Don't you mean your future?" There was bitterness in Austin's voice. "It's what you want, not me."

"Don't be a fool. This is what you're meant to be. I want you to forget the past and move forward. Now, go back and start networking."

"We better get inside before they do," I whispered to my daughter.

Abby and I scooted around the side of the building to the front door.

"What was that about?" Abby asked, once we were back by the refreshment table. "Do you think it has to do with Austin's senatorial run?"

I nodded. "Probably. But some of what Victoria said… I wonder if it is also connected to Melissa's murder."

CHAPTER 29

The next morning my phone trilled. Jason's name popped up.

"We're good to go with the diamond sting," he said. "I spoke with my bureau chief. The office is sending an undercover investigator to Krill's Jewelers tomorrow with a diamond ring to be cleaned. The diamond has been plotted, so when we get it back we can check if it's still the same stone."

"Who's going undercover?"

"There's an investigator from the police department who will be working with us. She's in her late forties, but her son is a theatre make-up artist. He guarantees he can make his mom look thirty years older than she is. She'll appear frail, and she'll act naïve—the perfect patsy."

After saying goodbye to Jason, I headed to the mall for another day of work at the Bay Cove Pet Shop. I'd notified the SPCA about the delivery of more puppies at the end of the week. I told them how this delivery service had a history of transporting sick pups. The SPCA planned to be there on Friday. They'd wait at the far end of the parking lot until I sent a text that the truck arrived.

Today, I simply planned to gather more information for my story.

Upon entering the store, I spotted Eliot, the owner. He appeared to be in a heated conversation with a man in a suit who held a dog carrier. I couldn't hear everything said, but I did make out the word "lawsuit."

Eliot motioned for Billy.

"Take this dog and put him in the back," Eliot ordered.

Billy unlatched the dog carrier and removed a beagle puppy. It wasn't a young puppy. Judging from his size, I would have guessed he was about six or six seven months old. Eliot made his way to the counter, pulled a checkbook out of a drawer, scribbled something, and handed a check to the man in the suit. The man grabbed his empty carrier and stomped out the door.

"What happened?" I asked Eliot.

"Dissatisfied customer. Wanted his money back." Eliot glanced at his watch. "This guy is a lawyer and threatened to sue. He had no grounds, but I didn't want the hassle."

Eliot turned and yelled to Billy, "Get the beagle and put him in one of the cages up front."

"But you said to put him in the back room," Billy called back.

"Now, I want him out here to be sold." Eliot pulled out a handkerchief and wiped the perspiration off his forehead.

Billy hesitated. "Don't you think—"

"Do it!" Eliot ordered.

Billy brought the beagle from the back room and placed him in a cage. Eliot glanced at his watch again and strolled through the store. After a few minutes, he returned to his office.

I bee-lined to where Billy stood.

"Why didn't you want to bring that dog back out?"

He shook his head. "It's not right. The store shouldn't sell this dog."

Ted, the other sales associate, was standing nearby. He apparently heard our conversation.

"That beagle has temperament issues," Ted said. "Eliot told me earlier she bit her new owner twice and drew blood. She bit Billy before she was sold, too. I'm not talking about puppy 'play' bites either."

"And Eliot is putting her back up for sale?"

Ted shrugged and strolled away. I exchanged glances with Billy who shook his head. "I hope no one with kids buys her."

Puppy mill dogs sometimes had aggression issues from genetic inbreeding and lack of early socialization. If this puppy was six months old, he had spent most of that time in a cage.

Billy left to fill food dishes. There was only one customer and Ted was with her, so I strolled around the store taking stock of all the puppies. I noticed the black poodle with the cough wasn't here. During the next hour, no one else came into the store.

Since I'd had a few cups of coffee before I arrived here this morning,

I needed to use the lavatory. It was in the back. I'd have to go beyond Eliot's office to reach it.

As I swung open the *Employees Only* door, I gasped.

Sprawled out in a box was the little black poodle.

Dead.

"Oh, no!"

Eliot, whose office door was open, sat hunched over his desk engrossed in paperwork. He looked up and said, "When I arrived today, I found him like this. Looks like a seizure."

My blood boiled, and I felt the heat rising through my body. But I couldn't show my feelings. I couldn't afford to anger Eliot and have him fire me before Friday's SPCA raid. I said nothing.

When I returned to the front of the store, I told Billy what I saw.

Billy shook his head. "Poor pup. Eliot doesn't care. He's mean. I don't know why he killed those snakes either."

"What snakes? What are you talking about?"

"Last month, he got a delivery of snakes right before closing. Most deliveries, like the dogs, are during the day, but the snakes always come at night. The truck pulls up behind the building. I don't know much about it, because Eliot never asks for help. He stays here after the mall closes and takes them out of the crates himself."

"Are they poisonous snakes?"

"No. We don't sell poisonous snakes." Billy shook his head. "I'm not particularly fond of any snake, but there's no reason to kill them."

"How do you know he kills them?"

"When the delivery came last month, it was about ten minutes after closing. The sales people had left, but I was still here cleaning up. Eliot seemed annoyed. He told me to leave and finish up in the morning. I was in the parking lot when I realized I forgot to give fresh water to the guinea pigs. Anyway, I rushed back to the store and let myself in—"

"You have a key?"

"I did. I'm usually the first one here in the morning to clean and make sure everything is set up before we open."

"What happened when you returned?"

"Since Eliot was in the back room, I wanted him to know I was here." Billy grinned. "Didn't want him to think it was a burglar." His smile quickly faded. "So, I went to the backroom, and I saw Eliot slitting open a snake."

"Slitting it open?"

He nodded. "Eliot told me this snake was sick, and he had to do it. I didn't believe him."

"Why?"

"Eliot seemed nervous. Like he knew what he was doing was wrong. I think he just got a thrill out of being mean. He told me not to say anything to anyone about what I saw. He said it might upset the other employees, and he'd fire me if I couldn't be trusted." Billy stared at the floor. "I need this job."

Billy looked up again and frowned. "He told me to leave. He promised he'd make sure the guinea pigs got water before he left. The next morning, when I got to the store, the guinea pig water bottles were empty. He never refilled them."

I digested all Billy had told me.

"Billy," I said. "When I asked you if you had a key, you said you did. Does that mean you don't have it now?"

"Eliot took it away from me the next morning. He claimed he'd be coming in early every morning, so he could let me in. He said mall security was concerned about too many keys distributed to employees."

I could feel the rapid beating of my heart race. Billy thought Eliot was mean. I agreed, but I also had another idea about what was going on. Snakes were sometimes used to smuggle drugs into the country. Packets of cocaine or heroin would be stuffed inside, and the snake's rectum sewn shut.

"How frequently do you get snake deliveries?"

"Once a month. It's funny. They come in a big crate that could hold dozens, but I've never seen more than three new snakes in here at a time."

"Do you know when the next delivery is scheduled?"

"No. But soon. The man is due."

"What man?"

"Two days before their delivery, a scary man comes to the store. He's real big. Heavy. He's got mean eyes too."

"What does the man do?"

"He goes to the back room to see Eliot. No one can get in there then. Eliot locks the door."

Billy paused. "I think that man may come today. It's been exactly a month since I saw him. I know because last time was my birthday."

"And it's usually a month between visits?"

"Yup. And Eliot is nervous today. He's always nervous when this man comes. And he glances at his watch a lot."

"Does this man come at a particular time?"

Billy nodded. "Always before noon."

Noon was twenty minutes away.

I needed to hear the conversation between Eliot and this big scary man. But how? No one would be allowed in the back area once Eliot's visitor arrived.

An idea popped into my head.

The other sales associate was with the only customer in the store. I bee-lined to the back and slowly opened the door to the *Employees Only* section. Once inside, I noticed Eliot's office door was partially ajar. He was huddled over his computer. He didn't notice me creep by.

I quietly opened the lavatory door and stepped into the small room, which was diagonally opposite Eliot's office. Instead of closing the door all the way, I left it open a few inches, enabling me to peek out.

Time passed.

Maybe he's not coming today.

I didn't know how much longer I could hide in here.

Then a door slammed. I peeked out at a man who probably weighed three hundred pounds. He looked like a fairy tale ogre, and he stood only a few feet away from my hiding spot.

Eliot emerged from his office. He locked the door connecting the *Employees Only* section from the showroom. Then he escorted the man into his office. I couldn't see anything, but I could hear them.

"Do you have it?" the man asked.

"Right here," Eliot answered.

"It will be this Thursday night," the man said.

Eliot and the man emerged from the office and left the back area.

I scooted out of the lavatory, through the back area, and into the showroom. The big man was exiting the store.

"Where's Kristy?" Eliot asked Billy.

"I'm over here," I called. "I'm checking the cat food in case a customer has a question."

He eyed me suspiciously. "There are two customers in the store. Ted is with one. You should be with the other."

"Okay." I scooted over to where a teenage boy was tapping on an iguana terrarium. I glanced at my watch. As soon as my shift ended, I had an important phone all to make concerning Thursday night.

CHAPTER 30

Upon leaving the pet shop, I drove to the Pendwell Wildlife Refuge where I was scheduled to interview the new wildlife rehabilitator. As I emerged from my car, I spotted a woman lugging a small cart through the parking lot. The cart was laden with bags and boxes. According to their labels, these containers held an assortment of wild animal food.

I stepped into the administration building and was greeted by Elena Salazar.

"Cassie Chipperwich—that's out new rehabilitator—will be right back," Elena said. "She had to load supplies in her car."

"I think I passed her."

"Cassie is still performing rehabilitation work out of her house, although now that's she's full time at the refuge, she's winding down at home."

"And she gets her supplies from here?"

Elena nodded. "Most wildlife rehabilitators do. We buy in bulk so we get the best prices. Then we sell to the others at cost. If we didn't have several rehabilitators on Long Island working from their homes, a lot of animals wouldn't get the lifesaving treatment they need. So, we try to help as much as we can. Oh, here she is now."

I spun around and found myself facing the woman from the parking lot. Tall, thin, with gray hair hanging loosely to her shoulders, and wearing no make-up, she appeared to be in her late forties.

"Cassie, this is Kristy Farrell from *Animal Advocate Magazine*. Elena introduced us, and then said, "See you later, Kristy. Remember, you're joining me on my trail walk with my youth group later." She vanished back into her office.

"I'm running a little late," Cassie said as we headed to the rehab wing. "I got a call earlier about some baby ducklings. They followed their mother and fell down a drainage pipe. Someone passing by heard the peeping from below the grate and called."

"What did you do?"

"I contacted the fire department to lift the grate. Then I removed the ducklings and reunited them with their mother. She was frantically pacing until they were all back together."

"Are the ducklings here?"

"Nope. None were injured. I transported them all back to the nearby pond. Now, why don't you ask me your questions while we walk," Cassie said.

"Elena said you work out of your home as well as here."

She nodded. "I converted my garage awhile back to accommodate my wildlife cases."

"What type of animals do you have there now?"

"I'm winding down, so I only have a few left. I have a turkey vulture, snapping turtle, Fowler toad…"

"A toad?"

"Yes. His leg was damaged in a so-called routine accident. At least the man who hit him with a weed wacker while gardening had the decency to bring him to me."

"It was an accident, right?"

Cassie sighed. "A stupid accident. That man should have been more careful. He should have checked the area first."

"Are those the only animals you have now?"

"I also have six baby cottontail rabbits." She frowned. "The bunnies never should have been brought to me. Some 'do-gooder' spotted the nest but didn't see the mother rabbit. He assumed the mother had been killed, but most of the time, mother rabbits disappear during the day and return later. People need to adopt a wait and see policy."

Cassie pulled open the door to the rehabilitation wing, and I was immediately greeted by the sounds of chirping, cooing, and scratching, accompanied by a mild stench of animal excretion.

I hadn't been in the rehabilitation wing in two weeks. I noticed a few of the animals who had been here earlier were gone, replaced by two new animals—a fox and a seagull. I asked Cassie about them.

"The fox was hit by a car and has a broken leg. He's expected to make a full recovery and will be released back into the woods." Cassie poured animal feed into a bucket. "The seagull may not be so lucky." She sighed. "Someone shot him. He's touch and go."

I focused my gaze for a few moments on the poor seagull. After an uncomfortable silence, I asked, "Any news on the missing animals?"

Cassie shook her head, frowning. "No. And I doubt there will be. The police don't consider it a top priority, and there doesn't appear to be any clues. Now, what else can I help you with?"

"I want to be sure I have the facts straight for my story. You were here as a part-timer for several years, right?"

"About eighteen months. The refuge needs someone to cover for their full-time rehabilitator on his day off and to help out when twenty-four hour care is needed. Now that I'm full time, Elena hired another rehabilitator to fill the part-time position I vacated."

"How did you originally wind up at the Pendwell Wildlife Refuge?" I asked.

"Elena. She recommended me to the director. At that time, the director was Melissa Modica."

I thought that odd. Considering the relationship between the two women, I found it difficult to believe that Melissa would take a recommendation from Elena. Was she pressured by Victoria? Didn't the board of trustees need to approve all new hires."

Before I could say anything, Cassie added, "Melissa was desperate. None of the other Long Island rehabilitators were available to take the job. There aren't that many of us."

Cassie then smiled for the first time since we met. "I know what you are thinking. Everyone knows Melissa and Elena didn't get along. So why would she hire me based on Elena's recommendation? Well, I'm a darn good rehabilitator, and Melissa heard of my reputation. She put her personal feelings aside and acted professionally. And the trustees approved her recommendation. Unanimously."

"How did you meet Elena?"

"We met when she worked at the Long Island Nature Museum. I was the rehabilitator on call, so they contacted me when a swan from the lake in the park was shot with an arrow. I gave it immediate medical care, transported the bird to the veterinarian who performed surgery, and then I provided the post-operative care, including tube feeding and administering round the clock pain medication."

"When an animal requires round the clock care, how does it work at a place like this?" I asked. "Does the rehabilitator sleep here?"

She shook her head. "Not usually, although it has happened in serious cases. Most often, the rehabilitator will come in at specific times during the night to give medication or provide an additional feeding." She picked up a bucket. "I need to get back to work. Do you have more questions?"

"No. This is fine." I said good-bye and made my way back to the main office, realizing that the person who stole the animals most likely had inside information as to the feeding schedule.

"Good. You're finished with Cassie just in time." Elena said as I sauntered into her cubicle.

To my surprise, Victoria sat in the visitor's chair in front of Elena's desk.

Victoria smiled and rose from her seat. "Hello, Kristy. I'm leaving. Enjoy Elena's trail tour and presentation."

"Let's go. The kids from the youth group should be assembling outside by now," Elena said. "I also want to get out of here now, so I can avoid seeing George."

"George?"

"He has several animal care books in his desk. He apparently forgot to take them when he left. He was supposed to come on Saturday and get them, but he couldn't make it. He's coming today to pick them up, and I'm not anxious to see him."

We headed outside her cubicle. Victoria hadn't left the building yet. She stood by the information rack arranging brochures.

"I've been so busy, I haven't eaten since breakfast," Elena said. "I'm going to grab some pretzels from our snack cabinet. Would you like some?"

I shook my head but grinned. "You have a snack cabinet? I'll have to suggest one for my office."

"We also have a small refrigerator and a microwave. We're so far away from anything, that no one ever goes out for lunch."

Elena headed to a small alcove in the back. She pulled open the drawer to a wooden cabinet and grabbed a box of pretzels.

"I'm not a big snacker. But when I do, I usually go for pretzels. They're my favorite." She shook the box and scowled. "It sounds like there is only one in here. That's strange."

"What's the matter?"

"The only one who eats these besides me is George, and I brought this box in the day before he was terminated. This is jumbo size. I know he eats a lot, but I can't believe he ate almost all in two days."

Elena opened the flaps and glanced inside.

"Omigod!" She pulled the flaps back down over the top.

"What's wrong?" I asked.

"There's a scorpion inside."

CHAPTER 31

Victoria, who still stood by the information rack arranging brochures, spun around and dashed back towards her future daughter-in-law. "A scorpion!" Victoria screamed. "Did it sting you?"

Elena shook her head. She placed the pretzel bar box on her desk, her hand visibly shaking. "Victoria, go to the rehabilitation wing and tell Cassie what happened. Tell her to get a glass container and come in here, right away." Her voice quivered.

Victoria zoomed out of the office. In a few minutes, she returned with Cassie who carried a glass container and wore a thick pair of gloves.

"We need to secure the scorpion," Elena said. Her voice was strong now. She had regained her composure.

Cassie nodded and placed the container, which appeared to be about ten inches deep, on Elena's desk. Then she turned the pretzel box upside down over the container, while using a pen to open the flaps. Once open, she poked the bottom and sides of the box with the pen until the scorpion dropped into the glass container. She pulled the empty box away and secured the cover on the glass container.

I frowned as a thought popped into my head. "Scorpions don't live on Long Island, do they?"

'They don't. At least not naturally." Elena replied.

It only took a moment to realize the implications of what Elena said. This wasn't the southwest where scorpions thrived and could find their way into someone's shoe, drawer, or pretzel box. This was New York.

Someone had deliberately placed the scorpion in the box.

"We need to call the police," I said.

"No!" Victoria said firmly. "This might only be a practical joke."

"Are you kidding me? Elena might have been killed." I argued.

"A scorpion sting, while painful, is not fatal to a healthy adult," Victoria responded.

"This one may be," Cassie said. Her face was grim. "Elena, take a closer look at this scorpion through the glass. Notice the color."

Elena bent her head down and peered into the container. Her eyes widened. "You may be right. Its dark yellow shade could indicate it's an Arizona bark scorpion."

"What's that?" I asked.

"The most venomous type of scorpion in the United States. While a sting from most scorpions is rarely fatal, one from this type can kill."

"Can you take this container to your professor friend at Dexter University whose specialty is desert life?" Elena asked Cassie. "He should be able to tell us if this is an Arizona bark scorpion."

"I'll do it right now."

Cassie exited with the container.

"Shouldn't you call the police?" I repeated my question from before.

Elena pulled her phone from her pocket.

"Don't call the police," Victoria pleaded with Elena. "Our director was murdered. And now, there's an attempt to kill you off. This could ruin us."

Elena held her phone tightly, but she appeared to be mulling over Victoria's comments. She nodded. "You're right. We can't afford another story. And we won't know for sure if it's an Arizona bark scorpion until Cassie returns."

I didn't like it, but it was Elena's decision.

"I better go and meet the youth group." Elena glanced at her watch. "The trail walk should have started five minutes ago. They're probably wondering what happened. Are you coming, Kristy?"

"I know I said I'd be joining you, but I'm going to beg off," I told Elena. Right now I needed to clear my head.

* * * * *

Before heading to my car, I decided to spend some time in the clearing, where I could sit and sort out my thoughts.

My heart was pounding, but as I inhaled the fragrance of the balsam pines, I began to calm down. When I reached the clearing, I plopped down on a large rock near the pond. Suddenly, the chirping of the birds ceased and not one was in sight. A rabbit hopped into the surrounding forest, and a squirrel disappeared up a tree. Silence. I gazed upward. A hawk soared above. I realized why the animals had taken off so quickly.

My thoughts returned to Elena and the scorpion. If someone deliberately placed the scorpion in the pretzel box, it had to be an inside job. It had to be someone who had access to the cabinet. And it had to be someone who knew pretzels were Elena's favorite snack.

Who would know this?

The employees would know. That included George Grogin—the employee Elena fired. Did he still have a key? Did he come back and put the scorpion in the pretzel box as revenge?

Victoria also had access to both the office and Elena's schedule. But Victoria supposedly adored her future daughter-in-law. And the image of Victoria handling a scorpion was almost comical. No one could think this was the action of Victoria. But I didn't totally dismiss that thought. I only pushed it to the back of my mind.

I began meandering down the path, back to the parking lot. When I reached my car, my phone trilled, jolting me out of my thoughts. It was Jason.

"There's been a new development in the Melissa Modica case," he said as soon as I answered. "The police just arrested George Grogin for her murder."

CHAPTER 32

"What?" I sputtered. "On what grounds?"

"When the police questioned George at his house, they spotted a gold necklace with the initial *M*. It was on his kitchen counter in plain sight. They asked him about it, and he admitted it belonged to Melissa."

"But that isn't enough evidence to arrest George, is it?" I asked. "Did he say why he had the necklace?"

"The clasp had broken, and he offered to fix it. This supposedly happened several weeks before her murder. He was usually good at fixing things, but he claimed he was all thumbs on this one."

"Melissa and George weren't getting along. Why would she ask him to repair something?"

"I don't know." Jason sighed. "But it's the neighbor's statement that's the most damaging."

"What do you mean?"

"A neighbor came forward and reported seeing George leave his house after eleven on the night of the murder."

I sighed. "Where is George now? In jail?"

"Yes. Bail hearing tomorrow. I understand his sister came up here from New Jersey and hired a lawyer. She's now scrambling to get money for bail."

"Who is the lawyer?"

"His name is Mark Mannerly. Just started a private practice. He worked for a few years for Legal Aid, but he's still a novice. I think he is all George's sister can afford."

Jason and I talked for a few more minutes. He told me the address of

Mark Mannerly's law office, which was two blocks from the courthouse. He also told me that the bail hearing was set for ten o'clock.

* * * * *

At around eight-thirty the next morning, I arrived at Mark Mannerly's law office. Since his office was in walking distance of the courthouse, I figured he might stop here before going to the bail hearing. I was in luck.

The door was unlocked, so I stepped inside. No one was behind the front desk in the outer room, but I heard voices coming from the inner office. Since the door to this office was ajar, I peeked inside.

Sitting behind a large metal desk was a man I judged to be in his early thirties. His face was angular and his hair black and curly. The nameplate on his desk read *Mark Mannerly, Attorney at Law.*

Sitting in front of the desk on a straight back chair was a large woman with coffee-colored skin and short ebony hair. I assumed she was George's sister.

I knocked.

"Who are you?" the man behind the desk called out. He frowned as his bushy eyebrows melded together, looking like a giant caterpillar.

"I'm Kristy Farrell," I said. "I'm a reporter for *Animal Advocate Magazine.* I recently interviewed George for an article I'm writing on the Pendwell Wildlife Refuge." I paused, then added what I knew would get their attention. "I don't think George murdered Melissa."

"Do you have proof?" the attorney asked.

"No. But it doesn't make sense that he would steal a necklace and leave it in plain sight."

"I'm George's sister, Verna Grogin," the woman said. "What you said is so true. And George couldn't kill anyone. He's the gentlest person I know. You've seen him with his animals, right?"

"Yes. But he does have a temper," I replied, recalling what Melissa told Linda Lau about his outbursts.

"That's only recently. He never was like that before."

"Before what?"

"During the last year, he seemed to lose his temper more than usual."

Verna frowned. "I think he was under a lot of stress. But he never would hurt anyone. Why he—"

"Don't say anymore, Ms. Grogin," the attorney interrupted.

Before I could speak, the office phone rang. While the attorney listened to the person on the other end, I continued to probe.

"Why do you think he left his house the night of the murder?" I asked Ms. Grogin.

She shrugged. "When Mr. Mannerly and I met with him yesterday, we asked. He said he went back to the rehabilitation center to check on some of the animals—the possums were vulnerable because of their age. But he told us he was home before midnight. George only lives fifteen minutes from the refuge."

"And he never mentioned to the police that he left his house to go to check on the animals?" I asked.

"No. He was afraid it would make him look guilty." She sighed.

"Do you think—"

"Mrs. Farrell," interrupted Mr. Mannerly, who had finished his call. He was still frowning, and he began tapping his pencil on his desk. "Do you have anything that can help prove my client's innocence?"

"Not specifically, but—"

"Then you'll need to leave. I must talk to my client's sister in private before the bail hearing. Furthermore, I'm instructing Miss Grogin not to say anything more to you. I'll be saying the same to George Grogin."

I bristled. "I want to help you find the truth. I believe George is innocent, and I'm aware that with powerful people, such as Victoria Pendwell, it's easy for someone like George to become an innocent scapegoat."

I turned, now facing George's sister Verna. "I'm an investigative reporter. I'm good at digging up facts. If I can help in any way, let me know." I handed her my card.

She grabbed the card, stuffed it in her bag, but didn't say a word. Mark Mannerly was still frowning. I was sure he would remind her to stay away from me.

I made my way into the outer office and was about to leave the building, when I heard Mark Mannerly say to Verna, "That was Dr. Mancuso on the phone before. He will meet us at the courthouse a little after ten. If bail is high, and we need more security, Dr. Mancuso assured me he would provide it."

Dr. Mancuso was the veterinarian for whom George worked before coming to the Pendwell Wildlife Refuge. I needed to talk with him.

But first I had to see George's neighbor—the one who saw him leave his house the night of the murder.

CHAPTER 33

I found the address listed for George Grogin. It was located in a community about fifteen minutes from the wildlife refuge.

The neighborhood consisted of a mix of Cape Cod and small ranch-style homes. Most were small but well maintained with manicured lawns, mature trees, and flower beds. I pulled up in front of George's house, a cape with a towering oak on the front left side.

I wanted to talk to the neighbor who reported seeing George leave his house the night of Melissa's murder, but I didn't know which one it was. Left? Right? Across the street?

The house on the left was a ranch, and a tall tree blocked this neighbor's view of George's front door and much of the driveway. This neighbor might see George's car drive off, but would not see George leave the house or get into the car.

I glanced at the house on the right and spotted a woman peering out a window behind heavy curtains. I hopped out of my car and knocked on her door.

Moments later, an elderly woman cracked open the door a few inches. She had white hair and crystal blue eyes—the bluest I'd ever seen.

She eyed me suspiciously. "Can I help you?"

"Are you the neighbor who reported seeing George Grogin leaving his house three Monday nights ago after eleven? If so, I'd like to talk to you about him."

"Why?"

"I'm trying to help him."

She hesitated, still peering through the door opening.

I didn't know how she would respond. If she liked George, she might answer my questions. But if she didn't get along with him, or if she believed George to be the murderer, she would probably slam the door in my face.

She pulled open the door. "Come in." She motioned me to a seat in her living room.

"I'm afraid I got poor George in terrible trouble," she said. "But I had to tell the truth."

"Of course."

"George is such a nice man. He helps me around the house. Do you know he made this rocking chair for me for my seventy-fifth birthday?" She pointed to the chair.

Before I could comment, her face clouded. "That was five years ago. He was fabulous at woodworking. But he can't do it anymore." She sighed. "Take it from me it's not easy getting old."

That statement puzzled me. George appeared to be in his early sixties. I knew several people in that age bracket who did woodworking as a hobby.

I needed to get the conversation back to the point of my visit. "How can you be sure it was three Mondays ago? That's a long time to remember."

"I remember because the next day I saw the television news about the murder." she said.

"When you saw him leave, did he appear upset or agitated?"

"I couldn't tell. All I saw was him leaving the house and getting into his car. It was no different than any other night."

"Any other night?"

She smiled. "You probably think I'm a nosy old thing. I have insomnia, so I'm up all hours. I see him leave the house late all the time. He has to take care of his animals."

Going to the wildlife refuge at night was a normal activity for George. But it still put him at the scene of the crime.

"You didn't see George return?"

"No. I took a sleeping pill after I saw George leave. I didn't wake up until seven the next morning."

"Thanks. I'll be leaving."

I was grasping at straws. There was nothing else I could ask. But something was bothering me. Something this woman had said. But before I could do anything, I needed to check my facts.

As I left the neighbor's house, a car pulled up in front of George's home. George and his sister Verna got out and headed up their walkway.

I ran toward them. "Did you get bail?" I asked.

"Yes," Verna replied. "George has never been arrested before and he's not a flight risk."

"I put up my house," George added. "Dr. Mancuso offered to lend us the rest, but we didn't need it. He's a good friend."

"Let's go inside," Verna said to George. She was frowning. "Remember what your attorney said. We shouldn't be talking to the press. We shouldn't be talking to anyone."

George didn't listen to her advice. He stopped and said to me, "I swear I didn't kill Melissa. I did go back to the preserve earlier to take care of some of the animals. But I didn't go into the woods. I was inside the building at the wildlife rehabilitation center."

"That's enough," his sister shouted. She grabbed his arm and he nearly stumbled as she pulled him toward the door.

"Please," I said. "I know your attorney asked you not to speak with me, and I respect that. But if you change your mind, please call me. You have my card. I'd like to be able to reach out to you if I find something out and—"

"If you have information, you can contact Mark Mannerly." Verna headed up the pathway to the front door.

George followed his sister, but first he turned toward me and mouthed, "Call me."

CHAPTER 34

Late that afternoon, I stopped at Mancuso Veterinary Hospital where George worked as a veterinary technician prior to his job at the Pendwell Wildlife Refuge.

I'd read on the refuge's website that Mancuso was the veterinarian on call when an animal in the rehabilitation center needed surgery. Wildlife rehabilitators were not trained to perform operations. This meant George would still have contact with Dr. Mancuso, although not to the same extent as previously.

Something was bothering me about George, and I hoped Dr. Mancuso might provide me with answers.

Having a veterinarian as a husband and as a daughter was an advantage. Both Matt and Abby knew Dr. Mancuso through professional veterinary organizations. Abby made the appointment for me, and she was meeting me at his office. She had told him I was a reporter, but the information I needed could help George.

As I stepped into the main office, I nearly bumped into the rear end of a whining Rottweiler. The dog was stubbornly refusing to move from his spot despite the effort of the animal attendant who was trying, with little success, to move him into an examination room. Meanwhile, from a safe distance, a West Highland terrier barked at a cat in a carrier who was hissing back. I turned to the receptionist and introduced myself.

"Your daughter arrived a few minutes ago and is waiting in Dr. Mancuso's office," she said over the yips of the West Highland terrier. "You can go down there too—last door on the left. Dr. Mancuso is with a patient, and he'll see you as soon as he finishes."

Upon entering his office, I greeted Abby and slid into a seat on the sofa next to her. After I updated her on the status of George and the murder investigation, we both sat back in silence. Abby fiddled with her necklace—a gold heart Jason had given her. The jewelry jogged my memory.

"When I interviewed Melissa, she wore a silver owl pendant. I'll bet she still had it on when she was murdered."

"Does that mean something?" Abby asked.

"One piece of evidence against George is a gold necklace with the letter *M* that the police found at his house. George claimed he was fixing the clasp for Melissa, but the police don't believe it."

"Do the police think he took it off the body the night of the murder?"

"I think so. But if Melissa wore the silver owl pendant, she wouldn't have had the gold necklace on too."

"What are you going to do?"

"I'll call George's attorney tomorrow morning and ask him to check if any of the crime scene photos of the body show the owl pendant."

"Will that clear George?"

I shook my head. "No. The most damaging evidence is the witness—"

"Good evening." Dr. Mancuso stepped into the room. He was a short, portly man with a ruddy face and a crop of coarse, rust-colored hair.

"I heard you offered to put up some of the bail money for George Grogin," I said after we exchanged pleasantries. "That was very generous."

"I feared George and his sister didn't have enough assets to cover it all. Luckily, they did." He sank into the swivel chair behind his desk and leaned back. "I know he's innocent. George couldn't kill."

"I'm aware he worked for you, but how well do you know him?" I asked.

"George was an excellent employee of mine for more than twenty years." He paused. "And he is a friend although I didn't see him much since he left here four years ago."

"How frequently had you seen him during the last few years?"

Dr. Mancuso shrugged. "About a dozen times—maybe a little more. He came here when he had wildlife that needed surgery."

"Did you notice changes in George?"

"I don't think so." He paused, furrowing his brow. "Well, I did notice that lately he was becoming a little forgetful."

I sat forward in my seat. "How?"

"The last time he was here, it was to pick up a hawk we had operated on. He would be returning it for post-operative care at the refuge's rehabilitation center. When he arrived here, he had to go back to the refuge because he forgot the transport cage." Dr. Mancuso grinned. "That's not something you should forget."

"What about his temper?"

"George didn't have a temper. In all the years he worked for me, I never saw him flare up at anyone."

I mulled that over in my mind, aware that recently he had temper outbursts involving members of the refuge staff. Only a few, but still...

"Was he always a bit uncoordinated?"

Dr. Mancuso stared at me. "He wasn't uncoordinated at all. He was—"

"I think I know what you're getting at, Mom," Abby interrupted. "You think George has a medical issue."

"Forgetfulness, occasional temper outbursts, stumbling... These are all recent developments with George." I pondered a thought for a moment before speaking. "For the last few years, I'm assuming you didn't spend enough time with him to notice any personality change or lack of coordination."

"You're right. I didn't. But if what you say is true, he could be ill. Those are classic symptoms of several serious ailments."

"Including a brain tumor," I said.

I turned to Abby. "I need to return to George's house and speak with him. Maybe this is nothing. But it could be something serious. He needs to have a medical exam."

"Will this help him with his legal problem?" Dr. Mancuso asked.

"If he's ill, it could be part of his defense." I hesitated and shook my head as I rose to leave. "But it won't prove he didn't commit the murder."

* * * * *

The next morning, I drove to George's house.

I knocked. Verna Grogin answered the door. "I told you—"

"Please." I put my foot inside before she could slam the door shut. "I need to speak to you and George about a matter other than the murder. It's about his health."

"His health?" She frowned but let me in.

"What's this about?" George came forward and joined his sister.

I talked to them gently, stressing that a medical issue was not definite, but it was a possibility.

George's shoulders sagged. "I had a feeling something was wrong. I've been getting these headaches."

"Oh, George," his sister cried out. "Why didn't you tell me?"

He shrugged.

"Thank you," his sister said to me. "I'll make a doctor's appointment. And I'll move into the house and stay with him at least until I find out what is going on—both medically and legally."

"Be sure to make that doctor's appointment immediately."

"I'll do that right now."

As I made my way to the door, she added, "I don't know a lot about health issues, but I am aware stress can make them worse. Do you have any idea how stressful it is to be accused of murder?"

George had been exhibiting these symptoms way before the murder. But I didn't respond to Verna's comment. I could tell she did not expect the question to be answered. After offering to be of assistance if they needed anything, I left.

Heading back to my car, I spotted a middle-aged man walking a bulldog. He wore a New York Met's cap—the man, not the dog.

"Are you a friend of George?" he called out to me.

"I know him," I answered cautiously. "What about you?"

"Yup. I live across the street. George is a great guy. I can't believe he was arrested for murder."

"It's all circumstantial evidence." Taking a long shot, I said, "You didn't see him, three Mondays ago, return to his house around midnight, did you?"

"No. Sorry. Why?"

"He needs an alibi for that time."

"Well, I didn't see him return, but I know he was home."

I could feel my pulse race. "How do you know that?"

"It was my wife's birthday. She and I had dinner in New York City.

141

After that, we had coffee and cake with her sister. She has an apartment in Greenwich Village. There was an accident coming home, and traffic was horrendous. We didn't get back until about ten minutes after midnight. Poor Bailey was hopping around the kitchen."

At the mention of his name, the dog looked up.

"It was a long time for Bailey to be in the house. He had to go out. So as soon as we walked in the door, I put on the leash and we went outside. He did his business as soon as we got down the steps. He's such a good dog."

"How do you know George was home?"

"He only has one car, and it was in the driveway."

I doubted George would have gone for a walk at midnight. But if he did, he was still several miles from the preserve.

"Didn't the police question you?" I asked.

"No." He shook his head.

"You mean they didn't knock on your door and ask if you saw anything?" I couldn't believe this.

"If they knocked, we weren't home. The next morning, my wife and I packed up everything including Bailey and went to visit our daughter in Maryland. We just returned today. That's when I heard about George. I didn't know he needed an alibi."

CHAPTER 35

"Why are you going to the wildlife refuge today?" Abby asked. I was talking to my daughter on Bluetooth while driving away from the Grogin house. I had called George's attorney and filled him in on the neighbor who could alibi George.

"I want to search for clues as to how that scorpion wound up in the pretzel box. And I want to go back to the clearing where Melissa's murder took place?"

"The clearing. Why? Melissa was killed nearly three weeks ago. There can't be any clues left now. What can you possibly expect to find?"

"I'm not sure. But I read the police report, and I have a few questions. I'm pulling into the parking lot now. Gotta go."

When I arrived at the clearing, a gray rabbit hopped into the woods and soon disappeared out of view. I briefly scanned the area where Melissa's body was discovered, but I knew I wouldn't find anything new here—I was sure the crime scene investigators had checked this section very carefully.

But it was the surrounding area that piqued my curiosity. There had been no mention of footprints in the police report. Surely there had to be some on the dirt path. It was too late now. Any footprints, of course, would be long gone. But I thought the omission odd.

I continued strolling around the clearing. I stopped and sat on a rock where I watched Freemont and two other turtles. Two swam in the pond and the other rested on a log. I wasn't sure which one was Freemont— they all looked the same.

A few moments later, I pushed myself off the rock, and rose up. I stretched and then made my way further up the clearing until I came to another path.

But this one was paved.

I ventured down this path, surrounded by pines, maple trees, and towering oaks. In less than five minutes, the path ended. It opened up onto the main road.

I stared at my surroundings, noting that directly across the road was Blackthorne Manor.

"That's why there were no footprints noted in the report," I mumbled. "The killer used the paved path."

I realized that both Melissa and the killer most likely parked in the Blackthorne Manor lot, crossed the road, and took the paved path to the clearing.

I needed more information. I bee-lined back to the administration building. Elena was there, and she let me in. I had lots of questions.

"Did Cassie's professor friend at Decker University get back to her?" I asked Elena as we headed into to her cubicle. "Did she confirm that the scorpion was an Arizona Bark Scorpion?"

"Yes. It was." She motioned me to sit down, which I did, but she remained standing.

"Any progress in discovering how the scorpion got here?"

"No, but I haven't had time to investigate. I don't think we'll ever know who did it." Her voice had coldness to it, and she appeared to lack her usual enthusiasm.

"Maybe you should—"

"Stop talking and listen," she said, sharply. Her dark eyes flashed.

"I just got off the phone with my former boss at the Long Island Nature Museum," she continued. "Contrary to what you were told, we still keep contact."

"I have no idea what you are talking about." Unfortunately, I did have a pretty good idea.

"Colin, my former boss, told me one of the docents let it slip that you were asking questions about me. You were prying into my past life."

I opened my mouth to say something but decided to wait until Elena finished her diatribe.

"The docent twisted the story she told you," Elena held up her hand and began ticking off her fingers.

"One, I did date Professor McCoy, who gave me the recommendation, but I was never his student. We met at the campus bookstore. I was working on my master's degree, and he only taught undergraduate courses. No impropriety whatsoever.

"Two, we did not—I repeat not—have a torrid love affair that exploded when we broke up. It was a casual relationship, and he broke up with me not the other way around. We parted as friends.

"Three, the recommendation from Professor McCoy got my foot in the door. I still had to be interviewed by both Victoria and Melissa. I also had to undergo scrutiny by the board of trustees."

"The docent didn't lie, but it appears she didn't tell me everything," I admitted. "Why do you think that? Didn't she know the whole story? Or do you think she wanted to make trouble?"

"This docent has an almost motherly interest in Colin, but he considers her a bit of a pest and brushes her off, sometimes with incomplete answers to her questions. She has also been known to twist things and exaggerate. As a reporter, isn't it your duty to verify the reliability of your sources?"

That comment stung me, and I could feel my face flush. I never took what people told me as fact. I used the information as a starting point to investigate.

"I always check my sources," I said angrily. "I'm not done with my story yet. You didn't see anything in print, did you?"

"Not yet. But that brings me to another issue. I know why you're digging so deeply into my background. The docent told Colin you were investigating the murder, and you considered me a suspect."

Gossip works both ways. While the docent did provide me with background, I should have realized she would gossip with others about what I told her.

"I never said I considered you a suspect," I said. "I only said that understanding the personalities of the people at the refuge would help form a picture that could be useful."

"The murder of Melissa has nothing to do with your story on the wildlife refuge. You're just a middle-aged busy body with too much time on her hands."

Middle-aged. That hurt.

I was about to argue that the murder could have a place in my story if it tied into the refuge, but I decided it would not be prudent to do so now. I would continue my investigation, but I needed to be more discreet.

"Okay." I said. "I get your point. Meanwhile, I have a question about the refuge." This question had more to do with the murder, but I hoped she wouldn't realize that.

Elena's arms were interlocked and placed across her chest defiantly. "What do you want to know?"

"I discovered a paved path leading from the clearing to the main road. How did that get there?" I asked. "I thought all trails were dirt, and nothing man-made was allowed."

Elena remained silent. Was she not going to answer?

"Okay. That's an appropriate question," she finally said. She had calmed down, but her rigid posture and tense facial expression told me this issue was far from over. Our dealings would be different from this day forth.

"Your statement is true now but not in the past," Elena continued. She slid into her chair. "When the Pendwell family owned the land, Clifton Pendwell—that's Victoria's husband—was involved with a community youth organization. He let the group use the clearing for camping. Before he died, he put in a path, so they would have easy access to the space, especially when bringing in camping equipment. It is the only paved path in the refuge. "

Elena's phone rang.

"I have to take this call." She glanced at her watch. "Don't you have an appointment with Victoria soon?"

"Yes. And I need to be going." I rose from my chair.

"A final warning," she said as I made my way out of the cubicle. "Back off. If you continue to pry into my life, you'll be sorry."

I couldn't believe she was now threatening me.

I still had time before my meeting with Victoria, so I drove out of the parking lot and headed down the road, where I made a left turn into the parking area by Blackthorne Manor. I stopped the car and sat there, pondering this new development.

Had the police surmised what I had guessed—that Melissa and the killer parked here, crossed the road, and took the paved path to the clearing? If so, had they checked out this parking lot? Was there video surveillance? I carefully surveyed my surroundings. I couldn't see any cameras.

The killer wouldn't come here if there was a chance of being caught on tape. The list of suspects flashed through my mind.

Thanks to his dog-walking neighbor, George had an alibi. Jeremy Toth wouldn't know whether or not this parking lot had cameras. Although I kept him on my suspect list, I didn't believe he murdered Melissa.

That left Victoria and Elena. Austin too. He might have questioned his fiancée or mother about the security system for the Blackthorne Manor parking lot. Then there was the unknown suspect—the father of Melissa's unborn baby. Did he have a connection to the refuge?

As I pondered the situation, I thought about the scorpion. Someone appeared to be after Elena now. Did that rule her out as Melissa's killer?

Or did Elena place the scorpion in the pretzel bar box to deflect suspicion away from herself?

CHAPTER 36

Victoria Pendwell had invited me to her house for tea.

She wanted to talk to me about her plans for the refuge, and she claimed her home would have fewer distractions than if we met in the administration building.

But I surmised the real reason behind her invitation. You always have more control on your home turf. Victoria wanted to schmooze.

Victoria knew I was uncomfortable with her decision not to contact the police regarding the scorpion, and I'm sure she didn't want to see anything about the incident in my magazine story. I'd no doubt that at today's meeting she would pull out all the stops to convince me of the wisdom of her reasoning.

I drove out of the Blackthorne Manor parking area and headed down the main road. I passed the traffic light, where the red light camera was located, and made my first right onto another road, continuing until I glimpsed the Long Island Sound in the distance. Near the road's end, I veered left onto Badger Lane, which led to the long driveway to the Pendwell estate.

The fundraiser I attended here had been held outside on the lush grounds. I hadn't been inside the manor house.

I rang the bell. A plump, middle-aged woman in a maid's outfit swung open the door. She had big, molasses colored eyes—like a basset hound.

"I'm Kristy Farrell. I'm here to—"

"Come right in. Mrs. Pendwell is expecting you."

The entrance hallway was exactly as I had envisioned. Oil paintings adorned the walls, a spiral staircase led to a second floor balcony, and a crystal chandelier hung from the ceiling.

148

The maid stared at me. "You look familiar. Have we met?"

She didn't look familiar to me. "No. I don't think so."

"Sheila!" a voice called out sharply. It was Victoria Pendwell. "I'll take Mrs. Farrell into the living room. You go to the kitchen and bring out the tea."

Sheila, still staring at me, wrinkled her brow. "You must have a twin." She vanished, presumably into the kitchen.

Victoria shook her head. "Sheila does excellent work, but she won't stop talking."

"Your home is magnificent. I love that painting," I said, pointing to a landscape on the foyer wall.

"Austin did that. Painting is his hobby." She smiled. "He won't have time for that when he's in the Senate."

As I scanned the room, I spotted several other interesting items, including a pewter bowl and a silver walking stick placed in an intricately carved wooden stand.

"The bowl dates back to the American revolution," Victoria said after I commented on its beauty. "The walking stick isn't an antique, but I do love it. My husband bought it for me in Spain on our last trip to Europe. I broke my foot while we were there. I used the stick when we returned to New York. For a short while, I still needed extra support when I walked."

She sighed. "Now it just sits in the corner. Shall we go to the living room?"

As soon as we were seated, Sheila served tea using a bone china set. After a few minutes of more general chit chat, Victoria got down to business.

"I hope you won't write about the scorpion incident. First, we had bad press on the missing animals and then the murder. Another story could ruin us."

"I don't foresee writing about the scorpion," I answered truthfully. "But let's talk about the missing animals. Has anything new been uncovered in the case?"

Victoria shook her head. "No. But it hasn't happened again. And we're taking precautions so it never does. We've put in alarms and added outside lighting. But enough about this. I want to talk to you about the Pendwell Wildlife Refuge plans for the future."

Victoria spent the next half hour filling me in on renovating Blackthorne Manor into an education facility. Most of what she told me I knew from my meeting with Elena.

"Ambitious plans," I said. "Sound like they will cost a lot."

"My son Austin is stepping up his role with the refuge. After his election, which I know he'll win, he plans to get heavily involved with our fundraising. He has some wonderful ideas for events. Let me tell you about them."

An idea popped into my head. Austin was on my suspect list, but I hadn't been able to question him. Every time we met, it was by chance, and Victoria or Elena, were always around.

This was my opportunity.

"If Austin has ideas, I'd like to talk to him directly."

Victoria frowned, but suddenly her eyes widened. I imagined the wheels turning in her head.

She realizes the public relations opportunity for her son.

"What an excellent idea," she said smiling. "I'll call right now and arrange an appointment. When is good for you?"

I gave her three dates. Victoria grabbed her cell phone, which sat on the end table next to the sofa.

"Austin," she said into the phone. "That lovely reporter from *Animal Advocate* would like to talk to you about your fundraising ideas for the preserve. How's Monday at eleven?"

That probably wasn't good because she suggested the second date I'd given her. Tuesday at two.

"Wednesday at five?" she finally said. I could hear the annoyance in her voice.

Victoria frowned. "That can wait… Fine. Five thirty… Plan to stay for dinner… We'll talk later." She finished her call and placed her phone back on the end table.

She smiled at me. "You're all set for Wednesday. You can meet Austin here at five-thirty. I know you said five, but I hope that's okay. I also thought it would be more personal to meet Austin at our home than in his law office. Would you like more tea?"

I thanked her but declined. I was a coffee drinker. One cup of tea was plenty.

"I should be going," I said.

Victoria's phone trilled. She glanced at the caller ID. "I should get this. Sheila will see you out."

I was dismissed.

Sheila escorted me to the door. On the way, I spotted a photo of a collie. It was in an exquisite silver frame.

"Beautiful dog," I said.

"He belonged to Mr. Pendwell. He loved that dog," Sheila said.

"I have a collie too."

Sheila stopped short. "Now I know why you look familiar. I've seen your picture with your collie and another huge dog in my veterinarian's office. You're Dr. Farrell's wife."

My photo with Brandy and Archie hung in the waiting room of Matt's Veterinary Hospital. Victoria Pendwell's maid was one of Matt's clients.

Dozens of thoughts squirreled through my mind. But the one remaining was that Matt never told me about Sheila. Did he not know where Sheila worked? Possibly, but I doubted it. Matt never liked my involvement with murder investigations. But to not tell me... I was disappointed and a little annoyed. We would be discussing this.

"This is so funny," Sheila said, jolting me out of my thoughts. "I have an appointment for my Gus tonight. It's to update his shots, and this is the only time available before I go visit my sister next week."

"But my husband doesn't work Thursday nights."

"I'll be seeing the other Dr. Farrell, your daughter. I've seen her in the office but never met her. Your husband assures me she's an excellent veterinarian."

"She is," I agreed. We said good-bye and I left. As I made my way to my car, an idea flashed through my mind.

A maid always knows the dirt about the family, pardon the pun. Victoria said Sheila won't stop talking. While driving, I phoned my daughter. I told her what I needed her to do.

"Mom, I'm meeting Sheila for the first time tonight," she said. "I can't ask her about Victoria Pendwell."

"Sure you can. Steer the conversation toward bosses. I've thought of a great segue. You could tell her what it's like to work for your father."

"That doesn't mean she's going to talk about Victoria."

I envisioned Abby rolling her eyes at my suggestion.

"Trust me. Once Sheila starts talking, she goes on and on."

CHAPTER 37

I was foraging through the refrigerator for Brie cheese later that evening when Abby barged through the door.

"Did you learn anything?" I asked, grabbing the cheese as well as a knife and a box of crackers off the counter. I made my way to the table. The two dogs followed me, but once I sat down and placed the food out of their reach, they scampered over to greet my daughter.

Abby pulled up a chair across from me. "Most of what Sheila told me we knew, but I do have more detail. Do you know what Austin would like to do with his life instead of becoming a state senator?"

"A game show host?" I said jokingly. "Seriously, I can't imagine."

"An artist. I understand he's a pretty good one."

"He is. But that doesn't help us much with the murders. Anything else?"

Abby nodded. "Do you remember the fight Victoria and Austin had outside the administration building the night of the owl prowl?"

"Of course."

"Well, they had a similar argument in the house the week before Melissa was killed. According to Sheila, Victoria accused Austin of doing something really bad. Something she claimed could destroy everything."

"What did he do?"

"I asked Sheila, but she didn't know."

"I know Victoria tends to be melodramatic, but this still has to be something worth looking into. I'm going to delve deeper into Austin's past." I sliced a small slab of cheese, shoved it on a cracker, and popped it in my mouth.

"Sheila also said Austin's engagement to Elena is pretty shaky."

I finished chewing. "On whose part?"

"Austin. He told Victoria he's not sure Elena is the right one for him. Also, he doesn't want to settle down yet."

"How did Victoria take that news?"

"Not well. Sheila says that lately, whenever Austin comes to the house, Victoria winds up fighting with him. She keeps reminding him that marriage to Elena is a good career move."

"Did Sheila say anything about how Elena feels toward the marriage?"

"Elena wants to be a Pendwell, but she's becoming frustrated with Austin. She knows he's seeing another woman."

"Does Elena know this woman's identity?"

"I think so."

"And Victoria?" I asked.

"She absolutely knows."

Abby chewed a slice of Brie before continuing. "Victoria invited one of the senior partners in the law firm to her home for cocktails. Sheila overheard most of the conversation. It seems Victoria wanted the blonde—that's what she called her—to be fired."

"Has that happened?"

"No. The lawyer explained that since Austin was romantically involved with the blonde, she might sue, claiming Austin promised advancement for sexual favors. Trust me. The law firm is not happy about this."

"What's going on here?" Matt paraded into the room. He'd been in the den watching the Yankees versus the Red Sox.

Abby provided Matt with a brief summary of the patients she saw tonight. When she started talking about Sheila's dog Gus, I interrupted.

"You never mentioned your patient worked for Victoria Pendwell," I said.

"Sheila isn't my patient. Gus is my patient." He grinned.

"You know what I mean."

Matt grabbed a beer from the refrigerator and shrugged. "I honestly didn't know she worked for Victoria Pendwell. I only knew she was a maid at some north shore estate. Sheila babbles on and on, and I don't pay attention unless it has to do with Gus."

I sighed. Matt knew the name of every dog, cat, and hamster he'd ever come across. He could tell you their medical history as well as their personality quirks. But humans? No way.

"Would you have told me if you had remembered?" I asked.

Matt ran his hand through his thinning hair. "Probably not. I don't like you involved in murder, and I don't want to encourage it. I'm going back to the den now. The Yankees are up by one run and it's the last inning coming up."

"Jason is probably watching the game too," Abby said, glancing at her watch. "I think I'll head home."

"I'll walk out with you," I said. "I'm leaving too."

"Where are you going at this hour?"

"The mall."

"The mall closes in less than twenty minutes and it takes ten minutes to get there."

"That's okay. I'm not going inside."

Abby stared at me quizzically.

I grinned. "I'll be in the parking lot."

CHAPTER 38

I pulled into the mall parking lot behind the Bay Cove Pet Shop. Most cars were exiting—these were the shoppers. The two dozen or so cars still there belonged to the sales help and managers. Staff usually stayed for at least half an hour after closing to put away inventory, check receipts, and perform other housekeeping tasks.

Time passed. Soon only a few cars remained in the parking lot. As I drove around, I noticed a black sedan and a large white van parked in the back near the fence. The vehicles looked empty, but I knew better.

While researching my wildlife smuggling story last year, I'd made a solid contact at the United States Fish and Wildlife Service. He was regional director of the agency, and his name was Ray Maxwell. When I was assigned a story on wildlife smuggling, I learned from him that stuffing packets of cocaine up a snake's rectum was one of the many unusual ways used to smuggle drugs.

I phoned Ray the other day and explained my current suspicions regarding the Bay Cove Pet Shop. I told him the next delivery of snakes was tonight. He notified the Drug Enforcement Agency, and the two law enforcement departments were planning a raid. Ray said he would be here too, and I was pretty sure he was in the black sedan.

"I better get this over with," I mumbled as I pulled up next to the car. I hadn't told Ray I was coming, and I felt he wouldn't be pleased.

I was right.

As soon as he spotted me, a frown spread across his face. "What are you doing here?" he asked accusingly as his window came down.

"I gave you the tip. I want to see it through."

"This is dangerous. These people aren't jaywalkers. If this is a drug smuggling operation, the smugglers are probably armed."

"I'm parking in that area," I said, pointing to the northeast corner of the lot, directly across from where I was now. "It's pretty far away from here. I won't leave that spot until your raid is over. If it is a drug smuggling operation, text me once you make the arrests and everything is safe. I'll come then and take pictures. This will fit perfectly in our magazine's *Animals in the News* section."

Ray didn't say anything, but he continued frowning.

"I promise I won't do anything foolish. And think of how my story will help increase public awareness as to the relationship between animals and drug smuggling."

He sighed. "Okay. But you stay in your corner of the lot. Lock your doors, stay down, and don't move until I text you."

"Got it." I sped off before he could change his mind. Ray Maxwell and the federal agents were in one corner of the lot, and I was now parked at the other end, which provided me with a partial view of the back entrance to the pet store. By now, there were a little more than a half dozen cars in the lot. Even after most staff leaves for the day, it wasn't unusual to have a few cars left.

About twenty-five minutes later, a truck pulled up. The driver jumped out. From what I could see, he appeared to rap on the back door of the Bay Cove Pet Shop. Someone swung open the door. It was hard to make out, but I was pretty sure it was Eliot.

Eliot and the driver headed back to the truck and picked up a crate. Using both hands to carry the crate, the two men were making their way toward the pet store when the black sedan and white van careened in front of them.

Four agents, wearing jacket emblazoned in the back with either *Fish and Wildlife* or *Drug Enforcement Agency*, hopped out of the van. I saw Eliot and the driver drop the crate. Two of the agents hauled the crate into the pet store. The two remaining agents made Eliot and the truck driver "assume the position" by the front of the truck.

A few moments later, an agent stuck his head out the back door of the store. I couldn't make out what he said, but I saw Eliot and the driver being handcuffed.

I had promised not to leave my spot until Ray texted me, but I was getting impatient. Finally, I received his message, and I sped over to where he stood.

"Your tip panned out," he said as I hopped out of my car. "The snakes are pythons, and our portable x-ray machines discovered packets inside them. Two of the snakes were dead on arrival, so we opened them up. Sure enough, the packets contain cocaine."

"What about the other snakes?"

"We'll try surgically removing and hope for the best. But snakes carrying drugs rarely survive."

I went inside and photographed the two dead pythons with the cocaine packets. My eyes were drawn to the remaining live snakes that would be checked later for packets. I shuddered at the sight of the slithering reptiles. I considered snakes sinister looking creatures. It was irrational, and I knew it.

I noticed there was a separate compartment containing two more live snakes.

"These are corn snakes, and they have no cocaine packets, so the store could keep them to sell," he said. "It's the smuggler's cover."

"What do you mean?"

"Although the snake deliveries are made after hours, it's still possible for a late working mall employee heading out to the parking lot to notice a truck or van. If someone spotted snakes being brought in, but never saw snakes in the store, it would be suspicious."

"What's going to happen to Eliot and the truck driver now that you arrested them?" I asked.

"It's a drug arrest. These laws are tougher than those regulating the smuggling of wildlife. Hopefully these guys will be in prison for a substantial time."

"What about the store?" I asked.

"The Bay Cove Pet Shop is shut down."

"And the animals inside?"

"We called animal rescue a few moments ago. They're coming now to take all the animals."

I didn't say anything.

"You look upset," Ray added, apparently reading my expression. "I thought this would make you happy."

"Oh, I'm delighted this place is now closed. But I also wanted to nab the puppy mill distributors who deliver sick dogs. The Bay Cove Pet Shop is due a delivery tomorrow morning, but if they're closed—"

"The puppy mill distributor won't know they've been shut down. Deliveries don't go through the mall. They come around to the back, where you can't tell if a business is open or closed."

"You're right." I nodded. "They'll knock on the back door, but law enforcement will be waiting in the parking lot like you are tonight. They can check the distributor's truck, and if the puppies are sick, as I suspect they will be, then legal action can be taken."

CHAPTER 39

Friday morning, I was back at the mall again in the lot behind the Bay Cove Pet Shop. This time, Abby slouched next to me in the car.

An SPCA van was wedged in the corner of the lot, its motor running. A large black sedan pulled in beside it, blocking the van's identifying logo from view.

"I'll bet you that's an unmarked police car," I said.

Abby nodded.

"Billy told me the puppies are usually delivered a half hour before the mall opens for customers," I said. I glanced at my watch. "It's time."

"Look!" Abby pointed to a truck that pulled up directly behind the pet store. A sign hanging off the back read *Caution—Live Animals Inside.* "I think they're here now."

The driver hopped out and rapped on the back door of the shop. No one answered because, unbeknownst to the truck driver, the pet store had been closed down and the owner arrested.

Within seconds, the SPCA van careened toward them followed by the unmarked police vehicle. A woman emerged from the van, followed by two men. They all wore jackets emblazoned with their organization's logo.

The woman showed something to the truck driver. I assumed it was identification. I couldn't hear the conversation, but judging by the shaking of his head and wild hand gestures, the driver was not happy. He lifted open the back door of the truck and he hopped inside accompanied by the woman from the SPCA. Two police officers emerged from the unmarked car and stood near the truck.

"Let's check this out," I said, jumping out of the car.

160

"Hey! Wait for me." Abby followed.

I identified myself to one of the police officers. I told him I was the magazine reporter who gave the tip to the SPCA.

"You can wait but stay back," the officer said.

After about twenty minutes, the woman from the SPCA emerged. I introduced myself, and it turned out she was the woman to whom I'd provided the information about today's delivery of puppies.

"You were right," she said. "There are about ten dogs in here. We found a dead Yorkshire terrier, and a crate with three French bulldogs, all of whom have severe diarrhea. There also appears to be several eye infections as well as respiratory problems among the other dogs. These puppies are sick."

"So, what is going to happen?" I asked.

"We're taking all the dogs back with us," she said. "They'll be treated by a veterinarian at our facility and then…" She paused. "Those that survive will be put up for adoption."

Those that survive.

"What about this distributor?"

"Legal action will be taken. You can count on it." Her face was grim.

I watched the puppies being carried out and loaded into the SPCA van. My stomach churned at the sight of those sick animals.

"This store was shut down last night." I said to the woman from the SPCA. I explained about the cocaine packed snakes and the drug raid.

"I'm well aware," she said, nodding her head. "We were notified. We came last night and rescued all the animals inside. The place is empty."

I said good-bye and told her I'd call if I needed more information for my story.

Abby and I drove back to her home in silence. Once in her house, Abby prepared Greek omelets for lunch, and I brewed coffee.

I shook my head as I handed her a steaming mug. "It's a business. These people have no more feelings for those dogs than for a tube of toothpaste. How can people be like this?"

"You would be surprised at the cases of abuse I've seen as a veterinarian."

"Your dad talks about them too."

"We had an issue with an abused dog a few weeks ago. Thankfully, he now has a happy new home."

"Was he rescued and put up for adoption?" I sipped my coffee.

"This case has a slightly different twist. The dog was rescued by a ten-year-old boy. The dog lived two houses down. The boy claimed the dog was always outside—no doghouse to protect him from the scorching sun, pouring rain, or freezing cold. The poor animal was skin and bones since he apparently wasn't fed on a regular basis. And his owner beat him too. The boy witnessed it."

"Did the boy report this to anyone?"

"That's what he should have done." Abby put an omelet on a plate and placed it in front of me. "Instead, what he did was steal the dog."

'Did the owner find out?"

"Oh, yes, and he wanted his dog back."

"What happened?"

"Luckily, law enforcement was able to prove the dog was abused. They were able to legally take him away from his brutal owner. Now the dog lives with the boy and his family. But not all stories have happy endings like this."

I took a bite of my omelet as I sat there thinking about the puppies I saw today. I could understand how a young boy would do what he did.

Then a thought flashed through my mind. "That's it."

"What's it?" Abby asked.

"I think I have the answer to something that has been bothering me for the last few weeks."

I recalled from last week that Cassie, the new full-time wildlife rehabilitator, only worked at the wildlife refuge until noon on Fridays unless an emergency came up. I grabbed my phone and hit my search engine. I searched for her home address, knowing that as a licensed rehabilitator this information would be readily accessible. It appeared she lived in a community about ten miles from the wildlife refuge.

"Abby. This omelet is delicious, but I don't have time to finish it." I took one last bite, grabbed my plate and placed it on the counter. "I'll call you later."

I sped off to find Cassie. When I arrived at her house, a large van was in the driveway. I pulled up in front of a neighbor's house and walked back. If Cassie was home, I didn't want her to see me.

The front garage door was shut, so I crept along the side until I was in the back yard. I heard the sound of a squawking bird coming from inside. The back door to the garage was partially ajar. I took a deep breath and swung it open.

They were in plain sight—a chicken hawk, muskrat, and red fox.

These were the animals stolen from the Pendwell Wildlife Refuge.

CHAPTER 40

Cassie, who appeared to be placing food in the muskrat enclosure, spun around. Her face paled.

"What are you doing here?" she cried out. Fear flashed in Cassie's eyes, and her lips were pressed in a rigid line.

"I have a hunch, and I think it's correct."

Her shoulders slumped. "What sort of hunch?"

I pointed to the muskrat. "The fox, the hawk, and the muskrat—you stole them from the Pendwell Wildlife Refuge. Where are the baby squirrels?"

"I released the squirrels a few days ago. They were old enough to live on their own. The muskrat and fox will be returned to the wild in another week. The hawk has to stay a little bit longer, but he'll be released too."

"What are they doing here?" I asked, although I was pretty sure of the answer.

"I brought these animals to my place to care for them."

"Is that because you didn't think they were getting proper care at the refuge?" I asked gently.

She nodded. "George was becoming increasingly forgetful. The—"

"George has a serious medical problem," I interrupted.

"I didn't know that. I'm sorry. He's a nice man. The animals I took were the most vulnerable. The remaining wildlife at the rehabilitation center was on the mend and scheduled to be released shortly. But these..." She fanned her arm, pointing to the hawk, red fox, and muskrat. "Unless their care was one hundred percent correct, they might have died."

"I understand." And I did.

"So what are you going to do?" she asked.

I'm a journalist. But nothing would be accomplished by my telling this story except embarrassing George and possibly causing legal problems for Cassie who was only trying to help the animals—and had succeeded.

"Nothing," I said. "The case of the missing animals will remain a mystery."

* * * * *

After leaving Cassie, I decided to pop in on George to see how he was faring.

"I'm glad you're here," Verna said when she swung open the door and saw me standing on her porch. "I wanted to talk to you."

"Did something happen?" I was relieved his sister was staying with him.

"Nothing like that. I wanted to thank you. I contacted George's doctor immediately after you told us you suspected George had a medical problem. The doctor saw us right away and arranged some tests."

"What did you find out?" I said a silent prayer.

"George does have a brain tumor."

I sucked in my breath. "I'm so sorry."

"But we may have caught it in time, thanks to you. It's in a spot that is operable."

"Is it cancerous?"

"We don't know yet. We have more tests scheduled for next week. Please sit down for a spell."

"I can only stay for a few minutes." I sank into an overly cushiony sofa. "Where is George?"

"Resting. I'd wake him, but—"

"Oh, don't do that. He needs his rest."

"Would you like coffee or tea?"

"Thanks, but no."

"How about a cupcake? This was on the porch when I woke up this morning." Verna pointed to a gift basket sitting on a nearby table. The basket held an assortment of vanilla, chocolate, and strawberry iced cupcakes.

"No, thank you, but they do look yummy."

She smiled. "The basket came without a name. There was a card attached, but all it said was *Get Well Soon*. We don't know who sent it. I thought maybe you did."

"No. I didn't."

"George and I haven't told anyone about his health issue yet. But someone found out." She shrugged. "Maybe there was another card, and it fell off during delivery."

"That's possible. You should look on the porch."

We talked for a few more minutes before I rose to leave.

"I'd like to keep in touch," I said. "I have the house phone number, but I don't have your cell."

Verna grabbed her phone and tapped a few keys.

"I just sent it to you," She escorted me to the door. "And I promise I'll keep you posted on George."

As I hopped into my car, I began wondering about the cupcakes. Someone found out about George's condition. Who was it?

CHAPTER 41

"I want lots of peonies," Abby greeted me as I stepped through the doorway into my kitchen later that day. Abby and I planned to spend the early evening searching for floral arrangement ideas for her wedding. She had arrived at my house before I returned and had set up her iPad on the kitchen table. She appeared to be scrolling down.

"Peonies always were your favorite flower." I pulled up a chair next to her. "See anything you like?"

"A few." She moved the iPad to the side and grabbed a magazine from a stack of bridal publications she had brought with her. "But before we start, there's something I want to show you."

She thumbed through the magazine. "Here it is. This is Victoria Pendwell's Palm Beach estate. Victoria held a wedding for her godchild here last year, and this bridal magazine did a feature on it."

I scanned the magazine spread.

"This place appears larger and more elaborate than her Long Island estate," Abby said. "How can she possibly have money problems?"

I shrugged. "Her money problems are different than yours or mine."

I flipped the page in the magazine. "You're right about her Palm Beach home. This place is gorgeous. Look at that tree." I pointed to a tree covered with magenta flowers. "I think they have trees like that landscaping grandma's Florida condominium."

"That's a bougainvillea. Aren't they gorgeous? They're popular in southern Florida. Lisa has several on her property too."

Lisa was a college friend of Abby who now lived in Florida. Abby had visited her for a week last year.

"Is that a bougainvillea?" I asked pointing to another tree, this one with pink flowers.

"It's hard for me to tell from the picture, but I think that's an Oleander. Lisa has one of those. I warned her to be careful because of her dog."

Before I asked why she needed to be careful, Abby added. "I wonder if Victoria will hold her son's wedding there."

"Whenever I see Austin and Elena together, they don't act as if they are in love. It's almost like an arranged marriage." I grinned. "And from what Sheila says, it probably is." I sat back in my chair and stretched. "I wish I knew more about Austin."

"You still consider him a prime suspect, don't you?"

"I can't shake the feeling that Victoria, Elena, and Austin are all mixed up in something. I just don't know what. I have an interview with Austin on Thursday. Maybe I'll come up with an idea."

"I'll ask Jason if he can dig up more on Austin."

"Dig up more? Who are you talking about?" Jason strolled through the doorway. He bent over and gave Abby a kiss.

"Austin Pendwell," I said, moving the magazine aside. "We know so little about him."

Jason pulled up a chair next to Abby. "Austin's life has been scripted for as long as I know. His mother has been grooming him for public office since he was a child. What's known about him comes from press releases."

Jason continued. "I don't believe he has any close friends—only co-workers and social acquaintances. But I do know some of his business associates. I'll see if I can find out anything new."

"Meanwhile, do you want to help me search for ideas for wedding floral arrangements?" Abby asked him. She grinned.

"The flowers can wait a few more minutes," he rose from his chair and started brewing a cup of coffee from my coffee maker. "I have news about the jewelry sting."

"What happened?" I asked. "Did you get them?"

Jason nodded. "Sure did. Our undercover investigator brought a diamond ring into Krill's Jewelers on Monday. She was disguised to look elderly, and she acted naïve. It worked. She left the diamond in the shop for a cleaning. She picked it up yesterday and then took it immediately to the jewelry expert our office used to have this diamond plotted."

Jason smiled. "The diamond she dropped off at Krill's was not the same diamond the store returned to her. The one they gave back was of considerably less value."

"What did you do?"

"When the store opened this morning, the police were waiting. They arrested the owner as well as the employee who did the cleanings. He was the one who did the actual switch."

"What about my diamond?" Abby asked.

"I don't know yet. The District Attorney's office is currently going through Krill's entire inventory. Hopefully we'll find it." Jason's face clouded. "That's if he hasn't sold it."

"I'm so glad the sting worked," I said. "I was afraid the store owner wouldn't find the undercover investigator gullible enough to take a chance."

"Look at these pictures." Jason grabbed his phone and showed me two photographs. One was of an attractive woman with short blonde hair who appeared to be in her late forties. The next photo was of a white-haired woman with a haggard face who was missing a front tooth. I would have guessed her age to be in the late seventies.

"That's our before and after shots," Jason said. "I couldn't believe this woman's son was able to age her appearance to such an extent."

"He's a theatre make-up artist. They do it all the time in movies and on stage."

My phone trilled. It was George's sister Verna.

"Kristy. I didn't know who else to call, but George is in the hospital. It's real serious. And the doctors don't think it has to do with the brain tumor." She sobbed, and then stopped. "He may have been poisoned."

CHAPTER 42

"I'll drive you to the hospital," Jason offered after I repeated what Verna said. The three of us rushed out of the house, piled into his car, and arrived at the emergency entrance twenty minutes later. Dozens of questions were shooting through my mind, but first and foremost was whether George would survive.

The smell of fear always permeated a hospital waiting room, and this was no exception. Verna sat in the corner, her head in her hands. She looked up as we approached.

"How is he?" I asked.

"I don't know. No one will tell me anything. He's with the doctor now." Verna's eyes were swollen from crying.

"What are his symptoms?" Abby asked.

"Vomiting, bloody diarrhea, stomach pain. He also said he felt lightheaded."

"That could be from a lot of things," Abby said.

"The cupcakes," I said as the image of the cupcake basket flashed through my mind. "You don't know where they came from. Did George eat any?"

"Yes. He had one earlier. It was chocolate cake with chocolate icing."

"Did anyone else have one?"

"I was going to eat one, but I never got around to it." Verna shook her head. "If I'd gotten pretzels or chips like he asked, this would not have happened. I just didn't have the time yet to shop—"

"It's not your fault. Do you still have the rest of the cupcakes?"

"Yes."

"We need to have them tested," Abby said. "If the cupcakes are poisoned, and the lab can determine the type of poison, hopefully they can start the right treatment for George."

"I can't go now. I don't want to leave George." Verna's eyes filled with tears.

"Give me your keys and I'll fetch them," I volunteered. Remembering I didn't have my car, I turned to my future son-in-law. "Jason will you drive me?"

Before Jason could answer, Abby said to Verna, "Were there any other symptoms you can remember?"

Verna furrowed her eyebrows. "This may sound silly, but there was saliva coming out of his mouth."

"I need to talk to the doctor now," Abby said. "I have a hunch as to what the poison might be."

"What?" I asked.

"Oleander. The Oleander leaf is highly toxic. The leaf could have been pulverized in a blender and put in the icing and cake to disguise the unusual taste. George's symptoms are classic symptoms of Oleander poisoning. I know that from my veterinary training. It's the same symptoms if a dog or other animal ingested it."

"Are you sure?"

"It's just a hunch, but a strong one. The gastric symptoms are common for many other poisonings, but when Verna added salivating, that narrowed it a bit more. But I wouldn't have thought of it if I hadn't spotted the photograph of the Oleander tree in the bridal magazine."

"You mean the Oleander tree in Victoria's Florida home, right," I said. "Victoria was there a little more than a week ago. She might have brought back leaves and mixed the poison with the cupcakes. But whoever sent the cupcakes knew George was ill. How would Victoria know that?"

"And why would she want to poison George?" Abby asked.

Jason, who up to now had been standing silently, spoke up. "I don't think you should pick up the cupcakes. If the cupcakes hold poison, we need to protect the chain of evidence. I'll call the police and see that someone from crime scene investigation goes to the house. We should—"

"Ms. Grogin," interrupted a nurse, "the doctor will see you now. Follow me."

"Is George okay?" I asked.

"The doctor will explain everything." The nurse opened the door to a small windowless room, furnished only with a sofa, a few chairs, and a table that held a pitcher of water and a stack of plastic glasses. No one sat down.

A few minutes later, the doctor arrived.

Her face was grim.

CHAPTER 43

"I'm sorry," the doctor said. "We couldn't save him."

Verna sobbed softly. I think she expected this ending.

"Do you know what caused his death?" I asked the doctor.

"They'll be an autopsy to determine that," she said, then added, "Ms. Grogin, when you feel up to it, there's paperwork you need to fill out. Just go down the hall to the last office on your left."

Jason was talking on his phone. When he finished, he said, "I called the police. They're on their way to the house to pick up the cupcakes. Two officers will meet you there, Ms. Grogin, so you can let them in."

"But I can't leave yet." Verna seemed to be in a daze. "I have paperwork."

"Why don't you give Jason the house key, and he can meet them," I suggested. "I'll drive you home in your car when you finish the paperwork. You shouldn't drive when you're this upset."

Verna agreed and handed her house key to Jason. He and Abby took off while Verna and I headed down the hallway to the last office on the left—Accounts Payable.

Thirty minutes later, Verna and I left the hospital. When we arrived at the house, Jason and Abby were waiting in the living room.

"The police took the cupcakes to be analyzed," he said. "And Abby told them about the Oleander."

Verna said she wanted to rest. I asked if there was anything she needed and she said no. Jason, Abby, and I left.

* * * * *

The next morning, I called Verna and asked if she was up for visitors.

"I want to get to the bottom of George's murder," I said.

"I have funeral arrangements to make this morning," she said. "But this afternoon would be fine. I want to get to the bottom of this too."

After the phone call, I spent most of the morning making macaroni and cheese, my favorite comfort food, to take to Verna. I wasn't a great cook, but this was one dish that almost always came out successfully.

* * * * *

Later that day, I was sitting in George's house having a cup of coffee with Verna.

"It's going to be a private funeral," she said. "Just a few cousins and a handful of other family members. Not many are left. I'm setting up a memorial service at my church too."

"When will that be?"

She shrugged. "I can't do anything until the autopsy is complete and the medical examiner releases the body. I don't know when that will be. I haven't heard anything about the cupcakes yet either."

"These things take time, unfortunately." I sipped my coffee. "The day I visited here, you said the cupcakes had arrived that morning. Do you know about what time?"

Verna shook her head. "They were here when I went outside to grab my morning newspaper. It was about eight in the morning."

"And you're sure no one knew George was sick?"

"Pretty sure."

"Pretty sure is not the same as sure," I said, gently.

"I know I didn't tell anyone," Verna responded. "I don't think George did either."

"Wait a minute." I remembered a conversation I had with Elena the day she discovered the scorpion in the box of pretzels. George was supposed to come in to get a few belongings he had left behind. But he couldn't. He'd gotten arrested that afternoon.

"Did George ever pick up the rest of his things from his office at the wildlife refuge?" I asked.

"No. The afternoon we returned from talking with the doctor,

George called Elena and told her… Oh, no."

"He told Elena he was sick and had to take a batch of medical tests, didn't he?" I asked.

"Yes."

Elena knew. And she might have told Victoria and Austin.

I was jostled out of my thoughts by a loud rap on the front door.

"Stay there and finish your tea," I said to Verna as I rose from my chair. "I'll get it."

I headed to the front of the house and swung open the door.

Standing in front of me were Detective Fox and Detective Wolfe.

Fox shook his head while rolling his eyes. But I did catch a quick glimmer of a smile on his face.

Wolfe puffed up, turned red in the face, and looked as if he could bite through an iron bar with his teeth.

"You! Why are you here?" he sputtered.

"I was paying a condolence call," I answered somewhat truthfully. "What brings you here? I know the autopsy couldn't be done this quickly,"

"The lab report on the cupcakes," Fox replied.

Wolfe shot him a look. "Keep your mouth shut, Fox. It's not her business."

I ignored him. "Were they poisoned? Was it Oleander?"

Fox looked at Wolfe, then turned to me, and said, "Sorry. I can't tell you."

Wolfe stomped into the living room. Fox and I trailed.

"What's this about the cupcakes?" asked Verna.

"They were poisoned. Oleander," Fox said. He turned, now facing Wolfe. "She's his sister. She has a right to know."

Good for him.

Wolfe scowled and muttered something under his breath that would have made my priest blush. Then he whipped out a pad and pen. "You claim these cupcakes magically popped up on your doorstep?"

Verna raised an eyebrow. "I didn't say magically. Someone dropped them off. But I don't know who."

"So you say." He jotted something on his pad. "We've only your word that it happened this way."

Verna looked confused. "I don't understand. I—"

"You will inherit everything from George's estate, right?" Wolfe interrupted.

"I guess so. But George only has a few thousand dollars in savings and his recent medical bills will take care of that."

"He owns this house, right?"

"That's true. But there is a mortgage."

"But the mortgage is almost paid off and is small. You could sell this place, and after paying off the mortgage, you would still realize a profit of more than one hundred thousand dollars."

I realized where Wolfe was heading. I couldn't believe it.

"You've got to be kidding," I yelled. "George's death is connected to Melissa Modica's murder. It has nothing to do with Verna."

Wolfe pointed a fat finger at me. "You need to leave. Fox, escort her out."

"I'm leaving," I said. "But Verna, don't say anything. You need to contact your attorney."

CHAPTER 44

Detective Fox escorted me out. But I wasn't ready to leave the premises—at least not yet. I stood on the stoop of the Grogin house determined to find out more about the poisoned cupcakes.

Glancing to my left, I spotted the white-haired woman who lived next door, peeking out from behind her curtain.

"She's definitely the nosy type," I mumbled.

Maybe she saw who delivered the cupcakes.

I rang her doorbell.

She moved the door, opening it about four inches. "Do I know you?" she asked, staring suspiciously at me with her glacier blue eyes.

"Yes. I visited you the other day and asked if you saw George leave the house on a specific night in May."

"I remember." She swung open the door. "Tell me what's going on. Police cars here yesterday. And now those two detectives—"

"How do you know those two are detectives?" I asked.

"Two men in suits? What would they be? Life insurance salesmen?" She grinned as she pointed to the unmarked police car parked in front of the Grogin house. "Everyone knows that make and model is the official car of the county police department. When I was younger and still driving, I always slowed down when one of these was on the road. What's going on?"

I guessed Verna hadn't told her.

"George passed away," I said as gently as possible.

A look of sorrow passed over her face. But she soon narrowed her eyes and asked, "How? You don't have detectives visit if you die naturally."

"You're right," I admitted. "George was poisoned. A basket of cupcakes was left on his front stoop yesterday. I was wondering if you saw who delivered it."

"I wondered what was in that basket. Do you think the cupcakes were poisoned?"

"They were. Did you see anyone?"

She nodded. "Yes. I caught a glimpse of the woman who brought them."

"Woman? You're sure it was a woman?"

"Sure looked like it."

"Can you describe her?"

"I couldn't see her face, but she had long, light brown hair and was on the chubby side. She was wearing a ratty, gray sweater too."

"Anything else? Did you see her car?"

"No. I watched her leave the property. She appeared in a hurry to get away. When she left, she headed down the street. Maybe she walked here."

Or more likely she parked her car away so no one would see it.

After saying good-bye, I made my way to my car. I realized the person who delivered the cupcakes didn't resemble Elena, Victoria, Austin, or Jeremy.

Who was this mysterious woman?

* * * * *

Matt was working until eight o'clock tonight, so dinner would be late. That gave me plenty of time to do my research. I poured a glass of wine, booted up my computer, and clicked on the document where I had listed my suspects in the Melissa Modica murder. What was I missing?

I heard the door slam shut and looked up.

"I'm returning the silver platter I borrowed." Abby said as she strolled into the room. She bent down to greet the dogs. "You look deep in thought, Mom."

"I'm searching for a tie-in between George Grogin and Melissa Modica. Lots of people had motives to want Melissa out of the way. But what was the motive for murdering George? He was making mistakes at work, but that's not a reason to kill him."

Abby grabbed a glass of wine and slid into a chair across from me. We both were silent for a moment.

"First Melissa. Now George. And someone tried to kill Elena too," I said. "That makes three preserve employees marked for murder. "

After Abby sipped her wine, she furrowed her brows. "Do you realize if George hadn't been fired, he might have been the one stung by the scorpion?"

I turned away from my computer and faced my daughter. "What did you say?"

"If George hadn't been fired, he might have been stung by the scorpion," Abby repeated. "You told me pretzels were his favorite snack, and he ate far more of them than Elena did. If he had still been working there, he might have gotten to the box first."

My mind wandered back to my conversation with Elena—what she said before she grabbed the pretzel box.

"I know that look on your face," Abby said. "You've thought of something."

"You're right. Maybe the scorpion wasn't meant to sting Elena."

"Do you think it was meant for George?" Abby blew a wisp of her dark hair off her face.

"Possibly."

"But he HAD been fired. If he was no longer working at the preserve, he wouldn't have access to the pretzel box."

"I remember something I read a long time ago. It was an article a colleague of mine wrote in *Animal Advocate* on venomous creatures. Let me check it out before saying anything." I turned back to my computer.

"What are you searching for?"

"Got it." I swung the computer so Abby could see the screen. "A scorpion can go twelve months without eating. Whoever placed the scorpion in the box of pretzels may have done so before George was fired, expecting he would be the next to reach for a snack."

Abby appeared to ponder this. "This makes sense," she said. "The attempt with the scorpions failed, so the murderer delivered poisoned cupcakes to George. But who could have done this?"

"Let's go down the list of suspects, starting with Elena."

"But she was almost stung by the scorpion."

I shook my head. "No. She wasn't. She didn't reach into the box. She checked it out first. It could be part of a scheme she concocted to take suspicion off herself."

"Makes sense."

"Then there's Victoria. She appeared visibly shaken at the mention of a scorpion in the box. But she worked as an actress before she married Clifton Pendwell. She's trained at feigning all kinds of emotions."

"What about Austin?" Abby asked.

"He's attended events at the wildlife refuge with Elena and Victoria. I'm sure he would have access to the facility. But why would he want to murder George?"

"Why would anyone want to murder George?"

Our thoughts were interrupted when the front doorbell rang.

"Are you expecting anyone?" Abby asked.

I shook my head as I rose and headed to the front door.

"This is a surprise. Come in," I said, swinging open the door and moving aside.

Detective Adrian Fox stepped into my house.

CHAPTER 45

"We need to talk," he said as he leaned down to pet Archie and Brandy who had run to greet him.

"How did you find me?"

"I'm a detective. That's what I do?"

I introduced him to my daughter, and the three of use sat down in the living room. I offered him wine, a soft drink, or water but he declined as I expected he would. The two dogs had followed us in. Usually when we had a guest, it meant food would be served, and dogs are so hopeful.

"What's this about?" I asked.

"First, I want you to know you're wrong for criticizing the police for investigating Verna Grogin as a suspect in her brother's death," he said, sternly. "Family members are always checked out first."

Fox leaned forward, elbows on his knees, fingers formed into a steeple. "That being said, I agree with you. I don't think she did it. I believe George Grogin's death is connected to Melissa Modica's murder."

"Why are you telling me this?" I sipped the last of my wine. I was definitely ready for another glass.

"Because my partner refuses to check this out." He scowled. "More than that, with regards to the murder of Melissa Modica, he refuses to investigate Victoria Pendwell, Austin Pendwell, and Elena Salazar, who is soon to be a Pendwell."

"How can he not investigate them? They're prime suspects."

"Wolfe has always cozied up to the rich and powerful, like the Pendwells. He goes out of his way not to offend them. He concentrated his investigation on Jeremy Toth and George Grogin. He hasn't followed leads on any of the others. I'm afraid this case is going to be unsolved."

"What about George's death?"

"Same thing. I talked to him earlier, and he doesn't think it's related to Melissa's murder or the wildlife refuge. He's not looking into the Pendwells."

"Are you able to investigate on your own?" The dogs had now settled down on either side of my chair. Archie's huge head was on my lap and I was running my hand through his thick, black fur.

He nodded. "Carefully, when Wolfe is not around. Based on your tip, I searched for a money trail from any of the suspects to Melissa. I found no evidence of any financial transactions remotely related to her murder. But Wolfe found out that I was snooping, and he was furious."

I wanted to ask him how there could be no money trail, but before I had a chance, Fox added, "Wolfe ordered me not to check anything else involving the Pendwells without talking to him first."

"Can't you go to your superiors?"

Fox shook his head. "The only reason Wolfe rose to detective is because of his connections to police brass."

"His uncle is Deputy Commissioner, right?"

"He certainly is. I've always treaded lightly with Wolfe, but this time…" He shrugged. "Maybe Wolfe's looking for a high-paying security position at Pendwell Industries when he retires. He's nearing retirement age."

Fox sat back. "It may be nothing. I honestly don't know. But he's making it difficult to investigate what I refer to as the Pendwell trio— Victoria, Austin, and Elena."

"What can I do to help?" I asked.

"Keep up your investigation. Victoria, Austin, and Elena all claimed to be home alone when Melissa was murdered, which is not unusual since it was midnight. But Wolfe's not pursuing it further." Fox coughed. "I think I will have a glass of water, if that's okay."

"Of course." I scooted into the kitchen and came back to the living room with water for Fox and a second glass of wine for me.

Fox took a sip of his water and continued. "We haven't checked with neighbors or Victoria's household staff. We never talked to the doorman at Austin's condo or viewed the security tapes at Elena's apartment building either. Maybe you could—"

"Nosy around a bit." I chuckled.

Fox nodded. "Let me give you my cell phone number. This way we can reach each other without Wolfe knowing." He pulled out his phone, I grabbed mine, and we exchanged contact information.

Fox rose from his chair. "I'll be investigating too. But Wolfe outranks me. And with him on my back, it's not that easy to do. You're a good investigative journalist," Fox said as he departed. He grinned. "Even if you are pesty."

"Drat!" I murmured once he was gone. "I knew I forgot something."

"What did you forget?" Abby asked. She hadn't said a word during Fox's visit.

"From all accounts, Melissa had come into money," I said. "But Fox said he had no evidence of this. I wanted to ask him how that could be, but he changed the subject before I had a chance."

"Detective Fox didn't say he had no evidence of Melissa coming into money. He claimed he found no evidence of any financial transactions that could be connected to her murder."

"So what are you saying?"

"Maybe Melissa obtained extra money from a legitimate source. A second job? Selling her possessions through an online auction site? Your blackmail theory may be a dead end."

I shook my head. "I don't think so. The gifts for her parents, the expensive camera she planned to buy, and her loan to Jeremy—that's too much money obtained too quickly."

I would talk to Fox about this later. Meanwhile I had other avenues to pursue. "I'm going to need your help, Abby," I said.

"Me. What can I do?"

"You know the Pendwell's maid, Sheila."

"I know Gus, her dog." Abby smiled.

"You also have started a relationship with Sheila. Most people love their veterinarian. She only met you once, but I'm sure she'd talk to you. Sheila may be able to help us find out if Victoria left the house the night of Melissa's murder."

"But Sheila doesn't live on the estate."

"But there might be someone who does. A caretaker, for instance. Sheila can point us in the right direction."

"I don't know if I can—"

"Call her about some dog-related issue, and then steer the conversation to the Pendwell household."

"I'll try," Abby reluctantly agreed. "Gus had a hot spot on his back. I gave her salve to treat it. I was planning on calling anyway—to find out how he's doing."

"Good. Meanwhile, I'll check out Austin's condo and Elena's apartment building. Who knows? Maybe a doorman or neighbor saw one of them sneak out in the middle of the night." I grabbed the notebook where I listed my appointments.

Abby grinned. "You do know there are apps on your phone for keeping your schedule, don't you?"

"I prefer hard copy." I scanned my appointment list. "I could try to squeeze it in tomorrow, but I'm pretty busy.'"

"Tomorrow's Sunday. Probably not a good day anyway. I'm betting the regular doormen in Austin's condo and Elena's apartment building have that day off."

"Good point. I'll visit them another day."

"Do you think they'll talk to you?"

"I'm usually pretty good at getting people to open up, but staff at condos and apartment buildings, do try to protect the privacy of their residents. If I could get Detective Fox to go with me, they would have to talk."

I placed my notebook back on the table. "Meanwhile, I have an appointment with Austin later this week. I intend to keep talking to the suspects. In the course of conversation, sooner or later, the murderer will make a slip."

"What about George's murder?"

"I believe if we find who killed Melissa, we'll have George's killer too…" An image popped into my head. "That's it!"

"What's it?" Abby asked. "Do you have an idea?"

"George Grogin," I said, excitedly. "We've been trying to determine why anyone would kill him. I just recalled something. On the night of Melissa's murder, George went to the refuge to care for the possums in the rehabilitation center."

"Yes, but he was home before the murder took place. He was cleared of that."

"But he may have seen the murderer on the premises and not remembered."

Abby nodded. "Considering his illness, it's possible he forgot."

"And it is possible he didn't see anything. But the killer couldn't take that chance. If there was a remote possibility that George saw something, the killer had to make sure George was out of the way."

CHAPTER 46

Sunday afternoon, I headed to one of Long Island's pet stores. But this one would have a different story than the one at the Bay Cove Mall.

The Rocky Shore Pet Store sold pet supplies. You could get a dog or cat there, but they weren't for sale. This store had partnered with a local animal rescue group, and every weekend, homeless dogs and cats were offered for adoption.

"Giselda is going to her forever home," said the store owner, a motherly-looking woman. Her name was Martha.

Giselda was around five years old and, like my Archie, was a dog of many breeds.

"She's a perfect match for the couple adopting her," Martha continued. "Their old dog died four months ago. This couple just retired, and they didn't feel they could handle an energetic puppy."

I stayed for about an hour. During that time, two puppies and three kittens from the rescue group found homes too.

"It's a win-win situation for everyone," Martha declared. "The animals find loving homes, and humans get great animal companions. Plus, it's smart business for me. Most of these people will continue coming back here for their pet food and supplies."

I wanted my story on puppy mills to have a positive note. While the shutting down of the Bay Cove Pet Shop would show a glimmer of hope, I hoped my inclusion of the work of the Rocky Shore Pet Store would provide an option for those in the pet industry. I went home and finished writing the story. A little before dinner, I emailed it to my editor.

Playing Possum

* * * * *

"Olivia said your puppy mill article is fabulous." Clara said Monday as I stepped into the *Animal Advocate* office. "But she wanted me to remind you that your feature on the Pendwell Wildlife Preserve is due by next Monday."

My face clouded. "Don't worry. I'll have it in on time." I had been holding off completing this story in case there was a break in the murder case—one that showed a tie-in between the director's death and the refuge. Unfortunately, the clock was running out.

I made my way to my cubicle and was about to sit down behind my desk when my phone trilled. It was Dominick, my future son-in-law's father.

"I have the results on the cost outlay for the renovation of the wildlife refuge," he said. "I showed the Gerber Engineering proposal to a former colleague of mine who specializes in environmental engineering."

"What did he say?" I asked.

"Inconclusive. The costs are on the high end but within an acceptable range."

"So no embezzlement or creative accounting?"

"That's the problem. It's impossible to tell. From what you said, the board of trustees didn't seek proposals from companies of equal capabilities. Without knowing what similar companies would have bid, we can't know how legitimate this one is. And of course, there is no way to tell if money was exchanged under the table."

Before I could question him further, Dominick added, "My friend did tell me that Gerber Engineering has a good reputation in the industry regarding the quality of their work."

"Thanks." I clicked off and sat back. No evidence of impropriety. Perhaps there wasn't any. Or was it only that I couldn't find it?"

I had to be sure.

I placed another call. This one was to Susan Hanson, the trustee who had given me the proposal for Gerber Engineering.

Since it was a weekday morning, she was in school. I left a voice message. She called back about an hour later.

"I'm on a break now," she said. "What's up?"

"After Gerber Engineering finished their work at the refuge, did you ever inspect it?"

"No. They completed it about eight weeks ago, and I'm ashamed to say I haven't been at the refuge since then, except to attend the night board meeting at Blackthorne Manor."

"Can we meet later today? I know it's short notice, but I have a few questions."

"Can't we do this by phone?"

"I need to show you something."

After a short silence, she replied. "Okay. How's four this afternoon. I only live a few blocks from Sand Crab Beach. Why don't we meet there?"

I knew the place well, so I agreed. The concession stand wouldn't open until next month, but we decided that would be a good spot to rendezvous.

I no sooner clicked off when my phone trilled again. This time it was Linda Lau.

"I finally reached Melissa's high school friend Erin Leahy. She's back from her camping trip," Linda said. "And she has agreed to meet with us Wednesday at six-thirty."

"That's fine. I'll have an early dinner and—"

"Six-thirty in the morning." Linda chuckled. "Erin jogs in the park before work. She'll meet us at the concession stand."

I groaned. I wasn't a morning person. But I agreed to the meet.

"I gotta go," Linda said. "I hope this works, but I'm not sure Erin will be much help."

Linda said good-bye and clicked off before I could ask her why she felt this way.

CHAPTER 47

"I'm leaving," I called to Clara as I whizzed out of the office.

"What's up? You look like a woman on a mission."

"I am." I slammed the door behind me.

I sped off in the direction of the Pendwell Wildlife Refuge. Bypassing the administration building, I headed straight into the woods, where I spent the early afternoon taking photographs. I had the Gerber Engineering proposal with me, and I referred to it several times.

A few minutes before four, I arrived at Sand Crab Beach. Susan wasn't there yet, so I spent the next few minutes gazing at the whitecaps on the bay. I felt the tension leave my body as I inhaled the fresh salt air.

Susan arrived a few minutes later. She suggested we head down the beach and talk while walking along the water's edge.

"Melissa said she had proof of financial wrongdoings by Victoria, correct?" I asked, getting right to the point.

Susan nodded.

"But a week later, she told you she was mistaken." I wanted to be sure of my facts.

Susan nodded again. She didn't seem talkative today.

"Why didn't you believe her?" I asked.

"Because Melissa was hesitant and appeared unsure of herself. She was evasive. Plus she couldn't wait to get off the phone with me."

"Could that be because she realized she made a mistake in accusing Victoria and was embarrassed?"

Susan furrowed her brows as she appeared to mull over what I said. She shrugged. "I guess it's possible."

I took a moment to digest this information. Susan couldn't be sure.

Dominick said his results were inconclusive. As far as kick-backs or padding of costs, we had reached a dead end. But I had one more avenue to explore.

I reached into my bag and pulled out my phone.

"Gerber Engineering was responsible for removal of invasive species," I said. "Some of the sites where these invasive plants grew were specified in the proposal. I took pictures at those locations this afternoon."

I handed her my phone and pressed on the icon for photos. "These plants appear to be flourishing. Can you tell me if they are invasive species?"

"Plants are not my specialty, but I'll take a look."

Susan scanned my photos. She shook her head. "Nope. I recognize these plants. They are indigenous to Long Island. As far as I can see, there is nothing here that doesn't belong in this region."

"When I had first seen these plants, I thought they were overrunning the area," I said. "My thought was that Gerber had not done all the work they had been paid to do. I guess I was wrong."

"Removal of invasive species was only one facet of the project. Gerber was also supposed to dredge the ponds and install collection devices to intercept storm water borne sediment," Susan reminded me.

"Can you go to the refuge and check out if they did?" I asked.

"I'll think about that." She glanced at her watch. "But I have to leave now. Let's head back."

We trekked toward the parking lot in silence. Why was Susan so reluctant to verify if the work had been done? I sensed she hadn't told me everything.

"Is something bothering you?" I asked.

Her gaze shifted back to the surf. "You should know I will probably be leaving the board of trustees."

"Why?"

"I've tentatively been offered the promotion I wanted. Very tentatively."

"That's wonderful, but—"

"The head of the school district called me into his office. He told me this new job would be a lot more work, which I expected. But before it would be formally offered to me he wanted to be sure I had the time to devote to it. He suggested I might want to curtail some of my outside activities."

I took a deep breath. "They want you off the board of trustees?"

"I'm afraid so. I haven't decided yet, but I really want this new position. And it's not like I do any good as a trustee. I'll always be outvoted."

"Does Victoria have someone in mind to replace you?"

Susan nodded. "His name is Griffin Barrett, and his background is in environmental studies, which is good." She smiled. "He is also Victoria's godchild."

Victoria had to have total control.

"I do want to help you," Susan added. "I decided I will drop by the refuge tomorrow afternoon. I'll check to see if all the improvements listed in the Gerber proposal were completed. No one will know what I'm doing."

"Thanks." We continued to make our way back to the parking lot in silence.

"You need to be careful," Susan said when we were about halfway there. "I was told by one of the other trustees to watch out for you."

"What do you mean?" I stopped walking and stood in place.

"Victoria told him you were out to get her. And her family."

I sucked in my breath. I knew Elena was furious at me for prying. But I hadn't realized Victoria was also aware of my investigation into the murder of Melissa. That was naïve on my part. Elena probably told her. Or Victoria had come to the conclusion on her own.

We had almost reached the parking lot. "I'm going to stay here a bit," I said.

Susan left. I turned and stood for a few moments facing the bay and watching a seagull dive into the water and zoom back to the sky with a fish in its mouth. The beach was colder and breezier than inland. I wrapped my arms around my body as the wind off the bay sent a chill down my spine.

I mulled over what I learned today. Victoria was more devious than Elena. Instead of confronting me, Victoria appeared to be a follower of the philosophy, "Keep your enemies close."

Had she been manipulating me all along?

CHAPTER 48

The next morning, I passed through the security check at the federal office building housing the United States Fish and Wildlife Service. Ray Maxwell, my contact at the agency, had arranged for me to meet with Melissa Modica's former boss.

When I entered his office, he rose up to greet me. He was a muscular man with short cropped brown hair and tortoise shell rimmed glasses.

"Just call me Lou," he said. "Most people can't pronounce my last name anyway."

I smiled. Ray had told me a little about this man. Lou had worked for the agency for more than twenty years. He was a straight shooter who was more interested in getting the job done than in office protocol.

I told Lou I was writing a story on the Pendwell Wildlife Refuge, and I thought Melissa's death might have a connection to her work there.

"I'll help you all I can, but I don't know how," he said, scratching his head. "What do you want to know?"

"Melissa worked here a long time, so you and your staff got to know her. I want to find out what she was like. Her personality? Her character? What ticked her off?"

He leaned back and furrowed his eyebrows, appearing to ponder this for a moment. "Melissa was a workaholic. Serious type. I wish she hadn't left. I think she wished that too."

"Why do you say that?"

"She didn't like her new co-workers. She used the word 'devious' to describe one of them."

"Do you remember which co-worker that was?"

He shook his head. "No. She never mentioned any names."

"Did she have any problems when she worked here?"

"Not at all. She got along with everyone here at Fish and Wildlife. She enjoyed the work, and she had friends, too."

"Friends? I heard she wasn't a particularly social person."

"That's true. She was no social butterfly, but she had two good friends. Their names are Gina and Dan."

I had a thought. "After Melissa left Fish and Wildlife to take the job at the Pendwell Wildlife Refuge, did she ever come back here to visit? Did she ever have lunch with her former co-workers?"

He nodded. "Three or four times. She was here about a week before her death. She was so happy and thoughtful. She brought presents for a lot of the staff."

"Presents?"

"She bought me a beautiful illustrated book on butterflies. I've always been fascinated with the Monarch." He pointed to a large book sitting on his credenza.

He glanced at his watch. "I need to attend a meeting in less than ten minutes. But why don't I introduce you to Gina and Dan. They probably can tell you a lot more about Melissa than I can.

"Gina and Dan are both attorneys," he said as he escorted me down the long corridor with its ugly hospital green walls. He knocked on a door with a sign that read: LEGAL DIVISION.

"Come in," a female voice called out.

It was a small office with two metal desks. I judged the age of the two individuals sitting behind those desks to be around thirty. Gina was petite with black hair and olive skin. Dan, blonde and fair skinned, had the build of a defensive linebacker.

"Let's go into the conference room, so we can talk in private," Gina said after Lou explained the reason for our visit.

Lou headed off to his meeting while I trailed the two attorneys back down the corridor to a large room furnished with an oval table surrounded by eight chairs. There was a credenza on the far end of the room with a coffee machine on top. Dan offered me a cup. Of course, I accepted. Dan made a cup for each of us, and then we sat down.

"Lou told me you were good friends of Melissa." I said. I had grabbed a seat across from the two attorneys who sat side by side.

"Office friends," Gina responded. "We'd go to lunch occasionally, but we didn't see each other socially after hours or on weekends."

"But at work we were close," Dan added. "We worked on several projects together, and we got along really well."

Gina nodded. "We backed each other up whenever we could. Not everybody is like that."

"As office friends, did you know anything about Melissa's private life? Her family? Her romantic interests?" I sipped my coffee. It was surprisingly good.

"No." Gina shook her head. "She mentioned her parents once or twice, but she never talked about the people she dated. Most of our conversation was about work."

"That's true," Dan agreed. "Occasionally, when we went to lunch together, the topic of hiking came up. We were all into that, so we'd share information on any new trails we used. That's about it. Right, Gina?"

"Pretty much. Melissa liked to run, and she would sometimes talk about the marathons she entered. But that was about as personal as she got."

I was sure I had hit a dead end, until I thought of another avenue to explore. "Was money important to Melissa?"

"Not at all. She lived simply."

"Gina's right." Dan sat forward and ran his hand through his blonde hair. "Melissa was just as happy with her ten year-old car as with a brand new luxury model."

"Exactly," added Gina. "She dressed nicely too, but she never wore expensive designer brands. Aside from good hiking boots, she was never into things."

I mulled this over in my mind. This didn't sound like a person who would use blackmail to extort money from someone.

"Whenever Melissa had a little extra cash, she would use it on others, not herself," Gina said. "I'm an amateur photographer. When we had lunch a week before her death, she brought me a beautiful silver frame."

"She gave me a box containing a variety of coffees," Dan added. "I know Melissa came into a lot of money, but she didn't have to do that."

"A lot of money. What do you mean?"

"From her raffle prize."

I stared blankly. "She won a raffle?"

"Melissa bought a raffle ticket from some wildlife organization. She won first prize. It was a high-end raffle. I think tickets were five hundred dollars apiece. But Melissa always gave generously to causes she believed in."

"What did she win?"

"Twenty-five thousand dollars."

That explained where she got the money for the plasma television, washer, and dryer as well as the loan to Jeremy. She wasn't blackmailing the Pendwells or anyone else.

My brilliant idea for a motive was gone. Air fizzled out of me as my balloon, once filled with hope, quickly deflated.

CHAPTER 49

It was dark outside when my alarm clock rang. Matt pulled a pillow over his head and rolled over on his right side. The alarm may have awakened him, but he'd be back asleep in seconds. I did not have that option. I was picking up Linda Lau, and we were meeting Erin Leahy in the park where she jogged before work.

I brewed my coffee, gulped down a cup, showered, dressed, brewed more coffee, and poured it into my travel mug. By the time I pulled in front of Linda's home, the sun had risen.

"I sure hope Erin can help us," Linda said as we sped off to the park. "She's a little..." Linda didn't complete the sentence.

"She's a little what?" I asked.

"Ditsy. Spacey. Don't get me wrong. She's a nice girl, but her thought processes can be off track. The only reason Erin and Melissa were friends was because of their love of running and the outdoors. That's why I don't know if Melissa would have confided in her."

"A pregnancy is a big thing. You were out of town at the time. Melissa probably felt the need to confide in someone. Let's hope it was Erin."

When we arrived at the park, I drained my mug and then hopped out of the car. The grass was still wet from the morning dew. Linda and I made our way to the concession stand where Erin was waiting. Linda introduced us.

"We have a few questions before you start your run," I said.

Erin grinned. "I finished my run about ten minutes ago. I'm about to have my morning smoothie now." She grabbed a green drink off the concession counter. "Do you want one? They're really good."

Linda ordered a strawberry/banana smoothie, but I declined. I ordered another coffee.

"Did Melissa tell you she was pregnant?" I asked, getting straight to the point.

Erin nodded. "Yes, she told me. She was planning on keeping the baby. I warned her how rough life would be as a single parent. She said the hardest thing would be telling her parents although she felt they eventually would support her. But she kept putting it off."

"Do you know who the baby's father was?" I grabbed my drink from the counter and plunked my money down.

She never said, but I could make a good guess."

"Who?"

"Austin Pendwell."

"Austin!" I nearly dropped my coffee. "She hated him."

"Hate is a strong word. She found him obnoxious."

"Then why do you think it was him?" I sputtered.

"Melissa agreed to go to dinner with him because she was at her wits end at work. She felt he could iron things out for her with his mother."

I stared at Erin, my mouth open.

"Melissa felt she could deal with Austin for two to three hours at dinner if he could help her with her work situation," Erin continued.

"It's a long stretch from having dinner with someone to getting pregnant."

"Melissa was upset. She needed to unwind, so at dinner, she had too much to drink. She almost never drank alcohol. She went back to his condo and…" Erin shrugged. "Things got out of hand."

"Did she tell him to stop?" I couldn't believe what I was hearing.

Erin shrugged. "She never said."

"Did you tell this to the police?"

"I tried to talk to a Detective Woof."

"Wolfe."

"Okay. Wolfe. I paid a condolence call to Mr. and Mrs. Modica at their house, and Woof—Wolfe was there. I told him about Melissa's one-night-stand with Austin Pendwell. Wolfe said he'd talk to me later, but he never did."

"And you didn't pursue this?"

"No." Erin looked confused. "I had second thoughts. I didn't know if she asked him to stop, so I wasn't about to ruin his reputation if the one night stand was something they both wanted."

"But you said she was drunk. And what about the possible paternity issue?" My heart was spinning.

Erin shrugged. "Same thing. I wasn't positive it was Austin who got her pregnant. It's only a guess. And Melissa had told me that she didn't want the baby's father involved in her life, and it was fine with him."

For probably the first time in my life, I was speechless.

"But the father did promise to provide financial support," Erin continued. "Melissa said he had plenty of money—which is another reason I thought it was Austin. It sounded like they worked it out. Melissa seemed happy."

Erin paused to gulp down what remained of her smoothie. When finished, she said, "As far as I was concerned, the money certainly wasn't a motive for murder."

As Erin walked away to throw her empty smoothie container in the litter basket, Linda and I exchanged glances.

"The money might not be a motive for murder," I said. "But the impact on Austin's political career would be."

CHAPTER 50

I stopped at Matt's veterinary hospital to drop off some magazines for the waiting room. Although I'm an avid reader, I couldn't envision anyone reading here. Watching the antics of the animals in the room was too distracting—and entertaining.

Upon entering the building, a distinctive odor wafted through the air. My eyes were instantly drawn to the animal care attendant cleaning up an "accident" in the middle of the waiting room.

I wasn't greeted by the usual assortment of barks, meows, and canine toenails scratching the floor. It was fifteen minutes until closing, and there was only one patient in the room—a toy poodle shaking nervously as it sat on the lap of a middle-aged man who was stroking the dog's back.

I said hello to Katie, the office assistant, and handed her the magazines.

"Matt has one more patient," she said, nodding in the poodle's direction. "But Abby is finishing up. She should be out in a few minutes."

"Good." I smiled. Abby was the real reason I was here. She'd phoned earlier and told me Sheila was coming in to pick up additional salve for her dog's hot spot. I wanted to find out what information Abby could glean. If I were lucky, Sheila would arrive while I was here, and I would be able to probe further.

A few minutes later, an elderly woman emerged from one of the examining rooms. She held a dog on a leash. The animal was white around the muzzle and had a belly almost touching the ground.

"He looks so sad," I said to Abby who had followed them out.

"He's a basset hound. They always look sad." She grinned.

"Did you talk to Sheila?" I asked.

"She hasn't come in yet."

"Did she miss her appointment?"

"There was no appointment. She's only picking up some more salve for Gus. I reminded her that we close at nine o'clock." Abby glanced at her watch. "She still has five minutes. Dad will probably be here for another half hour, but at nine we lock the front door."

At that moment, the door swung open and Sheila rushed inside.

"Whew! Made it with not much time to spare." She appeared out of breath and her hair was disheveled.

"Slow down. You're here now. Take a seat while I get the salve for Gus." Abby headed to the locked supply cabinet.

"I can't wait to get home and have a stiff drink," she said, shaking her head. She slumped down on one of the comfy chairs. "What a day."

"What happened?" I asked.

"I almost got fired."

"Why?"

Sheila brushed her hair away from her face. "I accidentally cracked the marble floor in the Pendwell entrance foyer."

"How did you do that?"

"I was polishing Mrs. Pendwell's silver walking stick, and it slipped out of my hand and fell on the floor. It left a huge crack in the marble."

"And Mrs. Pendwell wanted to fire you because of this?"

Sheila nodded. "Eventually, she calmed down and said she guessed one accident in fifteen years wasn't a lot. But she told me to forget about a raise. Can you believe that? I haven't had a raise since way before Mr. Pendwell died."

Abby returned and handed Sheila a tube of medicinal salve.

"Mrs. Pendwell has never been easy to work for, but she's been worse lately," Sheila continued. "I think it's a combination of money problems and Austin's Senate run."

"She does appear to be taking a big role in his campaign."

Sheila chuckled. "Her biggest role is in diffusing any potential scandal."

Abby sat down next to Sheila. "What type of scandal?"

Sheila smiled wickedly. "Mrs. Pendwell is playing up Austin's engagement to Elena Salazar, but Austin is known to be a lady's man, if you get my drift. Elena and Austin recently had a huge fight over Austin's latest girlfriend. She's some blonde who works in his office."

"I heard Victoria isn't pleased about that."

Sheila nodded. "You're putting it mildly. She and Austin had a big blowout. Mrs. Pendwell claimed this blonde is a political liability. Her father owns a bar and had his liquor license suspended twice for serving minors. He also had an incident where he served someone who was obviously drunk and didn't stop him from getting in a car. I understand there was an accident. Luckily no one was killed."

Sheila stopped talking to catch her breath, before continuing. "This is not someone Victoria wants connected to her son."

"But it's not the woman's fault that her father had problems," Abby interjected.

"No. But Austin's opponent would use this to throw mud. More importantly, if news of the affair became public, there would be sympathy for Elena."

I nodded. "I hear Elena is popular and has her own following among environmentalists."

"That's what Mrs. Pendwell keeps telling Austin." Sheila rose from her seat. "I'd better be going."

"Does any of Victoria's household staff live on the property?" I asked before Sheila left the building.

"There's a groom who takes care of the horses. He also serves as caretaker of the property since Mrs. Pendwell's stable has dwindled. Still, his major function is the horses. He has a cottage in back."

"Would he have been around the first Monday in May?" I was referring to the night Melissa Modica was murdered.

"I don't know. You would need to ask him."

"Abby and I will walk out with you," I said to Sheila. By this time, the man with the poodle had been called into an examining room with Matt, the office assistant had left the building, and the light by her counter had been turned off.

Once we stepped outside, Abby locked the front door. Matt and his patient could leave, but no one could enter.

Sheila said good-bye. Abby and I continued walking to our cars.

"At least we know the groom lives on the premises," Abby said. "But we didn't learn anything else."

"Not true. Victoria's motive has intensified."

Abby looked at me quizzically. "How?"

I told her about my conversation with Erin.

"Getting Melissa pregnant while engaged to Elena Salazar could end Austin's career before it started," I said. "Sheila has verified that Austin's political career is Victoria's number one priority."

CHAPTER 51

I had no idea as to how I'd get Victoria Pendwell's groom to answer my questions.

The next afternoon, I pulled into the long driveway leading up to the Pendwell estate. I parked on the side, as far from the house as possible, hoping no one would see me. I had an appointment to see Austin today, but I wanted to talk to the groom first. Sheila had told me his name was Manny.

I wandered to the back of the house, passing a five-car garage. Behind the Pendwell home were the swimming pool, hot tub, cabana, and deck, all overlooking the Long Island Sound. I'd seen this when I attended the fundraiser here last week. But at that time, I hadn't paid attention to the property adjacent to the outdoor entertainment complex. Now my eyes were drawn to this section, where I spotted an empty horse paddock, a barn, and a small cottage.

Glancing at my watch, I noted it was almost five o'clock. I hoped the groom had recently returned the horses from the paddock to their stalls and was now in the barn, settling them in for the night.

The barn doors were open. I entered, and I was in luck.

"Who are you?" asked a muscular man with a weather-beaten face. The man's handlebar mustache reminded me of a caricature of a sheriff from an old television western. He was brushing a chestnut colored horse on cross ties in the center aisle.

"You must be Manny," I said. "I'm Kristy. I have a five-thirty appointment with Austin, but I arrived early. Mrs. Pendwell told me about her horses, so I wanted to see them."

"You shouldn't be here without Mrs. Pendwell." He frowned.

"This stable is private property."

"Oh, it's okay with her," I lied.

He didn't look convinced.

"She said if I arrived early, I could mosey back here and take a look." I could feel my nose growing. I spotted a cell phone sticking out of his pocket, and I hoped he wasn't going to call her to verify.

He continued staring at me with a wary gaze but finally said, "Well, if you're sure it's okay with Mrs. Pendwell."

"Absolutely." Pinocchio had nothing on me.

"This is her favorite horse," he said, referring to the horse he was grooming. "He's a thoroughbred. The other chestnut in the stall is a Dutch Warmblood. Mrs. Pendwell rode him a lot in jumping competitions. Next to him is a dark bay quarter horse. He's used primarily for guests who come and ride."

"All three horses are beautiful," I said as I strolled around the facility, thinking of how I could bring up the questions I needed to ask. An idea popped into my head.

"I'd love to work with horses," I said. "But your job must be grueling. Horses need constant care. You must work long hours every day."

"It's true. Horses need to be tended to everyday. But I have Mondays off. Mrs. Pendwell has someone come in that day to take care of them." He chuckled. "One day he didn't show up, and Mrs. Pendwell tended to the horses. Can you believe she mucked the stables herself?"

"Amazing." It was an image I couldn't quite picture.

I didn't want to get side-tracked. "You're not here Mondays?" I asked.

"Not during the day. I leave the estate six o'clock every Sunday night and return Monday evening at six."

That means he would be here Monday nights.

"Where do you keep your car?"

"I don't have a car. I use the Pendwell truck for work. But on my day off, my cousin picks me up, and I spend my time with him. He's a groom at a horse farm about a mile away." Manny frowned. "You're kinda nosy."

I quickly changed the subject and started talking about horses in general.

"Horses are so fragile," I said. "My daughter owned a horse when she was young. We almost lost him to colic." This was true.

"Colic is a problem." He had finished grooming the horse and now led it back to its stall. "This horse here had colic back in March. I had to hitch the horse trailer to the Pendwell truck and take him to the veterinarian." He shook his head. "That was some night."

"A good thing you caught it. Are you usually around the stable at night?"

"There were signs of distress during the day, so I kept a watch on him. Late afternoon, I decided it was time to bring him to Dr. Weiss. But to answer your question, most of the time I close the stable at around six at night. The horses are usually good until the next morning."

I realized a way to segue the conversation, so I could get the information I needed out of Manny.

"Dr. Weiss and I were talking to Victoria at her fundraiser last week. I thought he said you had a medical emergency with one of the horses during the first Monday in May." Another lie, but I crossed my fingers, hoping it would help me discover if he was around the night of Melissa's murder.

Manny shook his head. "Nope. This month has been quiet. Good thing too." He flashed a smile. "My cousin bought a new television last month, and he gave me his old one which is bigger and better than the one I had."

"That's great," I said.

"Sure is. Once I close the stable up for the night, I head back to my cottage, eat my dinner, and spend the rest of the evening sitting back with my feet up watching my favorite shows."

He hadn't been outside the night of Melissa's murder. The location of his cottage was too far away from the garage and house for him to see anyone coming or going.

My hope of finding someone to disprove Victoria's alibi for the night of the murder had reached a dead end.

CHAPTER 52

I rang the bell at the front of the Pendwell home.

Seconds later, the door swung open. Standing before me was a tall, thin, young woman with an angular and unsmiling face. She wore a traditional maid's outfit.

"Where's Sheila?" I asked, fearing Victoria changed her mind and had fired Sheila.

"It's her day off," the maid answered briskly. "May I say who is calling?"

"Kristy Farrell. I have an appointment with Austin—"

"Mr. Pendwell is expecting you. Come in."

"Do you always work here on Sheila's day off?" I stepped into the foyer.

"Yes."

"Is Victoria here today?"

"I believe Mrs. Pendwell is at home."

Unlike Sheila, this woman was definitely not a talker.

"Mr. Pendwell is waiting for you in the living room," she added. "Please follow me."

As we continued through the foyer, I spotted the crack in the marble floor that had most likely been caused when Sheila dropped the silver walking stick.

Not too bad. Still to break the marble, that walking stick came down with quite an impact.

"Mrs. Farrell is here, Mr. Pendwell," the maid announced when we reached the living room.

Austin was sitting in an overstuffed armchair, reading the newspaper.

206

He dropped the paper on an end table and rose. His smile was polite but not warm. After we exchanged pleasantries, he said, "Let's go into my office. It's down the hall."

But before leaving the living room, he turned to the maid. "I'm expecting someone from my office in about a half hour. I'm sure I will be done with my interview by then, but if not, please show my guest into the living room to wait."

"Who are you expecting, Austin?" called out a sharp toned voice. Victoria Pendwell strutted into the room.

"Charlene Cooper. She's dropping off papers."

"If she is only dropping off papers, I can take them from her. There's no need for her to wait for you."

"I need to speak with her."

Victoria frowned. "You won't have a lot of time for office work. I forgot to tell you, but I invited Elena to join us for dinner tonight. She'll be arriving in less than an hour."

Austin's dark eyes flashed anger. "Then I'll make my business short, but I need to see Charlene." He turned toward me. His face was beet red, his fists clenched. "Shall we go to my office? It appears my mother has me on a tight schedule."

Austin's office was magnificent. It smelled of leather and books. A bay window overlooking the Long Island Sound let in natural light. Two walls featured built-in book shelves, and a third wall featured framed photographs of Austin with other members of the rich and famous set. In the center of the room, a Persian rug covered a portion of the hardwood floor.

Austin sat down behind a large oak desk, and I slipped into a leather wingback chair facing him. Next to my chair was an end table, which held what I believed was a genuine Tiffany lamp.

"Beautiful room," I said.

"Thank you. It was my father's office. When he passed away, I decided to use it. I have a small home office in my condo, but when I work away from the law firm, I prefer to come here. As you can see, I have an entire set of law books on these shelves."

I started the interview by asking Austin about his work with the wildlife refuge. He told me he hadn't been too involved in the past, but he was planning to up his game and play a major role in fundraising.

"What are some of your fundraising ideas?" I asked.

He hemmed and hawed. Apparently, he had no idea. I was surprised. He knew my interview was to be about his expanding role with the wildlife refuge, and I thought he would be better prepared.

"I plan to be a goodwill ambassador for the refuge. I'll use my family ties to convince wealthy donors to contribute." That was all he had to say.

I asked a few more questions. He responded to half of these inquiries by saying, "There are several factors to consider." For the other half, he answered, "I'll have to wait and see."

I decided to change the topic.

"Off the record," I said. "Do you think the murders of Melissa Modica and George Grogin will have an impact on your election?"

"I can't imagine it will." There was a momentary hint of anger in his voice, but he quickly gained control over it. "Although they both worked at the refuge, I barely knew Melissa or George."

"Really?" I smiled sweetly. "I heard you dated Melissa."

"Oh, right." He leaned back. "It was so long ago that I forgot. I believe it was when she first started working at the refuge."

I decided not to mention I knew about their dinner date a few months ago. I'd save that for another time.

So far, Austin had answered all of my questions willingly, but I wasn't sure how he would react to my next one.

"I'm assuming the police are looking at everyone even remotely connected to either the refuge or Melissa. I guess as long as you have an alibi for your time, you have nothing to worry about."

Detective Fox had told me Austin claimed to be alone at his condo. I wanted to see Austin's reaction to my statement.

"I was asleep in my condo," Austin said. His face was impassive, but he ran his hand through his hair in what I interpreted as a nervous gesture.

Austin rose from his chair. I was afraid he was finished with the interview, and I had wanted to be here when Charlene from his office arrived.

As I searched my mind for a way to stall, his phone trilled.

"Excuse me," he said, dropping back down on his chair and grabbing the phone.

"She's bringing the papers from the office. She should be here any moment," he said to his caller. "When I was in Florida, two weeks ago, I went over the proposed revision with the client."

He was in Florida two weeks ago! Had he been near Oleander trees?

The front doorbell chimed.

"I think she's here now. I'll call you back later." He finished his call and rose again from his chair.

"It's been a pleasure talking with you, Kristy." He smiled. "I'll see you out."

He escorted me back down the hall. When we reached the living room, a smile spread across his face.

"I'll be with you in a minute, Charlene," he said to a woman sprawled out on the couch.

As I expected, she was the blonde.

CHAPTER 53

I wanted to find out more about Austin's indiscretions. That evening, I drove to his opponent's campaign headquarters. The brunette, whom I talked with last time, had mentioned she volunteered there every Saturday morning and Wednesday night. I remembered her name was Diana.

When I arrived, the place was bustling with activity. I spotted the brunette, but unfortunately, all seats nearby were taken.

"Now what," I mumbled as I stood near the doorway, surveying my surroundings.

I could pretend to be a volunteer and sit somewhere else. When she got up to get coffee, use the lavatory, or stretch her legs, I could take her aside and talk.

But that might draw attention to me. There were more than two dozen volunteers stuffing envelopes. Someone was bound to overhear, and I didn't need that.

The posted schedule listed the hours for headquarters today from ten in the morning until nine at night. It was eight o'clock now.

Next to the headquarters was a small café. It was a warm spring evening, so customers were dining outdoors. I noticed a few tables facing the entrance to campaign headquarters. If I snagged one of these seats, I could catch Diana when she left—hopefully alone.

I departed and secured an outdoor table facing headquarters. I'd be sure to see her when she left.

"What can I get you?" the server asked. She was short and slightly overweight with frizzy blonde hair.

"Coffee. Black, please."

"That's all?" The server replied in a tone that meant I better order more or she would push me out in fifteen minutes.

I quickly scanned the dessert menu. "I'll have the brownie sundae."

I always kept a book in my tote bag for when I waited for an appointment. I pulled it out and began reading while keeping an eye out for anyone leaving the headquarters.

My order came.

"I shouldn't have ordered ice cream," I mumbled. I needed to stall and ice cream melts quickly.

Soon a few people straggled out of the campaign headquarters. At about ten minutes before nine, Diana strutted through the doorway and onto the sidewalk.

My table was close enough to the campaign headquarters that I could almost reach out and touch her when she strolled by.

"Diana," I called.

She turned toward me, furrowed her brows, and stared suspiciously.

She doesn't remember me.

"It's Kristy Farrell. I met you here two weeks ago. We were talking about Austin Pendwell."

She nodded, but her expression was wary.

"I have a question, I need to ask." I had several questions, but I didn't want to push it. "Join me for coffee."

"What do you need to ask?"

"It's about Austin."

She shook her head. "No. I've probably said too much already. After you left last time, I regretted talking. I can't afford to have anything about my prior relationship come out."

"Please. I promise I won't let anyone know we've talked."

She hesitated. I was afraid she would refuse. But she relented.

"Okay." She came around and joined me at the table. The server immediately approached. Diana ordered an espresso, and I asked for a coffee refill.

"I haven't been completely honest," Diana said. "About three days after Austin and I fought and broke up, he called me. I was about to hang up when he told me he had obtained an internship for me at a law firm. I was still angry, and I never saw him again socially, but I took the internship."

She hesitated. "That internship catapulted me into my current job."

"I assume this is another reason you didn't come forward."

She looked down, averting my eyes, and nodded.

"After you broke off with Austin, did you keep abreast of what was happening in his life?"

Diana smiled wickedly. "I was quite aware of what was going on. We're both part of the legal community, and have mutual acquaintances. Many of my colleagues deal with him professionally, and I hear about his shenanigans through the grapevine."

"Shenanigans?"

"He's a real Casanova. Most of the time, I didn't pay much attention. But when he dated Jillian Thom, my interest was piqued."

"Why?"

We stopped talking while the server delivered Diana's espresso and refilled my cup with coffee.

"Jillian is a lawyer," Diana said once the server left. "I know her pretty well."

Diana sipped her espresso. I could tell she knew more, but she was saying nothing. I needed to probe.

"Is there anything about their relationship that you should tell me?"

"It was pretty hot for a while. But they broke up. I understand Mama Pendwell didn't approve."

"Mama Pendwell? Do you mean Victoria?"

Diana nodded. "She's like a mama bear. Ferociously protecting her cub—although her cub is a thirty-three year-old lawyer."

"Why did Victoria object to the romance?" I swallowed more coffee. I should have ordered decaf. I would be up through the wee hours of the morning.

"Jillian's mother was once engaged to Clifton Pendwell. They broke it off two years before Clifton met Victoria, but Victoria never trusted her. At one time, she accused Clifton of having an affair. It wasn't true, but Victoria was always jealous."

Diana pushed a strand of her dark hair away from her face and continued. "Victoria was insecure. Jillian's mom came from the same social background as Clifton. Victoria didn't. She was an actress from a middle class background."

212

We sat silently for a few minutes. Diana drained her drink and said, "But I don't think pressure from Victoria was the real reason for the break-up. I think Jillian had an incident with Austin."

"Incident?"

"Once, when she was still dating him, I ran into Jillian in the courthouse. She had a black eye."

"What?" I almost spilled my coffee. "Do you think he hit her?"

Diana shrugged. "I asked her. She denied it."

"But you think—"

"I didn't know, but I had suspicions. Then two weeks after I saw Jillian, I heard she was appointed law clerk to one of the judges. She didn't have enough clout on her own to get that position, but the Pendwells did."

I leaned back, pondering all Diana had told me. Austin definitely had a reputation with the ladies. However, he appeared to be able to secure their silence.

But that might not have held true for Melissa Modica.

CHAPTER 54

Elena Salazar lived in a high-rise apartment building in a community that recently had revitalized its downtown. The area now consisted of upscale restaurants, trendy boutiques, and a scattering of apartment buildings meant to attract young people.

I met Detective Fox at the building entrance late the next afternoon. He was off duty but had agreed to come. We planned to verify alibis today.

"At least we won't get any interference from Wolfe," he said with a chuckle.

I smiled. Fox had told me Wolfe signed out of the office an hour early yesterday so he could go home and prepare for his colonoscopy this morning. He wouldn't be bothering us today.

"I know the security chief here," Fox said. "He's retired from the police force. I called him and he's meeting us in his office."

Once we were in the apartment building's security office, Fox introduced me to the security chief and then got right to the purpose of our visit.

"We need to see the security tapes from your underground parking garage for this date," he said, handing the guard a paper with the date written on it. We needed to find out if Elena Salazar left here after eleven that night. The apartment was about a half hour drive from the refuge.

Fox had obtained the license plate of Elena's car, as well as its make, model, and year. We huddled in the security room and viewed the tape for the hour before midnight, but there was no sign of Elena leaving.

"Maybe we should go back earlier," Fox suggested. "When Wolfe and I originally asked for her whereabouts the night of the murder, Elena claimed she had dinner with friends and arrived home around nine. She claims she didn't leave her apartment until eight-thirty the next morning."

The security chief went back further. Not only was there no record of her leaving, but there was no record of her coming home.

"She wasn't at home at all that evening." I frowned.

"Did she tell you she parked her car in the garage?" the security chief asked.

Fox shook his head. "Not specifically. But she claimed she was at the apartment from nine o'clock that evening."

"Then she may have parked in the street. Some of our residents, especially females, don't like parking in the underground garage at night even though we have cameras. If they find a parking spot nearby on the street, they use that instead."

"But street parking is metered." I said. I knew this because I barely scrapped enough change out of my bag to park here.

"The meter is only in effect until nine at night. After that you don't have to pay until nine the next morning."

Fox and I exchanged glances. As far as verifying Elena Salazar's alibi, we had reached a dead end.

Next, we headed to Austin Pendwell's condominium. This luxury building had a doorman.

"I'm Detective Fox," he said to the doorman, flashing his badge. He didn't introduce me, making it unclear as to whether I was with the police or not. I had dressed conservatively in gray slacks, white top, and navy blue blazer, hoping those we interviewed would assume I was a detective.

Fox told the doorman he was looking into the whereabouts of one of the residents on a specific date in May. He told the doorman the date in question, then asked, "Were you on duty that night?"

"Sure was," replied the doorman, a tall, distinguished looking man who stood ramrod straight.

"Do you remember what time Austin Pendwell came home that evening?"

I groaned. That was three weeks ago. How could Fox expect a doorman to remember that?"

"I do remember," the doorman said. "It was my first day back from my vacation. Mr. Pendwell had some packages delivered that day which I stored for him. He gave me a pretty nice tip." The doorman scratched his head. "I'm not exactly sure of the time he came home. I'd have to say between seven and eight."

"And he didn't go out after that?" Detective Fox asked.

"Sure he did. He was only home a short while. He changed out of his suit into casual clothes and left. That was about eight-thirty."

"When did he return?"

"It was almost one o'clock. I'm positive because I usually only work until midnight. But my replacement was running late—he was coming back from New Jersey and got stuck in traffic. Anyway, he called and asked me if I would work that extra hour. He arrived here at one, and I was about to leave when Mr. Pendwell returned.

Austin didn't have an alibi.

Fox grinned. "I think I'm going to visit Austin this afternoon and find out why he lied."

As we turned to leave, the doorman added, "He probably was with his girlfriend and didn't want his fiancée to know. That's usually why he comes home late."

Fox and I exchanged glances. "What do you mean?" I asked.

"Austin has this blonde girlfriend. A real looker. She used to come here all the time. Then one day, his fiancée shows up when the blonde was upstairs with him." The doorman chuckled. "He had me stall his fiancée down here in the lobby until he could get his girlfriend out the back way. He never had the girlfriend here again, but I think he spent a lot of evenings at her place."

"Why do you think that?"

"Because the night after this occurred, I heard him on his phone as he was leaving. He said he didn't want any more close calls. From now on they would meet at her place." The doorman shrugged. "It sounded like he was talking to the girlfriend."

"The girlfriend's name is Charlene Cooper," I told Detective Fox as we made our way out of the building. "She works in Austin's law office."

"I don't want to talk to her there. I'll get her home address and visit her tomorrow after she finishes work," he said.

"Can I tag along?"

Fox hesitated. "Not a good idea. The security chief at Elena's apartment building isn't going to say anything about our visit. And hopefully Austin's doorman won't mention it either. But this Charlene will certainly run back to Austin."

I nodded. "Right. So this interview has to be done by the book. No civilians."

Fox stared at the ceiling. "Now, I've just got to figure out how I'm going to do this without alerting Wolfe."

CHAPTER 55

That evening, as I stepped into my kitchen, my phone trilled.

"Austin was with Charlene when Melissa was murdered," Detective Fox said as soon as I answered the call. "Charlene claims he's been there every Monday and Wednesday this past month. Arrives at ten and leaves after midnight. And Elena's apartment is a good half hour from the wildlife refuge."

"Could she be lying? She is his girlfriend."

"Not anymore. They had a huge fight this Thursday and broke up."

"This Thursday! That was the day I interviewed Austin at the Pendwell estate. Charlene arrived as I was leaving," I said. "She was delivering documents."

"Apparently, he gave her the bum's rush," Detective Fox said. "He needed her to leave because Elena was on her way over."

"That's right. Victoria invited her for dinner."

"It seems Austin promised Charlene he would end his engagement. Charlene now realized he had no intention of doing that. She was always going to be nothing more than his mistress."

I got his point. If Charlene was no longer Austin's girlfriend, she had no reason to lie about his whereabouts.

"I believe Charlene when she says Austin was with her during the time Melissa was murdered." Detective Fox sighed. "I guess Austin can be eliminated as a suspect."

After ending the call, I slid into a chair by the table and began pondering the facts. Archie, the canine tank, laid his head across my feet.

George Grogin was dead. Austin Pendwell had an alibi. Jeremy Toth was still on my suspect list, but I considered him highly unlikely.

218

Victoria Pendwell and Elena Salazar were the prime suspects.

I was jolted out of my thoughts when the kitchen door slammed shut. I looked up. Abby had arrived.

Jason was attending a law seminar, and Matt was at his monthly poker game, so Abby and I were having dinner together. Nothing elaborate. I was sending out for pizza.

Abby bent down to greet the dogs, who had rushed toward her and were now doing what I called their happy dances. I wiggled my feet, numb from the lack of circulation caused by Archie's huge head resting on them. Then, I ordered the pizza and poured two glasses of wine.

When Abby headed for a chair, I said. "While we're waiting for the food to be delivered I need to call Jeremy Toth."

"About the engagement party?" Abby stared at me quizzically.

I shook my head. "No. I need to find out if Melissa said anything to him regarding Victoria or Elena. Something he might consider unimportant, but maybe could provide a clue as to Melissa's murder."

"But Jeremy and Melissa were estranged, weren't they?"

"After the break-up, from what I've heard, it was bad for a short while," I admitted. "But eventually they resolved their issues. They weren't lovers anymore, but it appears they had some contact. After all, Melissa lent him money for *Crepes Galore.*"

"That could be a simple business deal, but I get what you're driving at. Melissa and Jeremy were back to talking to each other. She might have said something."

"I know I'm grasping at straws, but it's worth a shot."

I called and left a message for Jeremy on his voicemail. A few minutes later, the pizza arrived. I was about to dish it out when my phone trilled. Jeremy's name popped up.

I explained my reason for the call.

"I've told you all I know—"

"Knowledge is one thing. Suspicion is something else. Do you think Elena or Victoria could have killed Melissa?"

"Honestly, I have no idea. Strangely, Melissa got along with Victoria in the beginning. It was only after Elena began dating Austin that Melissa and Victoria started fighting."

"Do you know what they fought about?"

"Elena constantly complained to Victoria about the way Melissa was running the refuge, and Victoria always took Elena's side. But a lot had to do with their two different personalities. Melissa and Elena were like oil and water."

"In what way?"

"Melissa was a hands-on administration, and she was a good one. She claimed Elena was all show and only cared about public relations and marketing. Instead of complementing each other's strengths and weaknesses, the two argued most of the time."

"You need a strong marketing campaign for a place like the refuge. I've talked to Elena. Her ideas were good."

Jeremy snickered. "They weren't all her ideas. Melissa told me most came from Victoria."

Victoria. That was a comment I hadn't expected.

"Remember," Jeremy continued. "Victoria was an actress before she married Clifton Pendwell. She has a flair for the dramatic, and she knows how to court publicity."

"Elena told me about many of her plans. She was organizing an adopt an animal program at the local schools and—"

"According to Melissa, that was Victoria's idea," Jeremy said.

"Elena just recently coordinated an owl prowl which was a huge success. I thought that was a pretty creative idea?"

"It was, but it wasn't Elena's. The owl prowl originated with Victoria too. In fact, it was in the works before Melissa died. But Melissa was a little hesitant to go through with it."

"Why?"

"Although Melissa loved the outdoors, her experience in the woods had always been in the day. She wasn't familiar with the wildlife refuge at night and wasn't sure how well the participants would be able to navigate. She was concerned with the liability of the refuge if someone got hurt."

Jeremy paused. "Victoria actually offered to take Melissa on a 'mock' owl prowl so she could see what it would be like. I don't know if that ever happened."

Mock owl prowl. Of course.

That's why Melissa was in the preserve at midnight. She was meeting Victoria.

CHAPTER 56

"It all fits," I said to my daughter. "Victoria killed Melissa. She lured her to the clearing under a false pretense—convincing her of the merits of an owl prowl."

"Are you sure?" Abby looked doubtful. "Victoria Pendwell in the middle of the woods at night? I visualize her in a large executive chair at board meetings ready to have her picture snapped for a fashion magazine."

I shook my head. "Victoria may be the image of someone who never gets her hands dirty, but that's not true. The Pendwell's groom told me that once when the barn help didn't show up, Victoria mucked the stalls herself."

"But midnight? Why not earlier? If she went at ten o'clock it would still be dark."

"Yes, but more cars would be on the road. Victoria probably realized there would be more chance of someone seeing her at an earlier time." I sipped my wine. "I'm guessing Victoria said she had an event that night and wouldn't be free until midnight. For someone with Victoria's social schedule, that wouldn't be unbelievable."

Abby appeared to mull this over. "You may have a point. I also remember what Dr. Weiss told us at the fundraiser about how Victoria worked at a stable as a teenager so she could ride for free. That's backbreaking and messy work. Maybe she isn't a princess."

"Her parents lived comfortably, but nothing like the Pendwells. She was an actress..."

I stopped talking as an image flashed through my mind. "An actress. Of course. We couldn't figure out who delivered the poison cupcakes to George Grogin's house because the description didn't fit any of our suspects. But as an actress, Victoria would know how to transform herself into different characters."

Abby nodded. "Just like the undercover investigator who went into Krill's Jewelers with a diamond ring."

"Exactly. I'm sure Victoria was the chubby woman with the long, brown hair. Probably a wig and extra padding."

We both remained silent for a few moments. My mind was processing these new thoughts.

"Do you think Victoria's motive for murder was Melissa's pregnancy?" Abby asked.

"I do. Victoria cared more about the senate seat than Austin did. And winning that seat wasn't a slam-dunk—it's a swing district. A scandal of any sort could cause him to lose."

I sipped the remains of my wine and poured a second glass. "She killed Melissa and then poisoned George because she thought he might identify her. She couldn't be sure he hadn't seen her."

But my happy moment at realizing the killer's identity faded fast. Abby must have seen the change in my facial expression.

"What's wrong?"

"I don't know how to prove she was the murderer."

"The night Melissa was murdered, Victoria claimed she was home alone," Abby said. "But no one can verify her alibi. That means she has none."

I shook my head. "Unfortunately, her alibi can't be disproven either. All we have is circumstantial evidence."

"Jason once told me most criminal cases are won on circumstantial evidence alone."

"True. But I don't think we have enough. We need to put her at the scene of the crime. And it wouldn't hurt if we had a murder weapon. But Melissa was hit by a blunt instrument. That could be anything. As for the cupcakes, how do we prove she poisoned and delivered them?"

"Sleep on it," Abby suggested. "You know how sometimes nothing makes sense, but after a good night's sleep, you wake up and all the parts fit."

CHAPTER 57

When I awoke the next morning, I didn't have a solution.
But I did have a plan of action.

My first action was to call Abby.

"You have Sheila's cell phone number, right?" I asked as soon as she picked up.

"Of course. I always get that for emergencies and—"

"Text it to me now."

As soon as she sent me the number, I called Sheila. I didn't know if she would have an answer to my question, but it was worth a shot.

Sheila picked up on the first ring. I was in luck. Not only did she have an answer, but it was the one I hoped for.

My next action would involve a trip to the Pendwell Wildlife Refuge.

The refuge was hosting its Spring Clean-up today. Volunteers would be traipsing through the woods, picking up litter.

Today's myriad of volunteers would include community organizations and youth groups. But also participating would be the men and women who volunteered at the refuge on a regular basis. Perhaps one of them had seen or heard something—something insignificant on its own, but important when added as the final piece of the puzzle.

I drained my coffee cup as Matt stepped into the kitchen.

"I'm headed to the post office later this morning," he said. "You mailed in the payment for your red light camera ticket, right? I heard on the news the county was raising the late fees, so you need to be sure it's in on time."

"I'm good. I mailed it immediately. I always..." I stopped mid-sentence as an image floated through my mind—an image of Victoria

Pendwell speeding through that red light camera on the night of Melissa's murder.

I explained my theory to Matt. "If Victoria was at the refuge, she had to pass that camera on her way home. There's no other road she could take,"

"Don't you think the police checked this?"

"No. The traffic light is not immediately after you exit the refuge. It's about a mile and a half away. You can head in another direction too. Or you could go down another side road, but none of those roads would lead you to the Pendwell estate. For Victoria to get to her house from the refuge, she would need to pass this light."

I quickly booted up my computer and pulled up a map of the area.

"Look." I pointed to the screen. "The two side roads before the traffic light are dead end streets. The first road after the light is the only one she could travel."

"But the light may have been green when she went by," Matt argued. He grabbed a mug and filled it with coffee. "Or if it turned red, she might have stopped." He grinned. "Most people do."

"Maybe. But Long Island's gold coast is sparsely populated. If she murdered Melissa, she'd want to get away as quickly as possible, and at that time of night, there were probably no other cars on the road."

Matt looked skeptical.

"Remember," I said. "The camera was only installed a few days before, so it's unlikely she was aware it was there. And the village police patrol the local side roads at night."

"I guess it's possible."

"I know it's a long shot," I added as I grabbed my phone and called Detective Fox. He didn't pick up so I connected to his voice mail. I left a message explaining my theory about Victoria and the red light camera. I asked him to check for violations at that location on the night of Melissa's murder.

Before leaving the house, I phoned Abby. I told her about my theory too.

"Be careful. You've been openly questioning people about the murder. Victoria may think you're getting close to solving the crime. Also..." She stopped talking.

"What?"

"It's not important."

"Something is on your mind."

"Tonight's the engagement party."

"Don't worry," I assured her. "I will be there on time." I smiled as I ended the call.

I wanted to get to the wildlife refuge as soon as possible, but Long Island traffic doesn't care what you want. The clean-up started at nine o'clock. I arrived at nine-thirty and headed to the registration table outside the administration building. I wasn't the only late-comer.

Elena was coordinating the event. She handed me a trash bag and a pair of vinyl gloves. I grabbed a map of the area from a stack sitting on the table and began my trek into the forest.

The refuge was full of volunteers, so I wandered deeper into the woods, searching for an area where help was needed. I finally found a section with only three volunteers. One of them was Brian, the graduate student I met at the board of trustees meeting.

He apparently recognized me, and we exchanged greetings.

"I've done so much research on this place for my thesis I felt I wanted to volunteer today," he said. "I also come here and hike quite a bit."

While we picked up litter, we talked a little about his thesis on non-profit organizations. He had finally completed it.

"During your research on the refuge, did you get a chance to talk to Victoria Pendwell?" I asked.

"I did." He nodded as he bent down and picked up an empty potato chip bag and put it in with his trash. "Victoria was helpful. Very knowledgeable."

"Has she ever spent time in the refuge? I'm not talking about the administration building. I mean the woods." I wanted to hear his answer.

"Absolutely. She loves nature. I've seen her on the trails several times."

We walked, talked, and picked up litter for the next two hours. Unfortunately, he had nothing of significance to say about Victoria. Neither did the two other volunteers who had finished about fifteen minutes ago. They had headed back to the administration building where refreshments were being served.

"I think we're about done here," Brian said.

I scanned my surroundings, noting all the trash had been removed. "Let's head back to the main building and grab a donut." I wanted to talk to the volunteers there.

"Hey, there's Victoria now." Brian pointed up ahead as we trekked down the path. Victoria was standing in a small clearing off the trail. Her trash bag appeared to be more than half full.

She wasn't decked out in her usual manner. She wore jeans, a sweatshirt, and hiking boots.

She also had the silver walking stick.

I mentioned the stick to Brian.

"Oh, yeah," he said. "She always uses that when she's in the woods. "Says the forest floor can be bumpy and unstable."

It dawned on me that it wouldn't be unusual for her to bring the walking stick if she met up with Melissa at night.

That stick had cracked the marble floor.

That stick could cause a fatal blow.

That stick was the murder weapon.

"Hello, Victoria," Brian called out.

She yelled back hello and flashed him a big smile, which quickly faded when she saw me. "Hello Kristy," she said, drily.

"We're headed back to the main building now," Brian said. "Our bags are full."

"I'll join you in a few minutes. I want to clean up this section." Victoria pointed to the east side of the clearing where a few soda cans had been left under a tree. "People come to enjoy the beauty of the woods, and then they leave their garbage." She shook her head.

Brian and I nodded in agreement and then turned to leave.

"Kristy, why don't you stay with me?" Victoria called. "I have something I'd like to discuss."

Instinct told me I should continue back to the administration building with Brian, but curiosity won. What did Victoria want to tell me?

Once Brian was out of sight, Victoria wasted no time. She dropped her trash bag and moved to where I was standing. Our faces were inches apart.

"You've been checking alibis," she accused. "You don't know who you are up against. If you continue, I'll sue."

"You can't sue, if what I say is true." I shrugged. "And I haven't said or written anything yet. I'm still checking my facts."

"I had nothing to do with this murder. Neither did my family."

"If you say so." I didn't want to antagonize Victoria out here in the woods.

But Victoria wouldn't let it go. "You're snooping. This has nothing to do with the story you're writing. It has nothing to do with the operation of this place."

"The crime occurred here," I said defiantly. "But you're right. Aside from the location, the murder had nothing to do with the operation of this wildlife refuge."

As soon as I spoke, I realized I shouldn't. I'd made the statement with such assurance that Victoria realized I knew the reason for the murder.

Victoria's face darkened. She appeared to me as a rat-like creature with furtive eyes seeking a way to escape.

Victoria then glanced down at her walking stick.

Her heavy, silver, walking stick.

She wouldn't, I reasoned. Brian knows she's with me. If I wound up dead, she'd be suspect number one.

I quickly scanned my surroundings, searching for a rock or anything else I might use as a weapon if needed.

"Mrs. Pendwell, you are under arrest for the murder of Melissa Modica," a booming voice called.

It was the voice of Detective Wolfe.

Wolfe and Fox marched up the path.

Wolfe cuffed a stunned-looking Victoria.

"You're tip panned out," Fox whispered to me. "Victoria got caught on the red light camera at twelve-twenty six. That's eleven minutes after Melissa's watch broke when she crashed to the ground."

"How did you know where to find her?"

"After I verified the ticket, Wolfe and I went to the Pendwell estate. The maid told us she was at the preserve for the clean-up. We've been searching for her for the past twenty minutes."

"How did you get Wolfe to do this?"

"He had no choice. The red light camera ticket is pretty damaging. He admitted she must have committed the crime."

"He's senior officer. That's why he made the arrest, right?" I asked.

"Wolfe is a survivor." Detective Fox grinned. "Now, of course, he'll take credit for solving the case."

CHAPTER 58

"Did you have a good time?" I asked Abby.

"Fabulous. Thanks so much, Mom. You too, Dad."

It was a little after midnight. We sat on the deck. My backyard was illuminated by more than a dozen tiki torches.

The engagement party for Abby and Jason had been a success. The caterer cleaned up quickly and had departed ten minutes ago. Before Jeremy drove off, he made sure the four of us had a final helping of crepes.

Abby bit into her Nutella crepe. After she finished chewing, she said, "Now that the party is over, I want to hear about your morning." She grinned. "You solved the case."

I had told Abby about Victoria's arrest, but with the afternoon preparations for the engagement party, I didn't have a chance to go into details.

"Detective Fox phoned me an hour before tonight's party," I said. "Victoria has lawyered up. She won't admit committing murder. But Fox has been talking to the chief of the homicide bureau at the district attorney's office. He feels they have enough evidence for a conviction."

"What about George's murder?" Abby asked.

"Remember this morning, when I asked you for Sheila's phone number?"

Abby nodded.

"It was a long shot that paid off." I said. "I know Victoria has a cook, but I asked Sheila if she ever saw Victoria bake."

Jason grinned. "Good idea. If she was mixing Oleander leaves in the dough or icing, she wouldn't take the risk of having someone else make the cupcakes."

"Exactly. Sheila told me Victoria rarely went into the kitchen, but about two weeks ago, she remembered her baking cupcakes."

"What about the scorpion?" Abby asked. "Do the police know who placed it in the pretzel box?"

"Not yet. But they believe it was Victoria. She thought George would still be working at the refuge. And George ate pretzels every day. Elena only grabbed one on rare occasions."

"That was still a big risk." Matt took a bite of his Bananas Foster crepe. "She had to assume her future daughter-in-law might grab a pretzel first."

I shrugged. "Detective Fox thinks she was desperate. She couldn't take the risk that George saw her. I don't know what time she arrived at the refuge the night of Melissa's murder, but if she got there early, he might have seen her car on the way home."

"So what happens to the Pendwell Wildlife Refuge now that Victoria has been arrested?" Abby asked.

I leaned back in my lounge chair and continued. "I read the organization's charter when I was first assigned to write the story. It states that upon the death or resignation of any trustee, a new one would be appointed by the remaining board members."

"Is Victoria going to resign?" Matt asked.

"Clifton Pendwell, who was a bit of a law and order guy, put in a provision that any trustee convicted of a felony must resign. I don't think he thought it would be his wife." I smiled. "But who knows?"

"Victoria hasn't been convicted yet," Jason pointed out. "And even if she is, it won't happen overnight. Trials take time."

"I know." I frowned. "I guess we'll have to wait and see how it plays out."

* * * * *

Two weeks later, Abby and Jason treated Matt and me to dinner at the Woodland Inn in appreciation for our hosting their engagement party.

"There they are," I said upon entering the restaurant and spotting the two seated in a back booth by the knotty pine wall. They were sipping wine.

"Victoria is resigning from the board of trustees," I announced once we were seated and the server took our drink orders.

"Detective Fox told me the other board members were pressuring her to resign," I continued. "With all she has on her plate, she doesn't have the time or interest in fighting it."

"I thought most of the trustees were her friends," Abby said.

"Her friends are dropping her like a hot potato."

"When she resigns, who will be the chair?"

"According to the charter, the vice president of the board will assume the role temporarily. He then has six months to call for an election among the other trustees. The vice president is Charles Moran."

"Charles Moran. The founder and CEO of Moran Tech Industries." Matt paused until the server placed a bread basket on the table. "Moran has enough money to make the Pendwells look like paupers."

"I heard from Susan Hanson, too." I grabbed a roll and began slathering it with butter.

"She's staying on the board."

I took a bite of my roll and continued. "Susan's school board chair apparently no longer feels the need to accommodate Victoria Pendwell. Susan got the promotion at work and was told she's smart enough to know how to manage her time. He said if she feels staying on the board won't interfere with her new job, that's fine with him.

"There's something else I found out," I added. "Detective Fox told me they confiscated Victoria's computer. Guess what they discovered?"

"I can't imagine," Abby said grinning. "Tell us."

"Victoria ordered an Arizona Bark scorpion on the dark web."

After the server delivered my pomegranate martini and Matt's scotch to our table, Abby asked, "What's happening with Elena?"

"She broke up with Austin," I said. "Guess who she's romantically linked to now?"

"Who?" all three asked in unison.

"Charles Moran." I grinned. "We haven't heard the last of Elena. For now, she's staying on as director of the wildlife refuge—a job she's good at—but I foresee her moving up rapidly. She'll probably wind up running a bigger and more powerful environmental organization. Or maybe she'll run for public office."

"What about Austin?" Abby asked. "I saw on the news that he's dropped out of the senate race."

I nodded. "He also resigned from his law firm. I heard he wants to move to the south of France and become a painter."

Jason frowned. "That may not happen."

We all looked at Jason.

"With all of the attention focused on the Pendwells, accompanied by their dramatic drop in power, one of Austin's ex-girlfriends came forward today. She's accusing him of assault. Apparently, he has quite a temper when he doesn't get his way. I think charges will be filed momentarily."

"I can fill in some of the gaps in Melissa's life before her murder too," I said after briefly thinking about the demise of the Pendwell dynasty. "Do you remember when Linda Lau told me about her last phone call with Melissa? She said Melissa seemed happy for the first time in a long while."

Abby nodded. "I recall you telling me that. But no one could figure out why. I assumed it was her newly found money."

"It was more than that. Linda had lunch with Erin yesterday. Erin said that once Melissa decided to keep the baby it was like a giant load had been lifted off her shoulders. She was looking forward to becoming a mother. She knew her parents would be horrified, but in the end, they would support her."

"It didn't seem as if her father would. But she knew him better than we did," Abby added.

"There's something else." I sipped my martini. "She also decided to quit her job at the wildlife refuge."

"Quit!" Matt called out. Jason's eyes widened. Abby paused from sipping her wine.

"She decided to apply to law school. She planned on using the money she won in the raffle to help finance it. She wanted to specialize in environmental law."

"Too bad that will never be," Abby said.

We all sat in silence.

Finally, I said, "Well, that's it for this time."

"This time!" Matt almost spilled his scotch. "What does that mean?"

"Just a figure of speech." This was the third murder I had solved. My mind flashed back to the two previous cases—one at the Rocky Cove Zoo and the other at the Clam Cove Aquarium. "You know what they say. Things happen in threes."

Abby grinned. "I doubt it. You're an investigative reporter."

"For a magazine focused on animal issues." I responded.

"But Mom. With you, somehow, it always leads you to murder."

ABOUT THE AUTHOR

LOIS SCHMITT has been a mystery fan since she read her first Nancy Drew novel. She combines a love of mysteries with a love of animals in her series featuring wildlife reporter Kristy Farrell. She is a member of several wildlife conservation and humane organizations, as well Mystery Writers of America. Lois received 2nd Runner Up for the Killer Nashville Claymore Award for her second book in the Kristy Farrell series, entitled *Something Fishy*. *Playing Possum* is the third Kristy Farrell Mystery. Lois worked for many years as a freelance writer and is the author of *Smart Spending*, a consumer education book for young adults. She previously served as media spokesperson for a local consumer affairs agency and currently teaches at Nassau Community College on Long Island. Lois lives in Massapequa, New York, with her family, which includes a 120-pound Bernese Mountain Dog. This dog bears a striking resemblance to Archie, a dog of many breeds, featured in her Kristy Farrell Mystery Series. To learn more, follow Lois Schmitt on Facebook and Lois Schmitt Mysteries on Instagram.

If you enjoyed reading this book,
please consider writing your honest review
and sharing it with other readers.

Many of our Authors are happy to participate in
Book Club and Reader Group discussions.
For more information, contact us at info@encirclepub.com.

Thank you,
Encircle Publications

For news about more exciting new fiction, join us at:

Facebook: www.facebook.com/encirclepub

Twitter: twitter.com/encirclepub

Instagram: www.instagram.com/encirclepublications

Sign up for Encircle Publications newsletter and specials:
eepurl.com/cs8taP

CPSIA information can be obtained
at www.ICGtesting.com
Printed in the USA
BVHW081117031221
623051BV00001B/25